LOSING LEAH

TIFFANY KING

FEIWEL AND FRIENDS
NEW YORK

A FEIWEL AND FRIENDS BOOK
An imprint of Macmillan Publishing Group, LLC
175 Fifth Avenue, New York, NY 10010

Our books may be purchased in bulk for promotional, educational, or
business use. Please contact your local bookseller or the Macmillan
Corporate and Premium Sales Department at (800) 221-7945 ext. 5442
or by e-mail at MacmillanSpecialMarkets@macmillan.com.

Library of Congress Cataloging-in-Publication Data is available.
ISBN 978-1-250-12466-1 (hardcover)
ISBN 978-1-250-12467-8 (e-book)

Feiwel and Friends logo designed by Filomena Tuosto
First edition, 2018

1   3   5   7   9   10   8   6   4   2

This book is dedicated to anyone who has ever felt like the world is crushing them. Our strength is found within and I know that each of us has the power to persevere. We will not let ourselves give in to the shackles that threaten to hold us down. We are stronger than anything that the game of life can throw our way. We are not alone.

PART ONE

1

MIA

POUND.

Smile. Pretend you're fine.

Pound.

Focus. You got this.

Pound.

Don't think about it.

Pound.

Stop being a baby. You've been here before.

"Mia, are you okay?" The voice is familiar, though it sounds like it's coming from the end of a very long tunnel.

I open my eyes, not even aware I'd closed them. I force a smile. My traitorous hand drops from its spot at my temple.

"I'm fine," I lie, though I'm nowhere close to being fine.

Fine is normal. Fine is not having your head split open with an invisible ax. Logically, it was just a headache. Plenty of people get headaches.

Pound.

Screw you, I silently cursed at my head.

It responded with another pound.

"Headache?" My boyfriend, Luke, asked the obvious.

"It's no big deal," I lied again.

My recurring headaches started the day my sister, Leah, was taken. They were sporadic. In the beginning I got them all the time. Sometimes they were tolerable and easy to ignore and other times they weren't.

Pound.

This one happened to be an insistent bastard. I knew what that meant. I'd been here before. Time was short.

"I already know the answer, but do you want me to come in?" Luke asked, pulling up in front of my house. He watched as I rubbed my sore temples, giving away the severity of the headache. I'd never shared the origins of my headaches with him or the things that triggered them. As far as he knew they were brought on because I studied too hard. "Nah, that's okay. I'll be fine once I take ibuprofen," I lied, ignoring the intense pain behind my eyes. I didn't have much time before the headache would engulf me, leaving nothing but darkness. Most days I could feel the truly bad ones approaching and could prepare, but today's headache had snuck up on me.

"Thanks for dinner," I said, giving Luke a quick kiss somewhere near the corner of his mouth before hurrying out of his car. I pasted just enough of a fake smile on my face to get him to pull away. His reluctance showed that I'd slipped. Tomorrow when I felt better, I'd lie and tell him it was a migraine. That's the diagnosis my doctor gave me years ago. I even had medication to prove it. He didn't need to know the little pills wouldn't help. That they'd never helped.

Pound.

Mother of all pounding suck.

The headache was growing quickly, taunting me from every side. I needed to get in my house sooner than later.

"You won't win tonight," I muttered, standing on my front porch as I fumbled for the keys in my bag. I should have saved time and fished them out while I was still in the car. That was a dumb move. The problem was Leah's disappearance long ago caused my parents to go overboard with security.

Sensors on every door and window.

Front and back doors equipped with enough locks to keep Fort Knox safe.

It was a lame attempt to keep monsters away, but also a huge nuisance.

After several failed attempts and a few choice curse words, I finally matched my keys with the right locks and pushed the door open. Not surprisingly, the house was quiet and empty. Mom and Dad regularly worked late and clearly Jacob wasn't home either. Thank goodness. I loved my brother, but he was a worrier. If he knew how bad this headache was, he would take matters into his own hands, maybe even haul me over his shoulder and lug me to the emergency room himself. Tonight his absence was a godsend. I could tell this headache was going to be a doozy.

My eyes were already having trouble focusing, which made entering my security code into the keypad by the door more of a chore than it should have been. Luckily, with enough blinking I finished in time, because my throbbing head would have exploded had the alarm gone off. The impending stairs that led up to my room looked as intimidating as a mountain. I slid along the wall for support, flipping on every light switch I passed. I was terrified of the dark. It was smothering and oppressive, like a mystical force trying to squeeze me in its grip. I usually slept with all the lights on in my room, including the night-light that used to belong to Leah. Not that it did much good once my eyes closed. There was simply no escaping the dark.

Pound.

Tiny razor-sharp tentacles were digging their way into my brain.

Fear gripped me.

I began to doubt I would make it to my bed before the shadows consumed me. My feet may as well have been encased in cement, as heavy as they were. Each step I took felt like a hundred.

Pound.

Somehow, I managed to pull my way to the top using the rail, and my foot found the last step. Leaning against the wall, I took a deep breath to gather myself, blinking over and over again to maintain focus. My room was at the end of the hall, but it looked like it was three football fields away. I needed to get to my bed. Everything would be tolerable if I could just make it there.

I shuffled down the hall like a zombie. "Almost there," I said, counting the steps in my head. Ten more and I would reach my door. Five more after that and my bed would be within reach. I wouldn't allow myself to think about the times in the past I hadn't made it. My energy and focus were better spent moving forward.

Four steps to my room. If it wasn't for the wall, I would have been on my ass already. The shadows were beginning to bleed together. I was almost out of time. I wasn't going to make it. Panic began to claw its way up my throat.

Two steps. I was so close and yet my head felt like a grape being squeezed in a vise.

One step. I could no longer see. Reaching out blindly, my hand closed around my doorknob. My body weight pushed the door open and I fell forward into my room, collapsing on the floor. Even if I'd had the strength to crawl to my bed, I doubted I could have pulled myself up anyway. Rolling over on my back, I closed my eyes, letting the darkness take hold. *You win* was my last conscious thought.

• • •

"Earth to Mia—are you in there?" Amber, my best friend in the world, asked the next day, rapping her fingers on my locker to get my attention. I was too busy searching for my Spanish book to answer right away.

"I'm sorry, what did you say?" I asked, unearthing my book from the cluttered mess that was my locker.

"I said, how'd you do on the test?"

"Not bad," I finally answered as I slammed my locker closed before any other books could escape. "I think I probably passed."

"Oh, please. You know you aced it. Since when do you not screw up the grading curve for the rest of us? I swear if I had a time machine I'd go back and smack the guy who came up with the idea to mix letters and numbers together and call it math. Obviously it was some sadistic plot to separate the brains from the morons in the world," Amber joked, shouldering her book bag. "One day you'll be working in some lab figuring out the secrets of the universe and I'll be asking people if they want paper or plastic. Unless I bag a rich dude, of course."

I laughed, elbowing her in the arm. "As if bagging a rich dude hasn't always been your plan. Besides, you'll be some starlet in Hollywood, going to all the cool parties. Everyone will want to be your friend and you'll forget about the nerd you befriended way back in elementary school."

Amber linked her arm through mine. "I wouldn't count on it. Best friends for life, right? Anyway, you know all my secrets. I could never dump you." She giggled.

"Best friends for life," I confirmed, smiling as we sidestepped a questionable wet spot on the polished linoleum floor on our way to her locker.

Luke and Anthony (Amber's newest boy toy—her words, not mine) were already waiting at her locker by the time

Amber and I made it through the herd of students who all seemed as eager as we were to get to lunch.

"'Sup, babe. Inside or out?" Luke asked, dropping a peck on my lips as he slung his arm across my shoulders.

I shook my head. Same joke. Different day. He knew I preferred to eat lunch outside beneath the sun and clouds, but he still asked. He thought he was being cute. He was right, of course, but telling him that would only inflate his ego. "Outside, of course," I answered. "I need to get my lunch, but I'll meet you guys at the normal spot," I said, smiling brightly at him.

"I'm coming too. You know you'll need help carrying the buffet table," he teased, making Amber snort with laughter. Anthony shot us a mystified look. This was only his second lunch with us and he'd yet to witness what my legendary stomach could hold when I wanted to pack it away.

The cafeteria line was busy as always, but Luke and I barely noticed as we talked about the upcoming football game on Friday. I paid for my lunch while he stressed about the college scouts that would be at the game and the importance of standing out. He was nervous. It was kind of adorable. He had nothing to worry about. Football came as natural to him as breathing, but if a little reassurance was what he needed to get pumped up for the game, I was more than happy to oblige my guy.

Amber and Anthony were at our normal spot outside when we finally made it from the cafeteria with Luke carrying two trays of food.

"Aw, what a gentleman—carrying your lady's tray too? Does he carry your purse also?" Anthony asked me, laughing at his own joke.

"When I'm wearing a matching shirt I do, and actually they're both hers, dickhead," Luke said, laughing as he placed the trays on the table. "I brought a lunch," he continued, pointing to the modest bag I held in my hand.

"Shut up." Anthony's eyes moved from Luke's face to mine, obviously thinking we were messing with him.

"I'm serious, bro. I got ten bucks though if you don't believe me."

"I wouldn't do it," Amber chimed in. "She can eat, like, twice her own body weight."

In typical alpha-male fashion, Anthony wasn't about to back down from a challenge. "Whatever. You guys are messing with me, and I'm calling your bluff," he said, slapping his money on the table.

"Suit yourself," I said, picking up my double cheeseburger with everything.

"I feel like I got hustled," Anthony said twenty minutes later as I popped the last French fry into my mouth. He'd watched incredulously while I plowed through a slice of pizza, the cheeseburger, fries, a chocolate chip cookie, and a pudding.

"Don't sweat it. You're not the first," I joked, downing the last swig of my Coke.

"I feel full just from watching you. Totally worth the money though." He laughed, rubbing his stomach.

Amber rolled her eyes. "Believe me. If she wasn't my best

friend, I'd hate her. I'm living on salads until football season ends. I'd give my left leg for a slice of pizza," she said, running a finger over my empty plate to capture a lone droplet of pizza sauce.

"I can help you burn off some calories if you need to," Anthony said, sliding his arm around her waist.

She slapped him on the arm. "I bet, you perv. I'm serious though. If Joshua drops me on my ass one more time, I'm going to throat-punch him."

"Maybe Luke should try out for the squad," I teased. "He'd never drop you," I added, giving Luke's bicep a squeeze. "What do you think? You ready to trade your football cleats for pom-poms?"

"I'd totally rock the skirts," he said, hiking up his shorts to flash us his hairy thighs.

"You'd have to wax that fur off, Wolfman Luke," Amber said, munching on her last carrot. "Why don't you come over to my house on Friday? Mia and I can get you all buffed and smooth."

Luke shook his head exuberantly. "Hard pass. I've seen what my mom looks like after she gets her eyebrows waxed. I'm out on that sadistic ritual."

"Aw, big tough football player afraid of a little girly wax," Amber cooed, making us both giggle.

"Give me a concussion any day. Right, my man?" Luke asked, looking to Anthony for support.

Anthony shrugged. "It's not all that bad," he admitted sheepishly.

Amber's eyes lit up with merriment. "You wax?" She chortled. "Where?" she asked, tugging on his shorts for a peek.

Anthony's face flushed bright red like he wished he'd kept his mouth closed.

"Gotta be the legs," I guessed, ducking under the table to check them out for myself.

"No, not my legs," Anthony answered, looking more uncomfortable by the second.

Amber and I exchanged an amused look. "You don't mean your boys, do you?"

"Say it isn't so," Luke said, shaking with laughter.

"Come on, man. You know there's no way hot wax is going anywhere near a guy's precious cargo," he choked out. "It's my pecs," he finally admitted.

"Your pecs?" Amber asked, raising an eyebrow. "You have hairy pecs?"

"It's not like I was Bigfoot or anything. I lifeguard over the summer and I like looking good." He blushed again, much to our amusement. "Now you know and we can change the subject."

"Not on your life," Amber teased. "We wanna see for ourselves."

"Absolutely," I added. "Show us the hairless wonder."

The halls were buzzing with activity as everyone scrambled to get to class before the fifth-period bell rang. "I'll meet you at the library after practice," Luke said, giving me a chaste kiss. "By the way, you look better today."

"I feel better. It was just a migraine. You know I get them sometimes."

"You study too hard."

"One of us has to," I teased, trying to take the focus off my head.

"Ouch, I'm wounded," he said, clutching his heart, making me giggle as he headed off to his afternoon classes.

Still smiling, I watched him leave. Today was a good day. My headache from the night before was long forgotten.

I was once again me.

A typical, normal teenager.

The twin who'd been left behind.

I was six years old when Leah disappeared from our front yard. I went inside to fetch us the cherry ice pops we both liked, and when I returned, she was gone without a trace. We were identical in every way, including our tastes in food. Where one of us ended, the other began. She was the other half of me, until in one instant, she wasn't. She was gone, along with my life as I knew it. Nothing was ever the same after she disappeared. How could it be? You keep doing the everyday things that make you a person—eating, breathing, moving. Some days you even kid yourself and pretend everything is okay, but deep inside your soul, you stop living the moment you lose the other half of yourself.

For the past ten years my family has pretty much gone through the motions at home. Holidays, birthdays—they basically come and go without any real hoopla. School has been my only solace. It provides sanity, purpose, an identity. At school I'm just Mia Klein. Not Mia Klein, the girl whose twin sister disappeared. To my friends, I stopped being that person long ago. The world moved on at school, while at home we remained shackled by the past.

2

LEAH

EVEN WITH my eyes closed I could tell the lights were on. I could hear the soft familiar hum of the fluorescent fixture hanging on the ceiling above my head. I wasn't ready to wake up yet. Not after the dream I'd had. The sun warming my skin. Gentle, flower-scented breeze playing with my hair. I missed it already.

As badly as I wanted to stay in bed, I knew I had to move quickly. She was already coming down the stairs and if she found me with my eyes closed, the day would start off bumpy. For now, the last remnants of my dreamtime escape would have to be tucked away in the back of my mind to be savored later. In one swift movement, I swung my legs off the small twin bed and jerked myself upright just as she entered the room. That was close. A second more and she would have freaked.

Stopping at the bottom of the steps, she hung the menacing leather strap in her hand on its usual spot on the hook just outside the doorway. My eyes drifted to the strap for the briefest of moments. That would have been my fate had she walked in and caught me still lying in bed. At least I had managed to avoid its sting first thing in the morning. If I was good the rest of the day, maybe I wouldn't have to endure it at all. I was already on the longest stretch I could remember without an incident. Of course, now I'd probably tempted fate and jinxed myself.

"Are you hungry?" she asked, giving me the once-over before heading to the dumbwaiter she kept padlocked except during mealtimes.

"Yes," I answered, pulling the blanket up on my bed and smoothing it out with my hand.

She paused, staring me down with a dead-eyed sternness. "Yes, what?"

"Yes, Mother," I answered.

"Do we need to cover manners again?" She made her point by indicating the leather strap hanging within her reach.

I shook my head, keeping my eyes purposely averted from hers. Any display of defiance would only elicit severe punishment. It was better to ignore the taunting reminder of my weakened will. "No, Mother," I said, casting my eyes to the ground in obedience. It had taken me a long time and countless beatings to get to this point.

In the beginning, I wept for my family, begging to be returned to them, but my captor's anger was swift. I fought the foreignness of my surroundings until eventually I lost every speck of my former identity. The monster who punished me time and time again slowly transitioned until she became *Mother*. When the flesh-eating leather strap didn't stop my tears, she would retaliate by giving me a shot in the arm. I spent most of my first few months in a dark slumber. Wonderful blissful darkness that allowed me to escape my harsh reality. She thought she was punishing me, but I grew to love the darkness. I coveted it.

"Very well. You can set the table," Mother finally said with pursed lips. "Did you sleep well?"

Obviously I had been forgiven for my faux pas. At least the day remained on the right track. "Yes, ma'am," I answered, reaching into the tiny cupboard above a single sink that sat against the wall near our dining table. I pulled out two plates and two glasses and sat them on the table. Our utensils were kept in the small drawer beside the sink. Mother unlocked the dumbwaiter and extracted the serving tray she used for our food. I then carried the tray to the table while she relocked the dumbwaiter door, giving the lock two tugs to make sure it was fastened. It was the same regimented routine day after day, unless of course I did something that deserved punishment.

The dumbwaiter had a lock for my benefit. When I was nine, I shimmied up the rope. My arms shook from exertion, but I finally made it to the top. I don't know what my plan was if I made it to the kitchen. Maybe just a glimpse out the window at the sun or a blue sky filled with cottonlike clouds.

The issue was Mother never allowed me to go outside. She said I suffered from a severe case of photosensitivity, an allergic reaction to the sun that would affect my immune system. At the time I guess I didn't care. I slid the dumbwaiter door open to find Mother waiting for me with a shot in hand. I don't remember much of what happened after that, other than when I woke up the dumbwaiter door had the new lock installed.

"You may use the bathroom," Mother said once the table was set and the food was in place.

"Thank you, Mother," I murmured, walking sedately to the bathroom though my bladder was screaming for release. The bathroom had no door, but was separated from the room with a single curtain. It offered little privacy, but I was always thankful for anything.

Once my bladder was empty, I stood at the sink and squirted a liberal amount of industrial soap in my hands. Mother was a nurse who had seen her share of unnecessary sicknesses brought on by a lack of cleanliness. She was fanatical about germs. Hands were to be washed and scrubbed thoroughly on the front and back sides, making sure to get under the nails. I went through the motions without a second thought. I'd done it thousands of times before.

Our meal was simple. Eggs, toast, one slice of bacon, and a glass of orange juice. Obesity claimed over a hundred thousand lives per year. Even though I had a slight figure, Mother wasn't willing to take any chances. Over the years I had learned to eat my food slowly, savoring each bite. My lunch would be a sandwich and a piece of fruit that already sat in a brown paper bag on the counter. It was my choice when to eat it, but it was all I got until Mother joined me for dinner. Patience was a virtue forced on me.

"Before I go to sleep I want to check over your schoolwork from yesterday," Mother said as I finished the last sip of my orange juice. "Did you complete your algebra equations?"

"Yes, ma'am. They were easy," I said, beaming with pride when she smiled at me.

"That's good. Math is an important skill. What about science? Did you finish your gravity formulas?"

I nodded, standing up to clear our empty plates from the table. With a little dish soap and the washrag, I cleaned and dried our dishes, handing over any of the items that belonged upstairs.

I joined Mother on the small couch where she was going over my class work. I knew everything was right. The answers came to me easily.

"Everything looks good," Mother said, closing up the file. "You will continue on conjugating verbs today in English, and I want you to finish your paper on the Civil War." She stood up. A small kernel of relief blossomed like a flower in my chest. Mother had always stressed the importance of education and it was one of the ways I could always please her. "I will see you at dinnertime. You may shower today, but no longer than five minutes. I will know if it is longer."

"Yes, ma'am," I said, standing with her.

She pulled me in for a brief hug. "You're a good girl."

I obediently returned the gesture. "Thank you," I said, readily accepting the praise. Hugs from Mother were a treat and few and far between. A warm tingle spread throughout my body. Making her happy was my one and only goal. I treasured these moments. They were my reward for being good.

As if she could read my thoughts, Mother stiffened and abruptly dropped her arms. The mood of the room changed to dread, like storm clouds moving in before a thunderstorm. I panicked, quickly going over the events of the morning in my mind in a dire search for any mistakes I had made. I knew I only had moments to figure it out and apologize for my transgression.

She stepped back, reaching for the strap I knew all too well. My time was up.

What did I do? What did I do? I racked my brain for an answer, but came up empty. What was I missing? It must have been something really bad. Mother hated to punish me. She had told me time and again that she only did it for my own good.

"Leah, what is that on your ceiling?" she asked, looking toward my bed with the strap in hand.

"My sun," I whispered, suddenly realizing the mistake I'd made. How could I forget to take it down? It was a weak sun anyway, hardly worth the price I would have to pay. I drew it in lemon-yellow crayon like a little kid and cut it out in a perfect circle with my plastic scissors that were useless for anything more than the thinnest piece of paper. It hung over my bed using two thumbtacks I had found years ago and kept hidden. I only wanted it to shine down on me while I slept.

"Your sun?" Mother asked in a shrill voice. "Do you miss the sun?" she shrieked, making me flinch. "Do I need to remind you of what the sun does to you? Or the fact that your own parents abandoned you because of your illness?"

I shook my head. "No."

"Then why would you hang one above your bed? You want to leave me, don't you? You can't wait to leave me all by myself." The leather strap followed her words, tearing at my body before I could protect myself. It snapped across my back like a streak of fire.

"No, Mother," I pleaded. "I don't want to leave you. I promise," I cried out as the harsh strap found my bare legs. My flesh tore away with every strike, leaving white-hot, painful, bloody contusions. "Mother, I love you."

She stopped in mid-swing, gasping from her anger-induced exertion. "You promise you won't leave me."

"I promise," I answered. It took all my strength to stop myself from whimpering as I spoke. Crying would only antagonize her again. Mother did not like to see tears. "I love you," I continued. The words felt hollow and disingenuous, but they were what she needed to hear. It was more my fault anyway. I should have remembered to take the picture down.

All of Mother's anger evaporated as quickly as it had surfaced. She pulled me in for a remorseful, tight hug. Inside I was screaming in pain as her arms circled the open wounds on my back, but I couldn't show it. I had gotten what I deserved.

"I love you too. I wish you wouldn't make me punish you," she said, pulling away.

"I'm sorry. I'll take the sun down."

She nodded, refusing to look again at the offending scrap of paper. "You understand why it upsets me?"

"I do. It was wrong. I shouldn't want anything to do with something that could hurt me so severely," I said, parroting the words I'd heard hundreds of times before.

She leaned over and kissed my forehead. "Good girl. Go take your shower," she said, shooing me toward the bathroom. "I think an extra five minutes will be okay," she added, smiling brightly like nothing had happened.

I responded to her smile instantly. Mother was a different person when she was happy. "Thank you," I said, closing the curtain behind me.

As I stripped out of my pajamas, I could hear her footsteps walking up the hollow staircase, followed by the sound of the dead bolts locking on the basement door. I switched on the shower and turned the water to a lukewarm setting. I braced myself before stepping inside, knowing that the water wouldn't feel much better on my tender skin than the leather strap that left me scarred. By now you would think I'd be used to the pain. Only when my head was under the flow of water did I allow the tears I'd been holding back to fall freely. In the shower they were not tears, but merely water from the showerhead, lost among the other drops of water combined with blood that circled the drain before disappearing forever. I couldn't cry for long though, and use up my precious minutes of shower time. The shower was one of the few times I felt like I was somehow in control. I got to pick whether the water was hot or cold. How much soap or shampoo to use. As long as I stayed within Mother's allotted time, I was the queen of the shower.

My mind wandered elsewhere while I scrubbed my skin that felt rough to the touch, calloused and scarred several times over after years of punishment. I never dwelled on the scars or what I had done to deserve them. The only important thing was that Mother had forgiven me. My living quarters were once again peaceful when I left the bathroom. Mother worked nights while I slept and then she would sleep during the day while I did schoolwork and read. She used to spend more time with me when I was younger, serving as the teacher for my elementary homeschooling years. As I got older I did the majority of my lessons on my own and she only checked my work. Any questions I had, I saved for dinnertime when she and I could discuss them. As for my spare time, I usually read or listened to music as long as Mother approved of my choices. Anything I knew about the outside world I learned through the countless books I'd read. My own memories of life outside my room were hazy and in most circumstances, gone.

I dressed in jeans and a T-shirt, placing my neatly folded pajamas at the foot of my bed. The bloodstains that covered them would be painful reminders of my transgressions that would taunt me until Mother saw fit to launder them. She had obviously come back down while I was showering, because my drawing and the two tacks were gone. In a way I felt sad, but there was no point in grieving over a piece of paper. It was nothing. Well, it ruined my streak of good behavior, so I guess it was something after all. Now I had to start over again.

I dolefully worked at conjugating verbs and then finished my Civil War paper before lunch. My goal was to have more time to read. Mother had never been one to buy me toys when I was younger; reading had become my biggest luxury. As long as I did my schoolwork and kept my living quarters tidy, I could have all the time I wanted. One entire wall of my room was lined with bookshelves. Mother had brought me cartons and cartons of books over the years and I devoured every one. It didn't matter what genre they were. They were my window to the outside world. Books fed my dreams at night and gave me the freedom of imagination.

My current read was about a girl who lost her memory. It had suspense and intrigue with a little romance mixed in. I enjoyed trying to solve the puzzle even though I didn't want to spoil the surprise at the end. The main character had amnesia, which in some strange way was something I envied. Being able to forget your troubles sounded appealing. I also liked the portions of the book that took place in a school. Since I've never been allowed to leave the basement, I had never interacted with anyone my own age. No school dances. No parties. No sleepovers. Nothing. It made me wonder if

I could relate to normal people. When I closed my eyes I could almost imagine walking through the halls, chatting with my very own friends. Maybe I would have a boyfriend or maybe I would even be a cheerleader.

I looked up at the piece of plywood that covered up the only window in the room. A smile tugged at my mouth, but I made myself return back to my book and the world that belonged among the pages.

MIA

I THREW off my covers, happy to have my head still free of the darkness from the other night. Judging by the morning sunlight peeking through the blinds, I was already running behind. I rolled over to glance at the clock, seeing that I had barely enough time to get ready before Jacob left for school. He would wait for me, but I didn't want him to be late. I showered in record time and pulled on my favorite jeans and shirt before grabbing my backpack and heading downstairs.

Jacob was standing at the kitchen counter with his cereal bowl tipped up to his mouth, slurping the rest of his milk. For whatever reason, that noise had always grossed me out. "God, Jacob. Get a straw or something," I said, wrinkling my nose as I popped two packages of Pop-Tarts into the four slots of the toaster.

"Ahhhh," Jacob said, wiping his mouth with his arm before placing his bowl in the dishwasher.

"Could you be any more of a slob?" While I waited for my Pop-Tarts, I grabbed a bottle of chocolate milk from the fridge. Normally I'd snag a piece of fruit too, but I knew I wouldn't have enough time to eat everything during the drive.

Jacob watched in amusement as I gathered my belongings, trying to balance my breakfast and my backpack together. "Isn't the older brother supposed to do all the eating in the house?"

I smirked at him. "Don't be jealous," I said, stacking one strawberry Pop-Tart on top of a blueberry one before taking a big bite. I liked mixing flavors.

Jacob rolled his eyes, but didn't deny my claim. He was a wrestler and had to maintain a strict diet to make weight. "So, are we going to talk about the other night? It looked like a rough one," he said, doing me a favor by carrying my backpack.

I shrugged, glancing over at the empty chairs in the living room as we left the kitchen. "Are they awake?"

"Yeah. Mom came down for coffee earlier. She asked about you. I haven't seen Dad yet though," Jacob said.

"Tell her I said hi," I answered sarcastically.

At one time the living room had been the life force of the house, with pictures of babies and toddlers littering the walls. The furniture was sturdy and perfect for making forts. That was when the room was filled with love.

After Leah's disappearance Mom cleaned out the room in a rampage, ripping out everything, including the flooring. The shag carpet was replaced with cold slabs of tile. Stark white paint covered up the bright yellow walls along with all the holes from the pictures that were taken down. The furniture was replaced with stiff chairs and furnishings that no longer welcomed children.

I remember at that time overhearing Mom weeping on the phone to my aunt Cindy that Leah's doll, Daisy, had been found. The authorities no longer believed that Leah was alive. I was so confused and too young to understand the true gravity of what had happened. I knew my heart ached and that I missed my sister, but wouldn't I have felt it if my twin was gone? We'd shared a special connection. I couldn't believe that she was truly gone.

"You should tell Mom and Dad how bad the headaches are getting," Jacob said as we climbed into his car. "Maybe they need to change your medication."

"It wasn't all that bad," I lied, polishing off my Pop-Tarts and taking a big swig of chocolate milk. I neglected to mention that it was my second severe one in three days. That was a need-to-know info drop and Jacob definitely didn't need to know.

Stopping at the corner of our street, he looked at me with his signature glare of annoyance. "Puh-lease. How dumb do you think I am? Two nights ago I find you passed out on the floor. Maybe you're not aware of this but normal headaches don't do that. Look, I let the matter slide yesterday because I got home late from wrestling practice, but now this is some serious shit, Mia."

"Maybe I like to sleep on the floor," I said dryly, looking out the window. I wondered what he would say if he knew the truth. He knew about the headaches, but nothing about the darkness that came with them that always terrified me. I didn't want him to think I was crazy, and I definitely didn't want him to tell Mom or Dad. They were just headaches. That's all. A small part of me wished they were more though. When I was little I believed they were a bond between Leah and me. I knew it was silly but I felt the headaches connected me to her.

"Mia?"

"Jacob, I'm fine. Can we just drop it, please?" I pleaded, imploring him with my eyes.

I could tell by the look on his face that he wanted to press harder. He took a deep breath, reaching over to pat my knee. "Sure, Mia, we can drop it." Jacob was overly protective where I was concerned. "Do you need a ride to the football game tonight?" he asked, pulling into the student parking lot.

"Um, maybe," I said, opening my car door. "Luke has to be there early and Amber has practice before the game. I might just stay after school though. I can always spend the time studying in the library."

"Sounds good. Just let me know, okay? Valerie wants to double, but I don't want to commit if you need me."

I took my backpack from him and slung it over my back. "You should tell her yes. I don't mind staying after."

"And I don't mind giving you a ride," he returned, jumping ahead to open the door for me as we approached the entrance of the school.

"I know you don't, but seriously, it's okay. I like Valerie. You should come hang out with us," I added. "Luke and I are doubling with Amber and Anthony after the game." I stepped around a couple making out just inside the door. The hallway was loud and chaotic just the way I liked it. Jacob made a face at my invitation. "What—you don't like Anthony?"

He shrugged. "Not particularly. He used to be on the wrestling team until he got all pretty and became a lifeguard," he said with disgust.

I chuckled, wondering if I should share what I had learned yesterday about Anthony and his pecs. The first bell rang. "Oops, I better go," I said, shoving the last of my Pop-Tart into my mouth. I'd have to tell him about Anthony's waxing routine later.

I ended up declining Jacob's invitation for a ride that afternoon. Instead I spent my time in the library working on my statistics homework. The library emptied out quickly after seventh period, but Miss Nelson, the librarian, knew me well and didn't mind that I stayed. She always hung around until after five anyway. Eventually, I trudged through my statistics homework and jumped on one of the computers to research a paper I had due in world history, but I couldn't bring myself to concentrate any further. The nagging feeling that I always seemed to struggle with began to dominate my thoughts again. My fingers danced curiously over the keyboard before typing the words "twin bonds" into the search engine.

The screen finished loading, displaying multiple search results. I clicked on the first link, not sure of what I was looking for. Was I trying to prove that my pain was actually Leah's? Could she feel anything about me? Maybe I was going crazy or at the very least I was being selfish. Leah had most likely died ten years ago and I was blaming her for my unexplained headaches. But what if Leah wasn't dead? What if she was just a regular girl going to school somewhere, living her life without having ever known that she had been abducted? I let the fantasy play out in my head for a few minutes. Maybe Leah was a cheerleader or goth, or maybe she was a brain like me.

Unfortunately, reality was harsh, and the fact of the matter was that if Leah were alive somewhere there would likely be nothing normal about her. She would know she was taken. If she could she would have reached out to us. Something in my heart told me Leah would do everything in her power to get to us. If she were free to do so.

There was no scenario that wasn't depressing to consider. Without clicking on any other links, I shut down the computer. Whatever answers I was searching for wouldn't come from the internet. I gathered up my things and waved at Miss Nelson before heading out. I figured I would go to the football field early to watch the players warm up and enjoy the last rays of sun. It would suck when daylight savings time ended. It never felt right for the sun to set by six. My favorite time of year was the summer months when the sun would shine until after eight every night.

My shoes slapped against the floor as I walked, echoing off the empty walls in the hallway. The noise was eerie. I picked up my pace, wishing the library wasn't at the far end of the building. I rounded the corner, relieved to be nearly outside. With all the lights off, every empty classroom I passed was darker than I was comfortable with. The sun may have still been out, but it was no longer shining on the side of the building where I was at. My eyes stared straight ahead, avoiding the long shadows in the classrooms cast by the furnishings. It felt silly to be afraid of the dark at sixteen years old, but my headaches had manifested the dark into something frightening.

Making my way past the science labs, a sudden noise coming from one of the rooms caused me to jump and I nearly dropped my bag. "Hello," I called out, clutching my heaving chest. If someone was trying to frighten me, I was prepared to lay them out. I was short, but tough. Jacob had been giving me self-defense lessons for years. I could put someone twice my size on their ass.

A faint scratching from the far corner of the room was the only response to my greeting. I stepped closer, peering as far into the room as I could without actually going inside. The darkness was heavy and impenetrable. I backed away slowly, pausing suddenly when it looked for a moment like the shadows moved. I stood like a statue. "Is anybody there?" I asked, getting no response.

Blinking my eyes, I focused on the spot I thought had moved when all of a sudden the shadows appeared to rise from the floor. They gathered together into one giant mass, moving toward me. I tried to turn and run, but my feet refused to respond. My brain literally screamed inside my head to move, and yet I remained frozen. The darkness slithered toward me like a snake, void of any light. A scream clawed its way up my throat as terror held me in place.

Move, a voice shrieked in my mind. I clamped my eyes closed, expecting the darkness to suck me in as it moved closer and closer. My heart roared in my eardrums like a freight train. *Move*, my mind shrieked again.

I forced my eyes open to find that the darkness had disappeared back into the shadows of the classroom. I blinked again to be sure, working to catch my breath as my chest pounded. "Nice going, you dork," I said, chastising myself. I couldn't believe I allowed my imagination to get the better of me. They were only shadows.

After a few more deep breaths, I was able to get my heartbeat back under control. I whirled around, anxious to get outside in the light and away from the dark classrooms. Everything inside me wanted to turn and look over my shoulder as I hurried down the hallway, but I fought the urge. It felt like a million eyes were on me, all whispering as I passed.

Reaching the heavy metal door at the end of the hall, I shoved it open, gulping the warm outside air like I'd been submerged. My lungs burned as I heaved in and out. Clearly I had held my breath while I raced down the hall. All thanks to my overactive imagination. If Jacob saw me now there was no way he would keep quiet.

The more distance I put between me and the building, the more ridiculous I felt. Between my headaches and being chased by shadows, I was practically begging for a trip to the doctor.

Amber and the rest of the cheer squad were already on the football field in front of the bleachers when I arrived. She waved at me before rolling her eyes at Trinity who was barking orders at the top of her lungs. I flashed an exaggerated thumbs-up, climbing to an empty seat on the third row where I'd have a better view of the action.

The metal bleachers were warm from the sun beating down on them all day. It was just one of the perks of living in a warm-weather climate. In other parts of the country people were probably already wearing jackets instead of shorts and T-shirts like we could.

"Did you see Joshua almost drop me again?" Amber asked, joining me while the squad took a break. "If he drops me tonight there's no telling where my foot might wind up, so make sure you're watching because it'll be good." She took a swig from her water bottle, waiting for me to comment. "You okay?" she asked.

"Sure, why?"

She pursed her lips, studying me intently for a moment. "I don't know. You look off or something."

I laughed, hoping it didn't sound as hollow to her as it did me. "Off? What does that even mean?" I asked, giving her a shove on the shoulder. "Are you a psychiatrist?"

She continued to watch me critically. "Say what you want, but I've known you too long. Did you and Luke get in a fight?"

"No. I'm fine, seriously. I think Trinity is trying to flag you down though," I said, nodding toward the rest of the cheer squad who were lining up in formation. I adored Amber and her intuitiveness, but I didn't want it directed at me. I had enough weird stuff happening without bringing Amber into the mix.

Amber looked like she wanted to say more, but Trinity blew her whistle stridently in our direction. "God, I'm going to shove that damn whistle down her throat. Maybe then it'll be less annoying," Amber grumbled, stomping down the bleachers.

This time my laugh was more genuine. I could easily see Amber making good on her promise.

By the time our team ran out on the field for warm-ups the bleachers had begun filling in around me. I flagged down my friends Tina and Jen when I saw them searching for a spot to sit.

"Girlfriend," Tina said, hugging me as she sat down. "I hope we slaughter Winter Park tonight, especially since they kicked our asses last year," she added, sticking her feet up on the row in front of us.

"Didn't you date that guy, Russ, from Winter Park over the summer?" I asked.

Jen giggled on the other side of her. "That's right. You did. He was a doucheball too. You should go sit on the other side of the field, traitor."

"A momentary lapse in judgment. Besides, he had a nice butt and I didn't know what an asshole he was until I went out with him. Plus, he was dumb as rocks."

"Football players usually are," Jen agreed.

"Not true. Luke's GPA is almost as high as mine," I said, standing up and cheering as the teams lined up for kickoff.

Talking became impossible once the game started. The crowd was charged into a near frenzy. Winter Park was our school's biggest rival. They were notorious for playing dirty. Last year they clipped Jimmy Clausen, our quarterback, in the ankle when the refs weren't looking. He sat out the rest of the game and the season with a broken ankle, ending our chances at state. Tonight was about retribution.

By halftime my throat was raw from cheering after Luke caught a long pass and ran it in for a touchdown, putting us up by seven points. Amber and the cheer squad did their parts too by keeping the crowd energized. Somehow Joshua and Amber managed to work out their kinks because I didn't see him drop her once. Little did he know he had saved himself from a throat punch, at least for one half of the game anyway.

"You're so lucky," Tina yelled into my ear when Luke caught another long pass. "Luke is the whole package. Cute and a football god. If we weren't friends I'd totally hate you."

"And probably try to steal him," Jen chimed in.

"I'm not that much of a bitch," Tina protested. "Now, if they're on a break it's open season."

"Well, paws off. Luke is mine," I said, giving her a nudge

with my hip. "I'm short, but I fight dirty," I added, holding my fingers up like claws. Tina laughed as I fished my hoodie out of my backpack. Now that the sun had gone down there was a slight nip in the air.

"Like I'd do that anyway. There's way too many fish in the sea. I—" She became distracted mid-sentence when the crowd erupted after our team intercepted the Winter Park quarterback.

Jen snorted. "Tina doesn't have the attention span to steal anybody's guy. Besides, Luke is so into you," she said, joining the crowd in performing the wave as it passed our section.

"Hey, I heard that," Tina, said sticking her tongue out at us. "She's right though. I know a lost cause when I see it. Luke is off the market," she added, winking.

Jen and I burst out laughing as Tina swung her arms over our shoulders.

The crowd in the bleachers remained relentless in their support of our team. With all the yelling and high-fiving going on, it was amazing that Jen and Tina and I could hold any kind of conversation at all. I stood up with my arms in the air when the wave passed our section again. As I sat down, something in the trees beyond the football field caught my attention, a movement of some kind. Peering past the bright lights, I held my hand over my eyes to cover the glare to try to make out what I'd seen. I thought it was probably the trees swaying since it was a bit breezy, but my instincts felt differently. It was as if I could see the shadows moving within the darkness. My heart began beating in a swift tempo that had nothing to do with the game.

"Did you see that? What a catch," Tina yelled, slapping me on the arm.

I never responded, but neither she nor Jen noticed. They were too caught up in the game with everyone else. Whatever was happening within the shadows was for me alone.

4

LEAH

SETTING THE tray down, I spotted the familiar small white pill next to my plate. I knew why it was there. The stupid paper sun that shouldn't have been worth this much grief. Unfortunately, Mother now knew that I'd been up after lights-out.

She told me the pills were for my own good. They would help me fall asleep while she was at work. That way she would know I was safe. I actually didn't mind taking them sometimes. The pills sent me into a deep slumber that felt like a security blanket. I could dream about anything without fear of Mother finding out.

On other days the pills were a nuisance that robbed me of what little freedom I had. Most nights I stayed awake in the dark for hours after Mother left for work. The lights were controlled by a switch outside the basement door where I couldn't reach. The darkness to me was a time of peace. In a world where I had no one else to talk to, the shadows became my friends. Like a blind person, I learned to navigate the darkness without sight. I knew every single space of my room by touch alone. Eventually, I would prove my obedience again and the pills would stop, but until then my freedom had once again been limited. "You're not eating," Mother observed, scooping corn up onto her plate. "I thought you liked meat loaf."

I forced my eyes away from the pill and the power it held. "I do," I said, picking up my fork and taking a big bite. It wasn't a lie. Meat loaf was my favorite meal. It was one of the rare occasions when Mother would be generous with portions and I would actually get stuffed. Having a full stomach always made me fantasize that maybe I was getting stronger. It was a silly thought. I wasn't strong. I wanted to be, but my muscles were weak. They'd always been weak. Mother said it was a side effect of my sickness. It could have been worse. I could be bedridden or dead. There was a time I'd wished for death, when my limbs had burned after one of Mother's punishments. Sometimes the vivid memories still haunted me.

"I thought we would watch a little television tonight," Mother said.

Like the little white pill, this was no surprise. Mother's anger may have been unpredictable, but her remorse was always the same. I knew she didn't mean to hurt me. She didn't want to strike me. She was only trying to protect me. Television was a truce, her way of apologizing. It was a rare treat that I secretly coveted. It was the one time where I did not need an imagination to see the outside world.

When dinner was over and the dishes were clean, Mother watched as I placed the little white pill on my tongue and swallowed. The effects would move through my bloodstream in less than hour. After looking in my mouth to verify that the pill was gone, she was satisfied. "Good job. You may go change for bed while I hook up the TV."

I hurriedly changed into the fresh set of pajamas that sat at the edge of my bed, not wanting to miss a moment of the magic. It didn't even matter what we watched. Every single second counted.

I slid onto the couch next to Mother and she put her arm around my shoulders. She had forgiven me. All I had to do was not ruin the moment by wincing from the still-fresh scabs on my back and arms. The wounds that would eventually scar were insignificant. All that mattered was that she was no longer mad.

Normally we watched educational programs, but on rare occasions, like now, she would put on an actual comedy or drama program. I'd read a lot of books over the years that mentioned television, but none of them had captured the essence of watching it live. Clearly, it was something that couldn't be translated on paper. That or the characters in the stories never appreciated a little TV time as much as I did.

After about twenty minutes, the effects of the pill began to take hold. My brain felt a bit mushy as the show came to an end. Mother switched off the television. Thirty minutes was all I ever was allowed. Not a minute longer. Tonight, I didn't mind. Sleep was already tantalizing me, making promises only I would understand. I was ready to sink into the darkness and let everything else fade away.

Mother helped me into bed and covered me up. I closed my eyes, hearing the sound of her footsteps on the stairs. I was asleep before she could even lock the door. As always, the darkness welcomed me into its warm embrace. Loving and gentle like an old friend.

• • •

The next few days came and went without change. Each night at dinner, the little white pill waited on my plate. I began to resent its presence. I welcomed my dreams, but the cost of losing my freedom was making me angry. The emotion was relatively foreign to me. Anger was something I had buried as a useless emotion years ago when I realized that it changed nothing. No matter how angry I got, my parents had never showed up to get me. I could get angry at myself when I did something to make Mother punish me, but it never stopped the leather strap from tearing me apart.

In spite of my reasoning, I still couldn't help feeling angry over the little white pill. It was robbing me of something I desperately wanted. Something that had become an obsession. If Mother found out, her wrath would know no bounds.

• • •

I woke up the next morning with a plan. It was dangerous, but worth a try.

"You look happy this morning," Mother said, placing one slice of bacon on my plate.

"I do?" I looked away, wondering what she saw on my face. She couldn't know what I was thinking. It would ruin my plan. "I slept well," I answered lamely.

"That's good." She looked pleased at my words and I regretted them almost instantly. The point was to stop taking the pills. If she thought they were helping she would keep them up indefinitely.

After breakfast, Mother gave me my homework assignments for the day and headed upstairs. I stood up and placed my favorite cassette into the tape deck I got as a gift on my eleventh birthday. I liked the music as a distraction from how quiet it could get in my room. I didn't have much of a selection to choose from and most of the cassettes showed their wear and tear. I was hopeful that Mother would give me more, but it hadn't happened yet. I learned long ago that Mother became angry if I asked for things like toys, books, or music. Instead she wanted the gratification of providing all my worldly possessions for me. What I liked was never even a consideration.

Humming along to my favorite song, I lifted the couch cushion and reached my hand down into the couch as far as it would go. My fingers fumbled around until they found what I was looking for. "Hello, Daisy," I whispered after extracting the crude doll I had made years ago out of one of my socks. The doll looked nothing like my old Daisy. She had no arms or legs and her features were drawn on with marker that had begun to fade years ago. Daisy's eyes were misshapen and her nose was crooked and too big for her face, but it didn't matter. I loved her. She was my friend, the only one who knew all my secrets. Best of all, Daisy never got angry with me, even when I shoved her deep in the cushions of the couch. She always understood.

Before I started my schoolwork, I sat with Daisy on my lap and whispered my plans into her hand-drawn ear. Daisy didn't cast judgment. She knew I would get into a lot of trouble if I was caught, but she also didn't tell me not to do it. That was why she was my best friend. She understood me.

Daisy sat with me while I did my schoolwork and while I finished another book. It was an epic fantasy novel that hooked me instantly.

"I'll clean up as soon as I finish," I told Daisy who smiled back. I forgot about my plan for the evening while I lost myself in a world that was completely different from my own. A world with dragons and sorcerers and one brave girl who held the key to saving the kingdom. The story was layered and intense and I felt a great loss when I turned the last page.

I sat on the couch after I closed the book. "Can you believe that, Daisy?" I asked, reliving the ending in my mind. I was so lost in thought I completely lost track of time until the sound of the lowering dumbwaiter jerked me out of my reverie. Fear sliced through me as I scanned my room. My schoolbooks were still laid out on the couch, Daisy was smiling beside me, and my book still sat in my hands. I scrambled to my feet and stacked my books quickly, placing them on my desk. I heard the locks above me being disengaged just as I picked up my mess from lunch and rushed it across the room to the trash can. Glancing around the room one last time, I felt confident everything was where it should be. The door opened at the top of the stairs and my heart dropped to my toes when I spotted Daisy on the floor in front of the couch.

Mother was coming. I could hear her footsteps. She would see Daisy and punish me. Racing across the room, I scooped Daisy up and leapt onto the couch, shoving her deep into the cushions just as Mother reached the last step. A thin line of sweat trickled from my neck and down the back of my shirt. My breath was slightly labored, but I forced myself to breath evenly. I wasn't used to so much exertion.

"Leah?" Mother questioned critically as she rounded the staircase and looked at me.

I didn't need a mirror to know that my face was flushed. My heart raced from the adrenaline pumping through my veins. Mother was sure to suspect I was up to something. "Yes, ma'am," I said, trying to keep my voice steady. My shoulders tensed, knowing how angry she would get if she thought I was hiding something.

"Are you feeling okay? You look peaked."

Peaked? I thought, relieved. That would work. I could do sick. It wouldn't even be a lie. At the moment I felt sick. My stomach was twisted in knots and my skin felt clammy. Even my head felt fuzzy. Maybe I really was sick. "Not really," I answered, lying back against the couch cushions. The dizzy feeling abated and the churning in my stomach loosened slightly.

"Damn. The flu is going around at the hospital. I might have brought it home with me. You should get in bed," she instructed, squirting sanitizer in her hands before placing her wrist on my forehead. "You're not warm, but you feel clammy. It's probably the flu. Bed," she instructed.

I nodded, sagging with relief. As I stood up the room spun slightly and I almost believed that I was really sick.

Mother clucked over me as I climbed into bed. "My poor girl," she said, smoothing a hand over my hair. I sighed with pleasure. "I'm going to go make you some soup."

"Thank you." I made my voice sound pitiful, almost fooling myself. Her footsteps faded as she climbed the steps. The locks were engaged and I could hear the dumbwaiter rising. Only when I heard her rustling around in the kitchen above did my heartbeat return to its normal rhythm. That was a close call that had the potential of going so much differently. My mistake today could never be repeated. What if Mother would have suspected something more? What if she had decided to search my room? I worked hard to cover all traces of what I'd been up to, but she could figure it out. I could not be so stupid again.

Mother returned shortly with a bowl of chicken noodle soup. I obediently opened my mouth as she spooned the hot soup into my mouth. I could have fed myself, but I knew it brought her pleasure to take care of me. Considering the close call I'd narrowly escaped, I accepted the soup without complaint.

"I knew I should have brought home a flu shot for you," Mother commented, catching a drop of the soup with the spoon.

"That's okay," I answered. "It's not too bad."

"You should stay in bed and rest tonight and tomorrow," she instructed, giving me a sip of juice.

"Yes, ma'am."

"Good girl. I'll check on you in the morning."

"Thank you, Mother," I said, closing my eyes, hoping maybe she had forgotten about the little white pill. Chances were I was setting myself up for disappointment.

I felt the bed dip as she stood up and I forced myself to breathe evenly. She probably just left the pill upstairs and planned to return with it. I wasn't in the clear yet. Her steps paused on the stairs. She could have been listening, waiting to catch me faking. I had no way of knowing for sure. The lock on the door upstairs disengaged and the lights went out to the sound of the door being closed and locked. My eyelids flew open. Either she really had forgotten or she thought my sickness would make me sleep without the assistance of the pill. I decided to do things differently. I needed to make myself stronger. Continuing to be weak would only hurt me in the long run. My other plans would have to be pushed to the side.

The darkness held me in its embrace while I waited for

the sound of Mother leaving for work. The wait would be longer since I'd gone to bed earlier than usual. I was patient though. Without the effects of the pills, I could wait all night if that's what it took. Tonight I would start the process of becoming someone else.

MIA

"**COME ON**, Mia. Don't be a wuss," Amber said in a loud whisper.

I jerked my head around to make sure the house was still dark behind me. "I'm not. Can a girl even be a wuss?" I muttered, eyeing the pile of clothes at my feet. This was a ridiculous idea. We'd be in a shitload of trouble if we got caught. I should have vetoed the idea immediately after Amber suggested it, but we were all still riding high from our victory. The Winter Park football team was sent home with their asses handed to them after Luke scored two more touchdowns, winning us the game.

We were all trying to come up with an epic way to celebrate when Amber suggested skinny-dipping in Principal Trout's swimming pool. It sounded like a brilliant idea at

Steak 'n Shake, but once we actually got to his house, common sense took over, for me at least. The house was dark, but the two cars in the driveway were a clear indicator that it wasn't empty. Luke and Anthony boosted us up over the wooden fence even though I was starting to balk.

"Come on, Mia. The water feels great," Luke said, quietly swimming to the edge where I stood. Thankfully the pool was dark, hiding the fact that he was completely nude. Luke and I hadn't taken our relationship to the next level yet and I wasn't ready to change that any time soon.

"Fine, but you guys have to turn around until I get in," I instructed.

His white teeth seemed to glow in the dark as he beamed up at me. "Done," he said, giving Anthony the same instruction.

Feeling like a fool, I shimmied out of my shorts and panties at the same time. Taking a peek over my shoulder at the house behind me, I pulled my T-shirt off up over my head and unclasped my bra, tossing them both on the stack of clothes at my feet. Suddenly I was out there, more than I had ever been. Goose bumps formed on my arms from the cool nighttime air. With my arms folded across my chest, I stepped into the shallow end of the pool. The water was warmer than the air outside as I waded in up to my chin.

"Okay, you can turn around" I whispered, treading water.

Luke swam toward me, smiling broadly. "Told you it felt nice," he said, reaching for my hand and tugging me toward him.

"You were right. I still think we're crazy though, especially you. If we get caught, Principal Trout can have you thrown off the team."

He chuckled. "Be honest. You're more worried about getting expelled," he teased, pulling me closer. The water was too deep for me to stand so I clung to his shoulders, trying to ignore the close proximity of our bodies. My eyes moved to the deep end of the pool where Amber and Anthony were clearly doing more than talking.

"They're too busy to worry about us," Luke murmured, dipping his head down. I sighed as his lips moved softly against mine, gently coaxing them to open. I let his tongue sweep inside my mouth, shivering at the sensations that raced up my spine. Luke and I had made out plenty of times over the past six months, but the absence of clothing made this far more intimate. I tried to keep a small measure of distance between us, but my legs seemed to float toward him on their own. Luke deepened the kiss. I gripped his shoulders, trying to hold myself in place. His tongue teased mine as his hands settled on my waist.

I broke away for a moment, surprised at how breathless I felt. Kissing Luke was always pleasant. Luke seemed to respect my boundaries. Amber lost her virginity over a year ago and had been on a nonstop sexual roller coaster since. Every single guy she dated expected it now. I didn't want Luke and me to get to that point.

Our spur of the moment skinny-dipping though had me thinking otherwise. I could tell by the look in Luke's eyes that he was expecting me to pull away. Oddly, I didn't want to. It felt good to be in his arms. Before Luke and I started dating, the only person who ever hugged me was Amber. Jacob and I tried a few times, but Mom and Dad weren't the affectionate type, especially after Leah disappeared. It just never felt comfortable.

Being in the pool, on the other hand, felt right. Even the darkness was less frightening wrapped in Luke's arms. I surprised Luke by looping my arms around his neck, allowing my body to drift closer until our legs tangled together. His eyes darkened. He liked it. It felt triumphant. Like when I aced a test. He lowered his head, ready to claim my lips again when a flash of movement in the trees at the back of the property grabbed my attention.

"Something wrong?" Luke asked when my head snapped backward. I stretched my neck, trying to peer around him. I knew what it was. A scream clawed its way up my chest as my eyes finally made out the hulking shape of a thick cloud of darkness rising from the shadows. It glided toward us, zeroing in on me. My head pounded as I reached for my temples. Why was it following me? I knew without a doubt that it was here to swallow me up.

A scream broke free from my chest, moving up to my vocal cords and escaping like a siren. Luke looked horrified. I could see his lips moving, but his voice was muted. His head whipped around, looking more concerned about the noise I was making than the dark cloud creeping past the edge of the pool.

Amber swam frantically to my side. I thought she would have been as terrified as I was, but even she seemed unconcerned about the ominous cloud that had disappeared back into the trees. I couldn't trust it though. I wouldn't. Luke grabbed my shoulders, distorting my screams as he shook me in an attempt to calm me down. He was right in my face, but I still couldn't hear him. We had to leave, to run and save ourselves. They would know this if they would stop worrying about me and see what was right in front of their eyes.

Lights came on, flooding the backyard. I looked in every direction, searching for any evidence of the monster that had tried to take me. My head pounded and I could barely see. Even in the light there was nothing but a few palm trees and a fire pit surrounded by lawn chairs. Where had it gone? Was it in the water with us? I jumped back in a panic. Looking up, I saw that we were no longer alone. The darkness was long gone, but our angry principal had taken its place.

Principal Trout was not happy to find four of his students naked in his swimming pool. Neither was his wife for that matter. Amber was convinced that if not for my freakish meltdown he would have called the cops. I lied, claiming I had seen someone peeking at us over the fence. Of course what I didn't mention was my freak show imagination and the sinister dark cloud of nothingness coming for me. It sounded ridiculous enough in my own head. If I voiced the truth they would think I had totally gone off the deep end. It was bad enough that I believed it myself.

Principal Trout gave us a stern lecture while his wife

passed out towels. His face was practically purple as he threatened expulsion and calling our parents. Luckily, in the end, Mrs. Trout persuaded him to let us off, reminding him how he had done similar things at our age. He grumbled something about those being different times, but grudgingly agreed to let us go. Mrs. Trout allowed us to get dressed in the house and then we did the walk of shame out the front door. My friends didn't say a word as we shuffled out the door. I couldn't blame them if they wanted to kick my ass. It was completely my fault we got caught.

My friends' reactions were the opposite of what I expected. When we got in the car they all burst out laughing hysterically. Our exploit had already reached epic status in their eyes. The fact that we had gotten away with Principal Trout seeing us all buck naked and me going batshit crazy seemed to pump them up even more. As a matter of fact, Amber and Anthony never mentioned my screaming fit before Luke dropped them off. All they seemed to care about was that we'd pulled off the ultimate stunt. Anthony had even taken a few pictures in the pool to prove it. I shuddered at the thought of them.

Luke pulled up in front of my house and turned off his car to talk to me. "Are you okay? You were pretty freaked out back there." He laced his fingers through mine and kissed the backs of my knuckles.

I nodded. It was beyond embarrassing to even think about it. "I guess it was like a knee-jerk thing, or whatever. Seeing some pervert spying on us totally scared me." The excuse sounded lame. There was showing concern when you saw someone peeping at you, and then there was losing your shit like a ghost had just floated out of the bushes. The two were easily distinguishable and I had done the latter.

Luke stroked his hands down my arms, rubbing and kneading them with his long fingers. It was comforting and one of the reasons I was so hung up on him. Luke had a sixth sense of knowing what I needed. All his concern was centered on me. A normal guy would have probably tried to make me feel bad for what happened. I could have gotten us in a lot of trouble. We were lucky that Principal Trout was a football fan, and that his wife had been so understanding. "I'm sorry you were so scared," Luke said. "If I would have seen him, I would have knocked his damn lights out. Nobody scares my girl." His hands moved up to stroke my neck. "Of course, I can't say I blame him for trying to catch a look," he said huskily.

I smiled. "Is that your way of telling me you snuck a peek?"

"I plead the Fifth," he said, leaning in to kiss me.

I laughed against his lips. It was sweet of Luke to try and make me feel better. His gentle concern for my well-being was comforting, like eating chocolate when you were stressed out. He pecked at my lips with soft butterfly kisses, moving down to my chin and across my jawline. Every touch to my skin left a trail of warm, tinkling pleasure that made me want to pull him closer. He was tender and careful not to become demanding. Tonight though, I didn't want tender. I wanted a real kiss. Something that would tease every nerve ending in my body and take me right to the edge. I slid my hand across his chest, yanking at his shirt to urge him to kiss me harder. I wanted to forget about monsters, shadows, and darkness. I wanted to feel safe. Luke shifted toward me in his seat. He had to be confused. I had never been this aggressive before.

We slid our bodies together as close as the middle console would allow. The emergency brake dug into my side, but I ignored it. Our hands moved with a purpose over each other. "I love you, Mia," Luke moaned, pulling away slightly. "You're killing me though." We were both gasping like we'd run a marathon. My chest pounded so hard I thought my heart would explode.

"I love you too. Was that too much?" I asked reluctantly. Luke was cool in the way he respected my boundaries, but I wasn't clueless when it came to guys. Eventually he would probably get sick of waiting for me to give him something I wasn't sure I was ready for.

"You surprised me, I'll say that. I meant what I said though. I do love you."

He squeezed my hand as I opened the car door, peering out into the dark. In my current state of mind I couldn't help staring at the trees and bushes around the house, expecting the shadows to reach out and grab me.

"Do you want me to walk you to your front door?" Luke asked when I hesitated.

I shook my head. My house was out-of-bounds. I never invited anyone inside. Even in all the years Amber and I had been friends, she had never been in my house. It wasn't only me either. We never had company of any kind over. We were a broken family that had never been repaired. Plain and simple.

"That's okay. I'm fine," I lied, forcing myself to get out of the car. I felt like I was losing control. The problem was I couldn't decide which scenario was more desirable—some kind of shadow monster that really existed and was hunting me, or imagining the whole thing because I was either having a nervous breakdown or maybe even had a brain tumor or something. Either way, I felt I was screwed.

Luke waited for me to unlock my front door before pulling away. I threw a wave over my shoulder as I walked inside. The downstairs area of the house was dark and closed up for the evening. As I dropped my keys on the side table and walked upstairs, I could hear my parents' muted voices coming from their room. I paused as I walked by, staring at the light shining under the door. My hand hovered over the doorknob, tempting me to walk in. I thought about crawling onto Mom's lap like I used to as a little girl after having a nightmare. I wanted to snuggle next to Dad, so he could hold me close and reassure me that monsters weren't real, that they weren't lurking under my bed or hiding in the shadows. It was a nice fantasy, but Dad stopped chasing monsters away ten years ago. Everything changed the day Leah disappeared.

"I'm home," I said, rapping on the door before moving on. If they wanted to know anything about me, they could ask. I was sick of trying to force them to be parents. I paused at Jacob's room as I passed. When he got home I could finally fess up and confide in him. Even if he didn't believe me, he would listen. Somewhere along the way Jacob had stepped into the role my parents abandoned. Losing my twin sister was hard enough, but without the comfort of Mom and Dad, it was unbearable. Without Jacob, I honestly feel like I would never have made it. Loneliness would have swallowed me whole.

LEAH

SWEAT TRICKLED along the curve of my neck, past the collar of my nightshirt, down each bump and rivet of my spine, and finally into my pajama pants. I was breathing heavy, but it was invigorating. It signified that I was doing something right.

I could only do twenty jumping jacks before tiring out, but I was still pleased with my effort. Five days ago, I'd barely been able to do five without collapsing. I was getting stronger. I could feel the difference in my limbs. In barely a week my body was already changing.

Once I finished a round of jumping jacks, I picked up the two stacks of books I'd bound with strips of cloth. With a set in each hand, I lifted my arms as many times as I could before my muscles quivered and I had to stop. Arms should not feel like cooked spaghetti. They should be strong and capable. Mine would have to be both for my plan to work. I had to keep going.

A couple of sets was all I could handle. I dropped the books at my feet and worked to undo the knots on the first stack. My fingers worked nimbly, going by touch alone in my pitch-black room. Thankfully, after my bout of "sickness," Mother decided not to continue giving me the little white pills. I seized the opportunity, vowing to be more careful this time.

The knots on my stacks of books eventually loosened and I made my way cautiously to my bookshelves and stowed the books where they belonged. I shoved the strips of cloth into the couch cushions, giving Daisy a light pat before extracting my hand. I would have liked to carry Daisy back to my bed. I had so much to share with her. So much I yearned to tell someone. Daisy was a risk though. A risk I could not take at the moment.

I made my way to my bed and lay down. My eyes remained open, even though seeing was impossible. I wondered if this is what it felt like for a blind person. Did they adjust to their surroundings as much I had? They had to. Like me, they were probably able to navigate their living spaces with ease.

Eventually, I forced my eyes closed, willing myself to go to sleep. I couldn't wake up tired two mornings in a row. Mother would start to suspect something. The sickness card could only be played for so long and I didn't want to take the chance of seeing the little white pills again.

As much as I tried, my mind refused to shut down enough to fall asleep. I was too excited about my accomplishments, anticipating a time when I could put them to use. A feeling of happiness spread through my body. I felt in control. It was a heady feeling and one I couldn't remember having before. I wasn't sure how to accept it. I fell asleep with a smile on my face, something that hadn't happened in years.

• • •

My smile was gone the next day. Mornings were when control was taken from me again. I could not dictate the moods of Mother. Even when I was good there were days when she seemed to find fault with the very air I breathed. Any number of insignificant things could set her off. Today would be one of those days.

I woke to her shrieking at me to get up. The first hit came by her hand when I accidentally bumped into her in my haste to make my bed. It was different from the leather strap. Her hand slapped across my face, jerking my head backward from the impact. The flesh of my cheek was on fire, but past experience taught me that if I reacted in any way it would only enrage her further. I had to act like nothing happened.

Breakfast started as a quiet affair after that. Neither of us spoke and I kept my head down, trying to chew my food although my cheek was swelling. I almost made it through without another infraction but because I was on edge, afraid of angering her further, I knocked over my glass and spilled juice all over Mother's lap.

"What is with you today? Laziness!" she screamed, jumping

from her chair. I immediately curled into a ball in anticipation of being hit. That was a mistake. "How dare you treat me like some kind of monster. Is that what I am to you? After everything I've done to protect you, to keep you safe?" Her fists rained down on my body in a fit of rage. Time and time again she connected on my back, shoulders, and legs. "Maybe you enjoy being punished, is that it? Do you know how much it hurts me to punish you? Why do you do this to me?"

There would be no protection from the physical pain, but I closed my eyes and my mind retreated to a place of shelter. A place where I could ride out the storm until she had worked out her aggression. I knew she had finished when I heard her grab a roll of paper towels from the small sink and throw them to the floor next to me before retreating up the staircase.

It felt like an eternity before I moved. I opened my eyes again, allowing my mind to ease back into reality and take stock of my pain. Pain was tricky. At times it was glaringly obvious, like from abrasions and contusions. Other times the pain lay in wait, striking just when you thought all was well. I'd become an expert at what the body could endure. I used to spend hours sobbing after one of Mother's punishments, cursing myself for causing it to happen. Tears would leak from my eyes until I had none left, then exhaustion would set in and take me. That never happened anymore. I just accepted my fate and moved on.

Today the pain was about a six out of ten. Six was tolerable. I'd had worse. When I was little all Mother's punishments felt like a ten, but over the years I'd developed a scale of severity of sorts. If one of her punishments reached a ten now it was excruciating, like the time she broke my leg. Tens shook me to the very core and made me want to give up which is why I never liked to think about them.

After a few minutes, I finally managed to pull myself up into a seated position. I didn't think I sat up too quickly, but my head spun slightly, threatening mutiny. I inched myself backward, cringing from a kink in my back. I had to use my right arm to propel myself along because my left arm felt bruised and sore to the touch. It was a long tedious trip across the floor. By the time I made it to my bed, I wondered if scooting to the bathroom would have been a wiser choice since my stomach was churning nauseously. I swallowed back the lump in my throat, hoping my breakfast would stay put. Puking would only add insult to injury.

Eventually I was able to hoist myself up on my bed. Several minutes passed as I tried to regain the air in my lungs and keep the contents of my stomach in check. I closed my eyes to keep the room from spinning. I knew I'd have to get up soon and clean the mess. There was no telling how long Mother would leave me alone. It could be all day and night or she could come back down at any moment. One thing I was certain of: Whatever had set Mother off earlier had nothing to do with me. Something at work had pissed her off and I became the target for her frustration.

I woke up realizing I had dozed for a short time, clearly remaining in one position for too long, judging by the stiffness in my joints. I inched up on my pillows, thankful that the room had stopped spinning. My head still throbbed, but tossing my cookies was no longer an issue. Now that I could take stock of my injuries, I tallied my throbbing head, a sore back, tender ear, and a bruise imprint of a shoe on my left arm, which explained the tenderness I felt while trying to scoot across the floor.

It could have been worse, so much worse. The bruise on my arm upset me the most since it would make it hard to continue my book-lifting exercises at night. The fleeting thought that she somehow knew what I'd been up to crossed my mind. Maybe my sore arm wasn't just a casualty of the fallout. I had to be wrong. It was a coincidence. A sore coincidence, but nothing more. As soon as my body wasn't so stiff, I would continue with my regimen, using only my right arm until my left could do its share again. For the time being, I suffered through my injuries to clean up the mess left behind from breakfast that morning.

Mother skipped bringing me dinner that evening, and breakfast the following morning. My stomach growled in protest, so I drank water to keep it satisfied. Finally I ended up scavenging through the trash for the few remaining scraps from our breakfast the previous day. Each hour ticked by at a snail's pace as I wondered if she would decide to forgive me by dinnertime. I tried whittling the hours away by reading, but every book I seemed to pick up had a mention of food in it and only made me hungrier. I decided after that to clean my room instead. Really it was just moving things from one spot to the next since my room was already spotless. It was a futile exercise, but served to keep my mind off my growling stomach.

By the time I heard the dumbwaiter being lowered at dinnertime I'd almost given up hope that Mother would return. I figured my final punishment would be starvation. I could hardly believe it when I heard the lock opening on the door, followed by Mother appearing at the bottom of the stairs with a smile and a bag of books. It was her form of an apology. I smiled back, eagerly waiting for her to unlock the dumbwaiter. I was so hungry I could have gnawed off my arm.

Mother actually helped me set the table while she chattered away the entire time. She was happy. Whatever demon had claimed her the day before was gone. I lapped it up like a dog, thankful to have her back.

"I think you'll like the new books I picked out for you," Mother said, offering me another roll.

I paused for a moment. She was offering me seconds. She had to be really sorry. "Thank you," I said.

"I told the sales clerk some of the titles you'd already read and she recommended a new fantasy series. She couldn't believe it when I told her you read almost two books a day," Mother said, beaming at me.

A smile stretched across my face. It felt good to please her. I just hoped I wouldn't make a mistake and ruin it. "I can't wait to read them," I said genuinely. "Thank you so much for buying me more. I'm such a lucky girl."

She reached over and patted my hand. "You're my little girl. I'd do anything for you," she said, giving my hand a squeeze. "Anything," she repeated. "I love you."

"I love you too, Mother." It felt like betrayal. I sometimes thought about my real mother, wondering why she had allowed someone else to raise me despite my sickness. Mothers were supposed to care more than that.

Mother's eyes got misty at my words. "That's my sweet girl. Now, I have another surprise," she said, returning to the dumbwaiter and removing another dish. "Dessert."

I couldn't believe my luck. Dessert was usually saved for special occasions. I fleetingly wondered if today was my birthday. It couldn't be. It was too soon. I knew it wasn't Mother's either.

"Chocolate chip," I said, gasping when she lifted the lid to reveal a plate of cookies. I remembered chocolate chip cookies from before Mother had saved me. The smell would fill our house every week when my other mom used to bake them for Jacob, Mia, and me. I hadn't had them since. It made me wonder if they were still a weekly ritual in my old home. Did Jacob and Mia still help Mom bake them?

I never allowed myself to feel jealous over Jacob or especially Mia. Life had dealt us our cards and it was not up to me to question how they were laid out. I was sure Mia thought of me also from time to time. Maybe even more often than that. Was it possible she had an illness like me? We were twins after all. How would our lives have been different had we stayed together? These were questions I would likely never know the answers to.

Mother and I ate the cookies in front of the television. Surprisingly, she let me have as many as I wanted. My eyes were bigger than my stomach and I ate until I felt sick. It was the best night I could ever remember having together. It was a night to be treasured.

That night I went to bed without exercising. Instead I lay there wondering if my recent rebellion had been misplaced. Mother loved me. Our relationship may not represent what I read in books or even what we'd watched earlier on TV, but I had to respect her for taking on the burden of caring for me.

My sleep was dreamless that night and I woke up the next day feeling at peace. I ate breakfast with Mother, worked on schoolwork, ate lunch, read, and then ate dinner. It was the same comfortable schedule I'd been following for years.

Lights went out at nine and ten minutes later I heard Mother leave for work. I climbed from bed and started my jumping jacks. I worked out for an hour, until sweat dripped down my neck.

I fell into bed in an exhausted heap.

7

MIA

MY ROOM was pitch-black when I pushed my door open. I
fumbled quickly around the wall for the light switch, not
wanting to deal with the dark a second longer. My eyes skirted
over my bed, past my desk, and across my window seat before
finally settling on my closet. The door was still open the way
I had left it that morning. Most of my shirts were hanging
haphazardly, ready to fall, while the others were already in a
heap on my closet floor. Still more clothes were tossed over
my desk chair and the foot of my bed. It looked like a tornado
had swooped in and strewn my clothes across the room. All
was normal.

I breathed a sigh of relief. Normal was good. My room was
always a bit messy since I wasn't exactly the most organized
person. I stepped over my favorite pair of sandals and kicked

a dirty pair of jeans off the bed. It was only a short-term solution, but I would clean in the morning. I fluffed up my pillows before climbing on the bed and switching on the TV for a little background noise. My real plan was to write in my journal stuffed under my mattress.

It really wasn't so much a journal as it was an open letter to Leah. Each page was filled with thought after thought in penmanship that had gradually changed over the years. It was a continuous flow of conversation that never ended. I didn't write in it every day, and sometimes I would only write a few words at a time. It was the only thing that kept me connected to her and made me feel like she was still a part of my life. Somewhere deep inside I wanted to believe that one day I would give her the journal and she could read about everything she had missed. The good and the ugly. Tonight's entry would be the ugly. I wrote with a fury, pressing hard on the page with my pen. The thin paper nearly tore as the ink bled into the slightly yellowed parchment. Thankfully I caught myself. I couldn't afford to tear the last remaining pages in the journal. There were only nine left. I had thought a lot over the years about the significance of reaching the end. Now that it was close, I wouldn't allow myself to dwell on it. The mere thought made my lungs shrivel and my throat close. My penmanship had become smaller and smaller in an effort to avoid it. It was hard to explain. Some people would consider reaching the end to be closure. For me, closure meant complete, never to be thought about again, and I couldn't go there. Psychologically I couldn't even wrap my brain around starting a second journal. The journal represented mine and Leah's lives. A person only gets one life. It sounded sadistic, but I couldn't help the way I felt.

The flow of words would not stop, filling two precious pages front and back and practically requiring a magnifying glass to decipher. Every detail from the past week found its way into the journal. My fears were transferred onto the page. It was easy to share with Leah. All my fears, dreams, and pain would be hers also. I told her everything about the ominous dark cloud that I had been seeing over the last week. My fear was tangible as I described it in detail. How it felt like a living, breathing creature. That it showed up in the shadows more frequently than not as the days progressed. I knew if she were here she wouldn't judge me. She would calm me. Convince me I wasn't losing my mind like I feared was happening. All my turbulent emotions poured out. My pain became Leah's as the pages absorbed everything I was feeling.

When I finally finished writing for the evening, I closed the journal and stowed it safely back in its place under the mattress. Sliding down to a more comfortable position, I settled in with my lights on and my television droning on in the background like I preferred. It was easier to fall asleep that way. I wasn't much of a dreamer while I slept and had a tendency to wake up in the middle of the night, so the TV provided some comfort.

I took a deep breath and exhaled, content that my thoughts had once again been purged. Maybe the darkness would be gone tomorrow now that I had confided in Leah. It was a silly thought, but one that gave me peace. Certainly no more silly than believing I was being taunted by something sinister.

The darkness wasn't gone the next day, or the day after that, or all the days that came later. It remained. Always there. In every shadow I passed. Lurking any place with the smallest absence of light. Haunting only me. The fact that no one else could see it made me question if it was real. Deep down I suspected I was unraveling.

LEAH

"WIDER, PLEASE."

I obediently opened my mouth as Mother poked around at my teeth. Every six months she would give me a complete head-to-toe physical, charting all my stats and measurements. I hated physical day. I'm forced to stand still for an hour and a half while I get probed and pinched, and anytime my numbers weren't to Mother's liking, her displeasure was evident.

I'd come to tolerate the physical pain of punishment. At times I think I even looked forward to it in a morbid kind of way, knowing I deserved it. Mother's physicals were a similar exercise of disciplined endurance. Despite hating the poking and prodding, at least I had her attention during the entire process. If I was good, I was awarded with a treat. Last time it was a chocolate bar. I was so excited when she gave it to me and yet I waited three days to open the wrapper. I was afraid I would devour it in one bite. When I finally opened it, the first thing I did was inhale deeply. The aroma of the rich dark chocolate was almost intoxicating. I wanted the treat to last as long as possible, so I would only eat small sections at a time before carefully rewrapping the sinfully good candy again. I managed to make it last almost two weeks.

With any luck today's treat would be another candy bar.

"Your teeth look good," Mother said, switching off her small flashlight. "No cavities," she added proudly, making a notation in my chart.

I beamed at her. "I brush hard every day."

"Not too hard though, right? I don't want you to damage your teeth."

I shook my head. "Only enough to remove all the grime."

She nodded in approval. "Good girl. How about your girl time? I've noticed you haven't used any of your monthly supplies."

I twisted a lock of hair around my finger. "It's not here yet."

Mother studied me critically for a moment. "Well, we know you're not pregnant," she finally chuckled, making another notation in my chart.

The way she laughed made me cringe. Of course I didn't want to be pregnant, but knowing it was never going to be a possibility made me ache. As long as I was here, living in seclusion, I would never have the opportunity for anything. I would never meet a boy, let alone hold hands with one, or know what it felt like to be kissed by one. I recently found myself scouring all my books, searching for the passages where the characters shared any kind of romantic contact. I would underline the passages, imprinting them to my mind so I could hopefully dream about them at another time.

"Don't worry, I'm sure you'll get it soon," Mother reassured me, mistaking my silence for concern about my period.

I smiled meekly, wondering if the time would ever come when I could approach Mother about the possibility of a life for me outside the basement. I appreciated the sacrifices she had made in order to keep me safe from my sickness and care for all my needs, but she wouldn't be around forever. Eventually, I would have to learn to live on my own. For now, I would continue to live vicariously through the characters in my books and hope for a better future.

Mother gave me a quick, unexpected hug. I burrowed into her, cherishing the warmth.

She pulled away as swiftly as she had reached out. I wasn't surprised. Mother had never been the most affectionate person. "Time to weigh-in."

I was never worried about my weight. I'd been under the curve on Mother's charts for as long as I could remember. The glass scale was cold beneath my bare feet, but I didn't flinch as I watched the digital scale scroll until my weight was computed. The numbers held little significance to me, but I couldn't help noticing the frown on Mother's face as she looked at the scale. She checked the chart and then the scale again. "Hop off and then back on again," she said, making a note on my chart. The digital scale scrolled for a second before computing my weight again.

A feeling of unease began squirming in my belly. Mother frowned again, grabbing her measuring tape. I stood still with my arms raised as she measured my waist and hips and then my chest. Each number was carefully documented next to my previous results. I couldn't resist peering over her shoulder as she recorded my arm measurements in the folder. Her displeasure was growing. The uneasy feeling in my stomach turned into a mass of squirming snakes as I saw the mistake I'd made on the paper.

I had ignorantly assumed that my nighttime exercise routine would go undetected. For a solid month and a half I put all my effort into my workouts. I would lovingly stroke my hand over my newly defined arms that no longer felt like cooked spaghetti, marvel at the tautness of my stomach that was no longer soft. My legs were my crowning achievement. They no longer shook from the slightest exertion. I had forced them to endure more resistance than I thought possible. I was so much stronger now. Every muscle in my body practically hummed with anticipation each night, eager to grow. It was so worth it.

That was before the same body I was so proud of was now betraying me. I'd been so naive. Mother was sure to notice the changes. Nothing ever escaped her watchful eye, and even if it did, the numbers would not lie.

The fraught expression on Mother's face became more

severe with each measurement. I wanted to cover myself, but there was no place to go. I couldn't lie or feign innocence. Her measuring tape felt like the blade of an ax resting against the back of my neck. I could almost feel the cold, heavy steel against my skin and wished it would finish the job. Mother would never forgive me for this. She would know. All my secrets would be revealed. Today there would be no reward. She would call what I had done betrayal. She would be right. I was supposed to trust Mother. Not defy her.

Mother remained silent as she slammed my chart closed and stomped around my room. I began to brace myself for the punishment I knew was coming as she methodically searched every square inch of my living space. Every secret I'd been hiding for the past ten years was exposed. My heart shattered as she pulled Daisy from the couch cushions and discarded her in the trash like an old dirty rag. Hundreds of pictures of the sun that I had drawn and hidden among the springs of the couch were shredded and tossed.

Mother practically growled as she moved to my bookshelves. I waited with bated breath, hoping she would not discover my darkest secret of all. She rifled through every book and tossed them to the side when the pages revealed picture after picture of a sun I would never see again. Each discarded book left a gap on my shelf, bringing Mother closer to my secret. I wanted to call out to her. Distract her. Anything to keep her away from the shard of metal I had been hoarding for months. The metal that I'd painstakingly pried away from the cabinet under my sink. It took countless hours of rubbing it against the block wall behind my bed to form it to the right shape and size to fit where I needed it. Another book hit the floor and my heart thundered against the cavity in my chest.

It reminded me of a time long ago when I tried to escape. When I still believed my other mom and dad might want me back if I could only prove I could keep the sun from hurting me. I had crept silently up the stairs and waited for hours by the door that always remained locked. My plan was immature and ill-conceived. Somehow I naively believed that if I could just surprise Mother and race by her as she opened the door, I would somehow be able to find the front door of the house and make it outside. I was so scared. The plan almost worked. Mother wasn't expecting me there when she opened the door, and her hands were full, so I did have the chance to slip around her.

Unfortunately, she cared less about what she was holding and more about snagging me. She was able to snatch me by my narrow wrist and jerk me backward. Her grip slipped though and I went tumbling down the stairs. When I woke my leg was encased in a white cast and Mother didn't talk to me until the day she removed it. It was the longest six weeks of my life.

Book after book was tossed to the floor and Mother hesitated before grabbing another. I held my breath. Maybe she had been satisfied. She already found Daisy and the drawings. I could take that punishment. She would be mad, but in the end, she would forgive me. Before my hope could fully blossom though, she reached for another book. The one I was hoping she wouldn't get to. My head dropped. Months and months of planning wasted. It didn't take a genius to figure out the tool's purpose. She walked over to the boarded-up window and lifted the tool to where it fit easily into the head of one of the screws. All the time. All the effort. None of it mattered anymore.

Mother's face changed, morphing into the monster that lurked deep inside her. I could only watch and wait as she reached for the leather strap hanging on the wall. Her hand closed around it before she bore down on me.

My body, which I had been working to become stronger, was no match for the leather strap. It tore at my tender skin over and over again, swing after swing. A lump formed in my throat, blocking any whimper of pain. My legs shook like a leaf. I was weak. I deserved every lash of the belt. *Weak. Weak. Weak.*

The words repeated in my head in a steady stream, building momentum like a train on a track. I imagined boarding the train, letting it carry me away to the darkness that I knew would shelter me. The words kept repeating as the train moved forward. *Weak. Weak. Weak.* I wanted to go faster, but an unexpected obstacle brought my imaginary train to a screeching halt.

My body felt like it was on fire. Not from the leather strap lashing at my skin. That was a different kind of heat. The sensation was coming from inside my body, buried within my soul. It pushed me to stand, even as Mother continued to swing at me with the strap. I tried resisting. I wanted to retreat to my safe zone like I'd always done, but the mysterious sensation would not allow me to falter. I could feel it taking over whether I wanted it to or not. My mouth opened and a scream erupted from my throat like a volcano. At that moment I knew what had taken over.

Anger. The very emotion I had dismissed long ago as useless.

Anger like I had never felt before. Anger balked at consequences. It never cowered in fear. Anger reached out and grabbed the leather strap before it could strike again. The strap bit into my palm, but that did not stop me from holding on with all my might.

Mother shouted at me to stop, but all I could see was the monster. Fury burned in the monster's eyes as it growled at me. It dropped the strap and launched at me, wrapping its hands around my throat before I could defend myself. My intake of air cut off as the monster's fingers closed tightly around my windpipe. I clawed and bucked beneath its weight, but it was no use. Darkness teased at my senses, but I continued to fight as long as I could. For once, I didn't welcome the darkness.

9

MIA

MY HEAD began throbbing as I left second period. For the briefest of moments I hoped that maybe it had nothing to do with the shadows that wanted to haunt me. Glancing in the direction I needed to go, I whipped around and headed the opposite way. I would be late for class, but it didn't matter. Taking the long way to my locker was the only option. I turned down hallway B and cut over to hallway C, glancing covertly over my shoulder the entire time. It was following me. Two months had passed since the first time I'd seen the ominous dark cloud. It no longer hid anymore. It was bold and followed me anywhere I went. I double-backed down the hallway before scrambling past the door of my second-period class to get to my locker. The hallways were crowded, but I welcomed the crush of coming-and-going bodies. Peering to my right, I could see that my attempt to lose the cloud had failed. The darkness cloaked the entire hallway, covering the walls and the ceiling.

My classmates were oblivious as they went about their business like it didn't exist. Their biggest worry seemed to be avoiding the tardy bell. I had accepted the fact that I was the only one who could see the dark cloud. I'd come to think of it as a creature, one that had yet to harm me physically, but seemed hell-bent on driving me insane. It no longer cared if it was day or night or if I was at home or school. All I knew was that it wanted to torment me. I rubbed my eyes hoping it would fade away, but the creature refused to disappear.

"Hey, did you find your biology notes?" Amber asked, emerging through the ominous cloud that blocked the entire hallway. It freaked me out to see her walk through the darkness unscathed. I wanted to grasp her shoulders and shake her until her teeth rattled in her skull. Did she have any idea what she had done? I would swim with alligators or walk barefoot over burning coals, even jump out of an airplane without a parachute before I would walk through the darkness. Deep-rooted fear gripped my senses anytime I thought about what lay beyond the shadows.

"You okay?" Amber asked, seeing the shudder that rippled down my body, leaving behind goose bumps on my arms. Her tone wasn't exactly condescending, but I sensed she was displeased with me.

It took my brain a moment to categorize her words and compute what she'd asked me. "I'm fine—and yes, I found the notes," I said, handing over the stack of papers I'd gathered the night before.

Amber reached for the folder with greedy hands. "Bless you. I know that old bat would like nothing better than to fail me."

I snickered, ignoring the ice-cold trickle of sweat running down my back as the darkness moved closer, testing the invisible boundaries I tried in vain to keep in place. I could feel the hairs on the back of my neck standing on end.

Holding a conversation was almost impossible with the creature invading my space. I scooted closer to Amber for good measure. I was sick of cowering away in fear, but I was more afraid of getting swallowed up.

"Are you listening to me?" Amber demanded, pulling at my arm in aggravation.

I forced myself to focus on her face. I couldn't blame her for being annoyed. The last two months had been rough. I was a different person. Fear had changed me.

It had become my constant companion. Sleep no longer held any appeal. Closing my eyes only accentuated my paranoia, so I fought it with every fiber of my being. I would lie in bed, watching reruns of old TV shows and infomercials. Any mindless program to keep my mind occupied.

Eventually, my erratic sleep patterns affected my appetite and I began skipping meals. I still went through the whole charade of lunchtime with my friends every day, but my mind was no longer in it. Amber and Luke knew something was wrong. Their confusion quickly eroded to frustration when I offered little to no explanation for my unusual behavior. I wanted badly to confide in them, but how would I put it into words when I didn't understand why it was happening to me?

My appetite and relationships weren't the only thing suffering. For the first time in my life my academic career was slipping away. Homework and test scores took a backseat to what was going on in my head.

I was slowly pulling away from everything and everyone who had been so important to me, and yet I couldn't seem to care.

Jacob was so busy with his own friends and wrestling practice that he hadn't noticed how much I had withdrawn. Luke was confused and hurt. I was starting to ignore his calls and had very little to say when we were together. He was certain that I had decided to end things with him. Amber was tougher. We'd been friends for so long that pulling away without her noticing was impossible. She knew something was wrong and she was hurt I hadn't confided in her.

"Sorry, I missed what you said," I answered. She huffed beside me as we headed to class. I sighed, but didn't say anything. I could feel the anger simmering inside her as we headed for third period. Her frustrations were ready to boil over. Her shoes slapped against the linoleum floor and she swung her arm in an exaggerated motion as she walked. I knew Amber well enough to know that she wouldn't remain bottled up long.

"What the hell is wrong with you, Mia?" she hissed.

Any other time I would have laughed. She was so predictable, like a ticking time bomb. There was no way I could continue feigning ignorance. She wouldn't fall for that again.

I shrugged. "I'm just dealing with some stuff," I said, making a point to not look over my shoulder at the darkness behind me.

She rolled her eyes, jerking me to an abrupt stop. "Is this still about the pool thing? Are you still mad at all of us? That was, like, two months ago. Okay, so we got caught. It's not like we got in any trouble," she said, blowing out an exasperated breath. "Do you want us to tell you that you were right? Is that what you need to hear?"

I started to shake my head and correct her until my mind registered what she had just said. "You guys have been talking about me?" This time it was my turn to be annoyed. How nice that my friends had taken it upon themselves to talk behind my back. "Are you and Luke going to hook up next, now that we're having problems?" It was a cruel thing to say. I knew it the moment the words left my lips.

Amber rolled her eyes. "You're kidding, right?"

I shrugged. I felt so confused lately that I wasn't entirely sure whether or not I was kidding. "I'm not mad," I said. "We could have gotten in a lot of trouble though. We're lucky Luke was a total rock star on the field that night, otherwise Principal Trout could have nailed us to the wall."

"But he didn't. Should we have listened to you? Sure, but come on. You have to agree, it was a rush," she implored as the warning bell rang.

I shook my head. Nothing about that night had been a

rush. She was right about one thing. I had changed, just not in the way she thought. I didn't blame any of them for the nightmare I was living, but it was only happening to me.

She stood in front of me, blocking my way into class. "You have to forgive us," she demanded.

I didn't know how to make her understand that forgiveness wasn't necessary. What I was going through had nothing to do with them. I was dealing with things they couldn't comprehend. And to make matters worse, I had no idea how to explain it. Pretending to care about the trivial things was too much to bear at the moment. "I do forgive you," I said, trying to appease her.

"Bullshit," she said as the second bell rang. We were officially late for class, which was another sign of how much I had changed. My perfect image was cracking at the foundation. I could see it, and by the look on Amber's face, she could see it too. The hallways had emptied, but our silent standoff continued. We were at an impasse.

Amber was the first to break. Sighing, she reached into her pocket and pulled out a pad of signed late passes that she always kept on hand. She tore off two from the top, handing one to me. I reached for it without question, but saw a flash of pain in Amber's eyes. There was a time when I would have balked at taking a pass from anyone other than a teacher, but now I did it without a second thought. Amber knew that and I knew it.

For a moment, I thought again about telling her the truth, not even caring if she believed me. Breaking it off with Luke would be hard enough, but our relationship was superficial in comparison to my friendship with Amber. Best friends were supposed to be forever. I glanced at the darkness to my left that was completely blocking the hallway. A ripple of fear crept down from the nape of my neck. Even if I could get the words out, I had no idea what to say.

Amber's face closed up. She stalked off toward third period without as much as a backward glance. Her movements had finality to them. A lump formed in my throat. I wanted to call her back, to beg her to not be mad, but I couldn't do it. I let her walk away. I crumpled up the late pass she had given me and chucked it into the trash can. As I walked down the hallway, I was well aware that the creature was following me. I didn't pause again at my locker or stop by the office to offer up some lame excuse they would likely buy. After all, I was the good girl, the one who was always on time for class and never missed a day. I got straight As and dated the perfect guy. I managed to do it all in spite of losing my twin sister and living in a house with a family that was a shell of its former self. My life had already been tragic enough. I had no idea what I had done to deserve any more.

I didn't head for the side entrance everyone else used when they wanted to ditch. I walked boldly out the front door, giving no thought to the possible consequences. I left my school behind without bothering to look back. I had one thought: Leah. I needed to connect with her the only way I could. I needed the journal tucked away under the mattress in my room.

10

LEAH

I WOKE to a buzzing noise in my ears. I couldn't see anything, but it gave me comfort to have my eyes open. Judging by the familiar spring poking me in my left hip, I knew I was on my bed. My throat burned like fire had scorched its way down my windpipe. My hands moved to see how tender it felt to the touch, but I was stopped by the rattle of a chain and the cold steel of a handcuff binding my right wrist. I jerked my arm toward me in a panic. The sudden movement made the metal bite painfully into my wrist. I gasped. Not from the pain, but from the surprise of being shackled. I yanked again, harder. The result was the same, only this time I did hurt my wrist. My hand closed around the chain, following it until I reached where it was firmly locked around the metal frame of my bed.

A slight whimper left my lips before I could stop it. Mother had never chained me up before. I knew she would be angry if she ever found out about my plan, but I only wanted to show her that it was okay if I went out at night. I never planned to hurt her or abandon her. I just wanted a chance to be outside, even if for a moment. If she would only listen, I would explain it to her.

My reasoning gave me some comfort. Surely Mother would understand. I closed my eyes, trying to ignore the burning in my throat. I reached with my free hand, searching the small table beside my bed for a glass of water. Mother would never chain me up without providing provisions. I fumbled around blindly on the table, refusing to give up hope. After a few futile seconds, I realized she had proven me wrong. It wasn't worth it to panic. Mother had to be planning on returning soon. This was my punishment for stepping so far out-of-bounds. Mother had her reasons and I had to respect them. She would understand when I finally explained everything to her. Maybe I could even try again to convince her to let me go outside under the cloak of darkness where the sun could not hurt me.

The idea gave me some comfort as I let sleep coax me back into its embrace. Mother would return soon.

• • •

Mother did return.

The basement lights came on, jerking me from an uneasy sleep. I tried to climb out of bed, but forgot about the shackle on my wrist that limited my movements. I sat up so

I could take in the rest of the room. My heart sank when I spotted my empty bookshelf. Every single one of my books had been removed. My couch was completely stripped. The cushions that hid Daisy from sight for so many years were gone. My heart pinched painfully in my chest at the loss of my beloved doll and friend. She was my one and only confidant and champion and now she was gone. I had no idea what I would do without her. I wanted to weep at the loss of my belongings, but I knew I needed to stay strong. I would earn them back. I would prove to Mother that I could be good.

I could hear her heavy footsteps as she descended the stairs. She appeared in the doorway and stopped, staring expressionless at me. I smiled tentatively as an initial apology, searching for any sign that the storm had passed. When she turned her eyes away, I knew all was not forgiven.

I remained patient as she bustled about my bed, roughly removing the blanket and sheet from around my legs and waist. I opened my mouth to apologize. The words were broken and scratchy, hurting my tender throat. Mother never acknowledged me, even when I begged and pleaded for her forgiveness.

She was all business as she tugged my pajama bottoms down and held the bedpan under my bare bottom. It was truly embarrassing. I was capable of using the bathroom if she would just let me up. My bladder couldn't resist the cold plastic and quickly emptied. After I finished, Mother set the pan aside and jerked my pants up without looking at me.

"Mother, I'm sorry," I pleaded as she carried the full container to my bathroom.

She flinched, but didn't answer, working instead to finish her chores. I could hear her rinse out the bedpan before flushing the toilet. A few minutes later she returned with the small cup I used when I brushed my teeth. I searched her face for any sign of forgiveness, but her expression remained as hard as granite.

She held out the cup. I croaked out a thank-you, clasping it tightly. I was afraid she might take it away before I could drink. The first few drops teased my dry lips. I parted them desperately, letting the cold water sooth my burning throat. The contents of the cup emptied long before I was ready. I wanted to ask for more, but she had already turned for the stairs before I could get the words out.

"Mother, I'll be good," I promised in a raspy voice.

It was as if I weren't there. Her only response to my plea was to switch off the lights, plunging the room into darkness again.

I tried not to cry, I swear I did, but I couldn't stop it from happening. Large tears streamed down my face, soaking the pillow on either side of my head. I could have swiped them away but I continued to let them fall. It had been a long time since I'd allowed myself the indulgence. Years of repressed moisture escaped my eyes at an alarming rate. I cried for the mistakes I'd made and for the sins I had committed. I cried for my sister who was stronger than I was. I knew if Mia were here she would be the perfect girl. She would never commit the countless infractions that seemed to come so easily for me. Mia was the good girl. She would never disappoint Mother.

I cried until I dozed off. It was a troubled sleep. The slightest noise would wake me again until eventually I gave up. Lying in the dark, I tried passing the time by counting. That lasted until I grew weary of seeing numbers in my head. I switched to recalling some of my favorite book passages. I would break them down scene by scene to see how much I could remember. My throat dried again to a dull ache with a burning sensation that heightened every time I swallowed.

I found myself yearning for light, even the smallest of beams. The very darkness which had always held me in its tender embrace was now betraying me as an enemy. Its oppressive torment was almost too much to bear as seconds and then minutes and then hours trickled by.

At least my other heightened senses picked up the slack. My ears zeroed in on the muted sounds above me—the creaking of the floor, the faint sound of running water. I was tempted to call out to Mother, but I knew better. I just had to wait. Wait for her return. Wait for her forgiveness.

I was in the process of trying to recite all the US presidents and vice presidents in order when my bladder began to clamor again for relief. I shifted in the bed, ignoring my stomach that cramped from hunger. Crossing my legs, I tried distracting my mind by thinking about anything that didn't have to do with water.

Sometime later, it could have been an hour. Or maybe it

was only a few minutes, I had no way of knowing, my bladder hit a new level of insistence. My mind played tricks on me, pushing me to stand when I knew I was unable to. The urge to get to the bathroom was so strong nothing else seemed to matter. I jerked on my arm, letting the cold steel dig into it. It was agonizing, but still I tugged. I knew my attempts were futile. There was no way my frail strength was any kind of match for the chain that bound me in place. My wrist was tender and raw with fresh abrasions from the cuff. I felt a thin trickle of liquid run down my arm. Without thinking, I moved my arm to my mouth, tasting the slight hint of iron in my blood. It was a reminder that I was still me.

Somewhere between trying to recite poetry and the words to my favorite songs, I lost my battle with bladder control. I would like to have said that I was embarrassed, but the truth was I felt nothing but great relief when it emptied. Mother would be upset over the mess, but my aching side practically wept with joy. I scooted myself as close to the edge of my bed as possible so the majority of the urine would flow to the floor rather than soak my mattress. My pajamas were, of course, soaked, but even that was a small price to pay. When Mother finally returned she would help me clean up since soiled clothes were not allowed. She could punish me again if need be. None of that mattered anymore.

Time continued to drift.

No Mother.

I slept.

No Mother.

I woke.

No Mother.

The same pattern continued over and over again. The second time I emptied my bladder was easier than the first. I gave no conscious thought to it when it happened. Without any food and water, I knew I had likely reached the point where I would have nothing left to give.

11

MIA

MY HAND wouldn't stop bleeding. Not that it was gushing. I watched with morbid fascination as steady droplets of blood bubbled to the surface of my hand before rolling down my palm, past my wrist and over my forearm. The blood left a crimson trail along the hairs of my arm before dripping off and collecting on the thick cream-colored carpet in my room. It was a brilliant red that would have made for a perfect shade of nail polish. I'd worn my fair share of red polishes, but none had captured the brilliance of blood with the way it glistened.

I knew I should get a tissue and Band-Aids, but I remained sitting on the floor with my journal propped up on my knees. The journal was complete. Every single line was filled. Blood stained the pages where my hand rested. The broken plastic pieces of my pen littered the floor around me. It had finally buckled under the pressure of my squeezing grip. For a time while I was writing I lost my head, treating the pen like an appendage. I wanted my own blood flowing from the pen to form the words on the pages.

The emotions I felt upon finishing the journal were as tangible as I expected. There was no relief that my open letter to Leah was finally finished. Even though she had been taken from us so long ago, I couldn't help feeling like she had only now truly left me. The memory of my sister was slowly slipping away, and yet the ache in my heart made me feel as though there was something more. Maybe I really was losing my mind.

A quick rap on my door distracted me from my blood-fascination trance. Before I could answer, Jacob pushed my bedroom door open and stepped into the room.

He took in the blood on my carpet and on my arm and without a word went into my bathroom. I could hear the water running, but didn't move. A moment later he returned with a wet rag. I watched with indifference as he gently lifted my hand and began to clean the blood away. He carefully washed the cut that was the source of all the blood, but I didn't even flinch. It was as if the cut belonged to someone else.

After he finished, Jacob wrapped the rag around my hand to capture any remaining traces of blood. "What's going on, Mia?" he asked, scooting back against my bed.

I shrugged. It was such a broad question. Even if I decided to confide in him, I had no idea where to begin. How did I tell my brother I was losing it? That some monster of darkness was dogging my every step, following me everywhere I looked. How did I find the words to tell him that I was still missing the sister we'd both lost so long ago? It felt wrong to pick at that scab, to reopen the wound that he'd worked so hard to heal. It was selfish on so many levels. I could not tell him any of it.

"Mia?" he probed.

I fixated on the small pool of blood on the carpet that was already drying in a deep rust color that no longer resembled the beautiful red color that had fascinated me earlier. Now it was an ugly color that no girl would want as a polish. "I'm fine," I finally answered when Jacob poked me in the side.

"Liar," he answered immediately, studying me critically.

I shifted on the floor so that I faced him. "Seriously. I accidentally cut my hand with my pen while I was writing, that's all. I was about ready to take care of it when you showed up."

He continued to eye me with the same doubtful expression he always wore when he knew I was hiding something.

I clamped my mouth closed before my tongue could betray my secret. Jacob had a way of getting me to talk. He always had, especially after Leah's disappearance. He was a natural-born listener. Even when my problems were juvenile and adolescent, he never judged me, and he was never condescending.

Jacob's powers of attrition once again overwhelmed my ability to hold firm. I barfed up all the secrets from my vault like an overflowing sewage tank that had to be emptied. I had to hand it to Jacob. He sat patiently listening as I spewed and spewed. He waited to comment until I had finished. I expected to hear him tell me I had lost it, and that I needed to lay off drugs. What else would explain the crazy shit I had admitted other than my brain had to be damaged.

"And you see this 'dark monster' everywhere?" Jacob asked, peering around my room. He would never say it aloud, but I was sure Jacob was skeptical since he couldn't see what I had described for himself.

I nodded, picking at the rust-stained carpet. "Crazy, right?" I didn't need to scan the room with him. I knew where my monster was every second and minute of the day. Without turning my head I knew it was lurking inside my small closet, spilling into my room, but I refused to look at it. "Are you trying to figure out how you can throw me into your car and drive me to some hospital?" I hated the insecurity in my voice, but the thought had to be going through Jacob's head.

He squeezed my good hand. "Well, that's definitely one option. But I was thinking maybe the better option would be to tell Mom and Dad. You could be really sick."

I snorted. "Gee, thanks for that one. I already know my head is broken."

"Well, duh, we all know that," he teased. "I'm not talking about that kind of sick, but something has to be wrong with your brain if you're seeing something no one else can."

"I can't tell Mom and Dad. They've already lost one daughter." I ignored the way he flinched at my words. "They've already lost one daughter," I repeated to make my point. "They don't need the stress of knowing something is wrong with their other daughter."

Jacob shook his head. "You don't always have to be the perfect daughter. It wasn't your job to replace Leah."

"Yes, it was," I said sternly. "I had to make up for the wrong daughter being taken."

Jacob looked shocked. His eyes darkened by a disturbed sadness. "Why would you say that? If you would have been taken, I would have lost my best friend."

I shook my head profusely in disagreement. "That's not true. You would have had Leah. Don't you see? Leah would have been the perfect sister, the perfect friend. I'm just the sad replacement." I felt moisture dripping down my cheeks. I reached up tentatively with my finger to touch the tears. I never cried. Crying was a weakness that I wouldn't allow myself. Crying would not bring Leah back. All it would do was reopen wounds that had never properly healed. After Leah was taken I wanted to cry so bad I felt like my chest would collapse from repressing my tears. I would lie in bed, biting my hand until the pressure would ease in my chest and I was able to breathe again. The crescent-shaped teeth marks on the backs of my hands held little significance other than as a means to suppress my other pain.

"Mia, I couldn't have made it without you. I miss Leah, of course, but you kept me going."

There was no mistaking the pain in Jacob's voice. I was the worst kind of selfish. The kind that kept me preoccupied with my own concerns while those I cared about suffered. I wasn't the only one who had lost Leah or a life that used to be. Jacob was a casualty too.

I reached over to pat his hand. The rag around my palm unraveled and dropped to the floor. My hand was still seeping blood slightly, but it was less vibrant. I knew the cut should hurt, but I could hardly feel it. I'd been blessed, or cursed, depending on your point of view, with a high tolerance for pain. Even when I used to bite my hand at night, the resulting soreness was slow to come.

"Jacob, I'm sorry. You're always so upbeat that I sometimes forget I'm not the only one who lost Leah."

He shrugged it off, but I could plainly see what I'd missed so many times before. "It's not like I was her twin and shared any connection like you two or anything. It just sucks. You know?" he said.

I nodded, wondering why this was the first time we had ever talked this openly. For the past ten years Leah's name had been taboo in our house. At times it was as if she never existed. That was why I started my journal in the first place. I needed the constant reminder of the piece of me that had been taken. Looking at Jacob, I realized my family and I had done a huge injustice by not talking about Leah. Not only to ourselves, but more important, to Leah as well. It was up to us to keep her memory alive.

Jacob and I leaned against each other. Both lost in our own thoughts, the silence swelled between us. "Do you think I'm going crazy?" I finally asked.

Jacob smiled wryly. "I think we're all a little bit crazy. Some of us are just better at hiding it. Do I think you're crazy because you're seeing dark, oppressive monsters?"

"*One* monster. Really, it's not a monster, I just think of it that way," I interjected.

He chuckled. "Sorry. One monster that's really not a monster. The point is, no, I don't think you're crazy. As a matter of fact, you might be the sanest person I know. I'm more worried about what could be physically wrong inside that skull of yours."

I dropped my head onto his shoulder. "So, you do think my brain is malfunctioning?" I asked, wondering if he could be right. Maybe this was all some elaborate hallucination my brain had conjured up because of a tumor that was slowly devouring my brain.

"I don't know, sis, but I think you should tell our parental units. If you don't, I will. It's one thing to keep something like bad grades or whatever from them, but this is something completely different."

I sighed. I knew he was right. It was something I probably should have done two months ago when the darkness first started following me. It just wasn't the kind of information I liked to share with them. Usually our conversations revolved around my accomplishments at school. We never discussed anything negative, and if we did, Jacob would step in and change the subject.

"I'll tell them. Not now though, okay?"

He cocked an eyebrow at me. "When?"

"Soon. Let's get through the holidays first. Christmas is only a few days away."

He didn't argue, but he looked unsettled, like he wanted

to continue pressing me. I knew he'd honor my wishes. Holidays were tough in our house. The first year after Leah was taken, we didn't even celebrate. Christmas came and went without a tree, lights, Santa Claus, or presents. Jacob, of course, took matters into his own hands. He snuck into my room early that Christmas morning and left me a small present on my bed. It was his favorite Green Lantern ring. The ring he had gotten the previous Christmas when we were all still a complete family. He loved that ring. I tried to give it back, but he wouldn't take it. He told me the ring would protect me. Taking his words to heart, I slid the ring on my finger. It was too big, but I still almost believed I could feel its power. I wondered what Jacob would say if he knew I still slept with it under my pillow.

12

LEAH

I NOW hated the dark, despised it for betraying me. For so long I loved it. I had come to truly think of it as a friend. I knew it made no sense. It was one thing to regard an inanimate object as a friend, like my doll, Daisy, but a whole other to give that title to something without substance, like the absence of light. I no longer cared. The darkness and I had an agreement and now it was no longer helping me. It was everywhere, and yet it refused to comfort me in the slightest or even let in the smallest traces of light.

I'd lost track of how long it had been since Mother came to check on me. I was weak from hunger and my throat was as rough as sandpaper. I even stopped daydreaming about food. My desire was gone. Everything inside me had started to give up. My body was broken and I was dying. I knew it with every fiber inside me. Why Mother had saved me so long ago only to let me rot away was beyond me. The urge I had felt to apologize had passed along with any feelings of rage. I just wanted death to hurry.

I curled up into a ball around the chain that bound me to the bed. It was the only comfortable position that allowed me some measure of warmth. The basement wasn't freezing, but the temperatures had dropped recently and my thin blanket was no longer sufficient.

I kept my head tucked under my arm with my eyes tightly closed. Sleep needed to be under my terms. It was silly, but it felt good to have a small measure of control. I wondered if this is what it felt like to be delirious. It wouldn't be that big of a stretch considering what I was going through. Sleep crept up on me to the point where I could no longer resist. My last coherent thought before falling under was of Mia. For years, I believed I would one day see her again, but I now realized that had been a dream. Mia and I would be forever separated.

MIA

JACOB RELUCTANTLY agreed, although under extreme protest, to wait until after Christmas to tell Mom and Dad the truth. Of course, I neglected to tell him that things were escalating.

The darkness was becoming more consuming, tormenting me everywhere I turned. Ignoring it at school had become damn near impossible; it had managed to fracture every relationship I had. My grades were all slipping and Christmas break was my only chance of catching up.

Jacob must have sensed how I was feeling, or maybe he was as scared as I was. The day after I spilled my guts to him, he woke up at the crack of dawn, hell-bent on torturing me. Before I could fully open my eyes, he dragged me from bed telling me to get my ass in gear, that we were wasting the day away. I was hustled out of the house with hardly enough time to pull jeans and a sweatshirt on. Let alone make my hair presentable.

"Jacob, the point of Christmas break is to sleep in," I griped as he shoved me in the passenger seat of his car. "Where are we going anyway?"

He excitedly pulled out of our driveway before I could finish buckling my seat belt. "You'll see," he answered, shooting me a wink.

"There better be coffee," I grumbled. "And doughnuts." I dragged my hair up into a messy bun on top of my head. Tendrils of hair escaped the bun, but I gave them no notice, tucking them behind my ear. My jaw clicked as I yawned widely. I was exhausted. I'd been up half the night keeping a watchful eye on the dark shadow that had taken up permanent residence in my room. The moment I closed my eyes, they would spring back open to find that the oppressive shadow seemed to have expanded just a little bit more. I was terrified about what would happen when it no longer had anywhere left to go. What would happen then?

A cold sweat broke out across my forehead. My hands became clammy and my heart thumped painfully in my chest. I inhaled and exhaled, trying to calm myself down, pushing the thoughts back. Instead I focused on the road ahead of us and not the sight I was sure I would see if I turned to look behind me. It would be there, following us. It was always there.

Jacob's secret destination turned out to be a tree farm. A

very sad tree farm. It was in the parking lot of a dying mall. Half the retail stores had abandoned the shopping center years ago, leaving it with a disarray of shops that seemed to change every few months. Judging by the slim pickings, waiting until two days before Christmas was not the ideal time to be out buying a tree. These trees were better suited for kindling than holding ornaments.

"A Christmas tree, Jacob?" I questioned, following behind him slowly. We hadn't had a tree since Leah. Hell, I wasn't sure we even had decorations anymore. "I'm not sure . . ." My voice trailed off as I eyed the pitiful selection around us.

"Yes, a Christmas tree," he responded, rubbing his hands together with determination. "It's time we start acting like a damn family and I don't care if that starts with just you and me. We're going to walk this lot and pick out a tree. Even if it's a sorry-ass tree," he added, lifting up a wilted limb of a tree that dragged along the ground. "And then we're going to take it home and decorate it. We're going to string so many fucking lights on our tree that this darkness asshole you've been seeing won't be able to touch it." His teeth clanked together as I threw myself in his arms, hugging him hard. My unexpected display of affection startled us both.

We weren't huggers as a rule but at that moment it didn't matter. Ten years of lost affection were made up for in one instant as I conveyed what his words meant to me. I'd been all alone in an ocean of turbulent water for so long. It was as if someone had suddenly thrown me a life preserver. Jacob was that life preserver. He returned the hug without shame. Neither of us cared that we were in the middle of some crappy mall parking lot, standing in the center of a dying tree farm. For that brief moment we weren't a broken family. We were a unit. Jacob and I.

The sound of someone clearing their throat broke the moment. I turned to see an older man wearing a straw hat and dirty overalls watching us with appreciation. "Can I help you?" he croaked. The sound of his voice suggested that he had spent the better part of the last fifty years inhaling two packs of cigarettes a day.

"We're here to get a tree," Jacob replied.

"Figured as much. But I was about to ask if you two wanted a room?" he said, raising his eyebrows at us suggestively.

I wrinkled up my nose. "Eww, no." Gross. Okay, no more hugging in public.

Jacob's face turned pale and then green before answering. "Really, dude? She's my sister," he said with disgust, stalking off to look for a tree. I could still hear him grumbling two rows over.

"Not my place to judge," the old man wheezed as he shuffled off.

Not sure if I should gag or laugh, I trailed after Jacob in search of the perfect tree that needed a home. This would be our Charlie Brown moment.

An hour later we were pulling back in our driveway with the least saddest tree we could find strapped to the roof of Jacob's car and a bagful of Christmas lights.

"What are you going to tell Mom and Dad about the tree?"

I asked. Together Jacob and I undid the ropes that we'd used to bind the tree to the roof.

"You mean 'if' they ask?"

"Good point." Chances were Mom and Dad wouldn't care either way. A part of me hoped they would. Even if it made them feel something, even if it made them sad, or even if it made them spitting mad. Anything was better than the constant nothing.

Jacob hoisted the tree easily onto his shoulder. I carried the bag of lights, ignoring the nagging feeling that I was being followed. Constantly followed.

It took most of the morning and early afternoon to decorate the tree. Jacob continued with his onslaught of cheer. He was jovial and loud and had Christmas music playing in the background as if he had researched how to be festive. He kept up a constant stream of forced conversation and trivial questions that led to mindless rabbit-hole discussions. He never gave my brain a chance to dwell on my problems. What he hadn't counted on though were the memories that assailed us both as we dug through the ornaments. Ten years of forgotten memories slugged us in our chests with the force of a jackhammer. We weren't prepared to see the ornaments from a different lifetime. By the time we were done both of us had tears in our eyes.

When we finished the tree was no longer empty. Jacob bent down to plug in the lights. He made an exaggerated drumroll noise with his lips before switching the lights on. We stood back to survey our work. Jacob was definitely right, the tree was bright—it lit up half of the room. The only problem was it still wasn't enough, and we both knew it. Maybe it would never be enough. The darkness Jacob had worked so hard to get me to forget was still there waiting for me in the shadows.

LEAH

THE LIGHT flickered on, making my eyes burn. I pulled the blanket tighter around my face, but it was a weak shield. The light was unrelenting. I had wanted it so badly after being left in the dark for days. Now the light flooded the room, making my head spin. I couldn't remember why I thought I had missed it.

My senses, which had been cut off so abruptly, felt overwhelmed. The sound of footsteps on the stairs pounded like they were walking on my own head. If my weakened voice would only work I would beg the noise to stop. I curled up tighter in my cocoon. Whether Mother had forgiven me no longer mattered. I wanted this life no more.

I could hear Mother's voice over the buzzing in my head. She was singing to me like she used to when I had first come to live with her. Years ago her crooning had given me comfort; now it was poison to my ears. I was a void, an empty vessel.

She tugged at my arm, but I made no movement in response. The shackle around my wrist clicked open and dropped to the floor. My arm fell listlessly to the bed.

"My poor baby is so weak," Mother clucked, smoothing her hand across my forehead. My head lulled to the side, insensitive to her affection. "It's okay. Mother will take care of you. First, I need to clean you. Don't worry. I'm not mad that you soiled your clothes. You've been a sick girl."

My eyes remained closed and unresponsive. I did not flinch. I did not move. I was dying. Mother had to know that. Would she be sad when I was gone? My thoughts became muddled. I had just woken up and yet still felt that I could drift off into a deep slumber.

The sound of running water jerked me awake. How much time had passed? I had no idea. Reality and dreamland had become one and the same.

"Drink," Mother said, appearing at my side with a cup of water. If I would have been stronger maybe I would have flinched, but my reflexes were as weak as the rest of my body.

The cool cup touched my lips, but they refused to part. My body was no longer thirsty. Couldn't she see that? I was gone.

"If you don't drink, I'll have to hook you up to an IV."

I watched her with dreary eyes, giving no reply.

She sighed and rose from the bed. "Fine. We'll have to do

this the tough way. I will not let you die because you refuse to drink. You are mine. I have no intention of letting you go."

Her words floated in the air between us as the significance of their meaning hit me like a bolt of lightning. The buzzing in my head intensified, drowning out the sound of her footsteps as she walked upstairs. She was wrong. My body had already given up. My mind yearned for peace. She could not take that from me.

I willed myself to move. My limbs protested, but I forced them to cooperate. With legs like limp noodles, I rose to my feet, fighting the dizziness that came from being upright for the first time in days. I sagged against the wall, breathing heavily. Time was of the essence. Using the wall for support, I forced my feet to move. My steps were sluggish, with a strong urge to stop. I ignored them. They could give up when I got to my destination.

Somehow I made it to the stairs. My intention had been to climb them, but their height was daunting before my eyes. I would not make it to the top before she returned. I knew it without a shadow of a doubt. There was no place to hide. I reached for the only hope I had. My hand hesitantly closed around it. I was not strong enough for this. Mother would not allow it.

Her footsteps were nearing the stairs. It wasn't too late to return to bed. My body wanted to sag to the floor as indecision filled my head. Down the steps she came. *Tap. Tap. Tap.* I tightened my grip, worried that I would fall. Her foot reached the last step.

I could see the surprise on her face as she rounded the doorway, only to be replaced by shock as I swung the strap. The very strap that had battered and bruised my body for years. The hardened, brass-plated buckle that was fastened at the end of the heavy-duty leather strap caught Mother across the temple. I should have felt remorse when she crumpled to the floor. I had done the unthinkable, and yet I felt nothing as I stepped over her body.

Soon it would be over.

All I had to do was get up the stairs.

Each step was taller than the last. I gripped the railing hard in my hand, using every bit of strength my body would muster to pull myself up. The open door was within sight, but so far away at the same time. It had always remained closed and there it was open, taunting me. Mother believed I was too weak to leave her. Little did she know I would find the strength. I just needed to make it to the top. My legs shook from exertion, but they kept working, allowing me to crest yet another step and bringing me closer. I could hear the first stirrings of movement behind me. I needed to hurry. It took two attempts for my foot to clear the last step.

I could hear Mother on the steps behind me. She was angry. My punishment would be severe if she caught me. It didn't matter. I lunged forward into the kitchen I had only seen one other time. The room was nothing like the prison I had spent the last ten years locked in. Bright with sunlight, it gave me hope that I would get to see the sun one last time. Joy filled my heart, filling me with adrenaline. I couldn't stop now.

Mother was seconds away. With a sudden surge of strength, I slammed the basement door closed and engaged the locks as she crested the last step. My window of opportunity would be short. Mother had keys. She would unlock the door and crush the very last bit of existence I had left.

I stumbled toward the front door, fighting off the relentless fatigue in my muscles. I was so close. My hand closed around the doorknob, but when I turned, nothing happened. "No, please!" I screamed, hearing Mother coming through the basement door. My hands shook feverishly, fumbling with the locks until finally I was able to pull it open.

Sunlight bathed my face, immediately blinding my vision. I waited for the pain that I was sure would come. It would be a welcome ending. I tripped down a small set of steps, barely staying upright if not for the porch rail. I still couldn't see. The end was close. Soon I would sink into the darkness once and for all.

"Leah, stop!" Mother shouted behind me, but she was too late. I stumbled out to the road where the sun's rays reflected off the black asphalt like a beacon. I was almost home. My body ached more than it ever had before and I wondered if it was the sun already killing me.

I heard the sound of screeching tires and cars crashing together. My body hit the pavement like a rag doll, but I felt nothing. A sea of yelling voices surrounded me. Horns and sirens swelled inside my ears. The sounds jumbled together like white noise. I opened my arms, welcoming my old friend, the darkness. The voices continued to pull at my senses, intrusive and annoying. I wanted to swat them away like pesky insects, but my arms were leaden. Then I remembered Mother. Where was she? I could feel my body moving and I opened my mouth to protest. I did not want to go back to the basement. I couldn't go back.

"It's okay, honey. We got you," said an unfamiliar voice as I was lifted onto a bed. I could feel the bed moving beneath me, followed by the shrill sound of a siren. Unexpected terror filled me. I had been through this before, not knowing where I was going, what was happening. "We're going to give you something for the pain," the same soothing voice spoke again. "You're safe now."

I shook my head. There was no pain. I felt nothing. What was safe? Did she know the sun had harmed me? I couldn't make sense of anything that was being said.

Time lost all meaning. My brain was mush. Eventually, I stopped hearing any sound. I had reached my bliss. I wanted to thank them, but my tongue was thick and uncooperative. I stopped trying to figure things out when my eyes closed.

I woke up suddenly as my eyelids were pried open and a bright light shined in my face. Tubes stuck out of my arms and the familiar IV needle protruded from my hand. The whole thing had been a dream. I never hit Mother with the strap, never made it outside. Mother had been right. I was hers.

"I'm sorry, Mother," I said, wondering if any more trouble was coming. It was not her face that peered down at me. An older gentleman in a white coat smiled as he patted my arm.

"You're going to be okay, young lady. Your parents are on their way."

Parents? Clearly I was still dreaming. It was the only explanation. I would wake up and Mother would be here. She would be mad, but that was okay. At least I got to feel the warm sun once, if only in my dreams. Strangely, the pain I remembered from before was gone. My world was back to normal.

The sound of voices startled me again sometime later. I was still too groggy to comprehend them, but a cool hand clasped mine as the voice spoke again. It sounded familiar. One that I hadn't heard in a long time. I had to still be dreaming. My fingers wanted it to be real. They closed tightly around the hand holding mine. The illusion would disappear as soon as I opened my eyes. A part of me wanted to keep this dream as long as possible. I could hear the voice murmuring, thick with tears.

My eyes fluttered open of their own accord and I recognized her instantly. She was older, her face lined more than I remembered and covered in tears, but the smile was the same. "Momma?" I croaked.

"I'm here, sweetie," she wept, stroking my forehead.

15

MIA

THE DARKNESS had become more consuming. It smothered my room, blocking out all light. There was no way to fight. It wasn't something I could push away. I did the only thing that seemed rational at the time and slipped on Jacob's Green Lantern ring that no longer felt quite as big on my finger, and pulled my blankets up over my head. I clamped my eyes closed, telling myself the darkness couldn't get me under the blankets. I pretended the tugging sensation I felt at my feet wasn't real. It couldn't be. I wanted to wake up Jacob but I was too terrified to even move. The darkness wanted to snatch me away, like a monster from the scariest of horror stories. Why didn't I listen to Jacob and tell Mom and Dad? They could have helped me.

My room became oddly cold. I shivered uncontrollably,

clutching my blanket tightly around my body. The tug at my feet grew stronger, but I refused to peek. Deep in my heart I knew the time to run and hide had passed, but I couldn't bring myself to face it. My heart thundered fiercely in my chest like a runaway train. I wondered, maybe even hoped that my heart would give out before the darkness could take me.

The seconds ticked by, measured by my steady pulse. No longer able to take the torture a moment more, I slowly began to pull the blanket away from my face. Inch by inch, until I could feel the cold air on my forehead. It kissed my eyelids as I tugged the blanket down over the peak of my nose. Finally, after what felt like an eternity, my face was completely uncovered. My eyes remained nailed shut. I couldn't decide if it was more terrifying not to look.

The moment I opened my eyes, nothing would ever be the same again. I could feel it.

My eyelids did not open slowly when I removed the blanket. Instead they popped open abruptly, as if I no longer had control over my own body, exposing the darkness at once.

Fear is a monster. Once you let it in, it eats you from the inside out.

In spite of that, fear was not the enemy. My enemy was the absence of everything. A scream rose in my throat but never found an exit as the darkness finally took what it wanted most. Me. The darkness had won.

16

LEAH

MY HEAD was a mess. Nothing made any sense. I faded in and out to the sounds of machines beeping loudly around me. The prick of a needle going into my arm made me gasp. Voices shouted over each other, making it hard to discern what they were saying. At times it was as if I was floating. Time had no sense of meaning. Each moment I managed to pry my eyes open a different face peered down at me. I called out for Mother but she never seemed to be there. Tubes were shoved in my nose and suddenly I could breathe easier.

I slept.

I woke.

More machine beeps again. This time I opened my eyes to see faces that felt vaguely familiar. Their lips moved but their words confused me. I called out for Mother again. My heart raced, causing my pulse to thump madly against my skin. There were too many voices. I covered my ears and clamped my eyes closed. Every bone in my body felt leaden and heavy. I just wanted to sleep, to be left alone without anyone talking over me, or poking me or prodding me. I just wanted them to stop. I needed space. A moment to process everything. It was all too much.

The words refused to come, stuck somewhere in my lungs, which had become a fist, squeezing any available air. I couldn't breathe. My chest heaved as gasps of air wheezed out of me.

"Breathe, honey. Just breathe." The familiar face appeared again at my side, stroking a hand over my forehead to soothe me.

"Where's Mother?" I asked, trying to look beyond the many bodies in the room. "Mother. Don't be mad."

Then the familiar face broke. One minute it was beaming down at me, the next it looked at me like I'd killed her. Before I could understand what I did done wrong, her face disappeared from sight. Grief seeped in like a wave washing away everything in its wake.

"You're okay, sweetie," a young nurse said as she adjusted a dial that caused more air to pour through the tubes in my nose. "Just breathe."

Fresh oxygen flooded my lungs. I inhaled deeply, working to regain my composure. "You're okay," the familiar voice murmured. Although I recognized her face, I hesitated to put a name to it. She stroked my forehead again with a gentle touch, tears flowing down her cheeks. I had so many questions, but my eyes felt heavy and refused to stay locked on hers. I fell unconscious before I could get the next word out.

She's there each time I'm awakened, always on the outskirts, silently hovering. Her presence was comforting amid the unfamiliar sounds around me, but my eyes refused to stay open for more than a few seconds at a time. During the brief moments I would awaken there always seemed to be a new nurse or doctor peering down at me. I found it hard to keep up. After so many years of having only Mother seeing to my needs it was unsettling to have so many people constantly around me, the buzz of voices, knowing that I was being talked about. And yet the gist of their words was just beyond my comprehension. I craved the peace of my basement. At least there it would have been quieter, less chaotic.

The firm grip of a blood-pressure cuff around my arm is what finally woke me on a bright morning. I glanced around my room and found that I was alone except for a nurse. I had expected to see the woman with the familiar face again, but as far as I could tell she was nowhere around. Had my mind played tricks on me? Maybe she had never been there at all. The thought occurred to me that maybe I had been taken to Mother's hospital? I braced myself, anticipating the moment she would walk through the door, sure to be angry over all the trouble I had caused.

"Well, hello there," chirped the nurse taking my blood pressure, seeing that I was awake. She beamed down at me. "How are you feeling?"

"Okay," I croaked, surprised that my voice was so rough.

"Here you go, honey. You're severely dehydrated." She held a cup of water out for me so I could sip from the bendy straw. Her cheerful tone and caring bedside manner was a steep contrast to Mother's. My own mouth turned up in a smile in response. "We have you hooked up to fluids but your throat is going to feel very dry for a while."

I drank greedily from the cup, not sure I could ever remember a time I had been so thirsty.

"Not too fast," she said, pulling the cup back slightly. "We don't want you to get sick."

I released the straw from my lips like she wanted but still felt like I could have guzzled a gallon of water if she would have let me. "We" don't want you to get sick. That was what she had just said. I couldn't help wondering who the "we" was. Actually, I had a million questions buzzing around in my head. Before I could get my tongue to wrap around them though there was a knock on my door.

"Mother," I whispered. A tremble radiated throughout my body. I knew I needed to apologize but I wasn't ready yet. Bile rose in my stomach and I wished I were alone. The bright, cheery nurse shouldn't have to see my punishment, to witness my shame.

"Can I come in?" a rich, female voice asked.

I let out a breath, sinking back in my pillows.

"Hello, I'm Dr. Marshall," the woman said as she entered my room. She held out a thin hand with long fingers and a perfectly sculpted manicure. I stared at her hand for a long moment. Oddly, I'd never shaken another person's hand before. She smiled patiently, waiting until I was ready. I tentatively reached out my own hand and placed it in hers. My hand looked pasty and dead in comparison.

I watched apprehensively as she settled into the chair next to my bed.

"How are you doing?" she asked conversationally, like we were old friends.

I stared at her mutely. There seemed to be no right answer to the question. Everything was very confusing at that moment.

"I talked to your doctors and they tell me you're going to make a full recovery, considering." Her eyes clouded over briefly on the last word.

"Are you one of my doctors?" I asked. My voice was still croaky and I wished I had more water.

"I'm a psychologist here at the hospital. In cases like yours, the hospital likes to bring in someone of my expertise early on. We're going to have a lot of chats, if that's okay with you?"

I nodded as I rubbed my wrist. I didn't think Mother would like it, but I didn't mention that.

"I imagine you'll be glad to have your IV removed soon."

I looked down at the tubing attached to the needle in my hand and absently scratched at it. Up until then I hadn't given it much thought. It was more tolerable than the handcuffs that had bound me to the bed in my basement room. My eyes shifted to my other wrist covered in a thick gauze bandage.

"I work in the medical field, but I've always hated IVs," Dr. Marshall rattled on in spite of my silence. "And what about when they're trying to find your vein with the needle?" She shuddered for emphasis. "Do you hate needles too?"

I shrugged my shoulders again. I ran her question through my head. Was I afraid of needles? It was a trivial thing considering there were worse things to fear. Mother gave me shots and I always knew that I needed to hold still. I did dread it when she would appear with shots in hand. Did that mean I was afraid of needles?

"Mother wouldn't allow me to be afraid of them. I held still because I was told to," I said.

Dr. Marshall remained indifferent, more curious than anything. "Mother?" she inquired. "Is that the woman you were staying with, Judy Lawson? You call her Mother?" she asked, jotting something on the notebook that sat on her knees.

"Yes," I answered though I didn't know that was Mother's name. I remember one time making the mistake of asking Mother what her name was and she slapped me in the mouth in response, insisting that Mother was all I needed to know. After that I never ever considered bringing it up again. "Is that wrong?" I asked as the doctor continued to make her notes.

She looked up from her notepad. "Nothing you say is wrong. I know you're confused. I'm only here to help you. Can you trust me to do that?"

My fingers plucked nervously at the blanket beside me. I

was afraid of the trouble this would cause and I wasn't sure Dr. Marshall understood that, but I wanted to trust her. I nodded again.

She smiled brightly at my words. "Very good. We're destined to be friends by the time we work all this out."

I smiled tentatively. "I've never had a real friend," I said.

Her face clouded for the briefest of moments before spreading back into a smile that didn't quite reach her eyes. She could not fool me. I may not understand a lot of things, but studying facial expressions had been a means of escaping punishment. Mother's moods could be read like pages in a book.

"I'm honored to be your first."

I instantly responded to her smile, feeling more at ease than I had since arriving at the hospital.

"I think if we're destined to be friends though, we should be formally reintroduced. Hi, I'm Dr. Alexandra Marshall," she said, holding her hand out again. "You can call me Alexandra."

I couldn't hold back a smile. Something about her made me feel like I could trust her. "I'm Leah," I said, shaking her hand like a pro.

I watched as she released my hand and jotted something on her pad. Had I done something wrong? My eyes moved to the paper, but the way she held it made it hard to make out her words. "I see. Well—Leah," she said, pausing on my name. "What do you remember about the day you were rescued?"

"I left," I answered simply. "Mother was angry, she probably still is. I knew the sunlight was bad for me. She warned me but I had to see for myself. Is that why I've been so sick?"

"Judy Lawson told you the sunlight would make you sick?" she asked, twirling her pen.

"Yes. In technical terms it's called Erythropoietic Protoporphyria but that's a pain to say. Basically, I'm allergic to the sun."

"Were you always allergic to the sun?"

"Since I was little," I answered uncomfortably. I didn't want to admit that my parents had given me up because of my sickness. "Mother knew how to take care of me."

"Speaking of which, there are some people here who are pretty anxious to see you," Dr. Marshall said, almost as if she had read my mind. "Are you excited to see your family?"

I shrugged. "They gave me up when I got sick. I'm not sure how I feel about seeing them. I can't wait to see Mia though," I said with open honesty and excitement.

Her face shifted into a forced smile.

"I see. Tell me about Mia."

"Mia is my twin sister," I said, barely able to get the words out.

"Your twin?" Dr. Marshall asked. "Did Judy tell you about Mia?"

I shook my head. Why would Judy tell me about Mia? I was old enough when she took me to live with her to remember my family. "I could never forget Mia," I said with conviction.

"I understand. Why don't you tell me a little about Mia."

I nearly laughed out loud in relief. It would be a piece of cake to talk about Mia.

"Mia is amazing," I started, feeling happy for the first time in days. "We're twins, but she's everything I'm not. She's funny, smart, and she's always good," I said, wishing my voice would stop shaking. It wasn't like I was admitting that I wasn't necessarily good, but she might have drawn that conclusion. Would she be less inclined to be my friend if she learned all the bad things I'd done? Probably.

I pushed the negative thoughts back in my mind and continued describing Mia, the perfect twin.

There were so many things I knew about Mia. I talked in great detail, proudly boasting over all her attributes.

"You seem to know a lot about your sister," Dr. Marshall said when I finally finished.

"Of course I do. She's my twin," I said indignantly. Did she really think I wouldn't know my own sister?

Dr. Marshall nodded, jotting again in her notebook. "I have to admit, I'm a little confused. Some of the things you remember about Mia don't match up with your time with Judy Lawson."

I looked at her blankly, wondering what her point was.

"For example, you mentioned that Mia is a straight-A student, but you were six years old when you were taken. Your parents tell me that the school year had just started when you disappeared. That's a little early for grades, isn't it?" Her tone remained soft and careful. "How do you know Mia is a straight-A student?" she gently prodded. Her question caught me off guard and I couldn't help recoiling away from her.

My head began to pound painfully.

Pound.

Pound.

Pound.

I rubbed my temples, searching for an answer that would make the throbbing subside.

"You also said that Mia likes to volunteer when she's not doing schoolwork or hanging out with her friends." Her words continued to pierce my head like a knife.

Pound.

Pound.

Pound.

I couldn't concentrate. "She's my sister. I have to know these things," I mumbled. None of this was making sense.

Pound.

I massaged my temples harder. Her questions were ridiculous. I had the sense that she was trying to trick me, but I had no idea why. Everyone knew Mia was a straight-A student, and all the other stuff I had said too. Why would I lie about that? All she had to do was ask around.

Pound.

"Leah, honey, do you understand that Judy Lawson kidnapped you?"

Pound

Pound

Pound

My head was splitting open, making speech no longer possible. I could only gape at her. She was wrong. Mother took me in when nobody else wanted me. I shook my head defiantly.

"Sweetie, Judy changed your name. You are Mia Klein. There is no Leah."

17

MIA

A SCREAM never left my throat.

The blackness I'd feared for so long seeped into my open mouth.

I could not breathe.

It was everywhere.

I could feel it spreading throughout my body.

Consuming me.

I tried to close my mouth to stop it, but my body no longer belonged to me.

The darkness filled every part of me.

And I ceased to exist.

PART TWO

18

"DOES YOUR head hurt?" Dr. Marshall asked sympathetically.

I couldn't answer her. My world was spinning out of control. Didn't she see that? Her lips were moving, but the roaring in my head allowed no sound to enter. I tried to process her words, but they made no sense. Mother cared for me all those years. How could she have . . . No, it just wasn't possible. She told me time and again that Mom and Dad didn't want the burden of me. Could she really have taken me from my family? I wanted to lash out. Lash out at Mother for what she had done. Lash out at Dr. Marshall for telling me.

I slammed my eyes closed, hoping for some sort of relief. Instead, images filled my head, playing like a movie. Images of me playing outside with Daisy and then suddenly being shoved in a car. Images of the days that followed of me screaming and crying for Mom and Dad. Images of the shots and the drugs that kept me medicated that she had given me and the sickness that had followed, which had been blamed on my allergy to the sun. Lies. All lies.

And Mia.

My Mia.

My twin.

It wasn't possible.

How could I have imagined my sister? My amazing twin who I loved more than anyone in the whole world.

I wanted to hurl. If my stomach hadn't been empty I would have. Instead all I could manage were uncontrollable dry heaves, twisting my stomach until it felt like it was being ripped from the inside out. Someone reached for my arm, trying to calm me, but I fought them off. I was inconsolable. I wished I had never left Mother's house. Why did I leave? In one swift moment I had lost everything I believed in.

When I woke hours later the sun was no longer shining through my window. The blinds were still open, so I could see the stars sparkling in the night sky. I couldn't remember ever seeing stars before or how beautiful they were. They weren't warm like the sun, but they held my attention just the same. My mind drifted to Dr. Marshall, but I pushed it to the far recess of my mind. I wasn't ready to accept her uninvited truth. I physically ached from my loss.

I was so deep in thought I didn't notice the chair next to my bed shifting.

"Hi, honey."

The woman with the familiar face had returned. I mean Mom, I guess. I knew who she was. Mother led me to believe she didn't want me and then suddenly she was here. She did want me all along, so did my father. I didn't know how to wrap my brain around this revelation. Thinking about it made my head start to pound painfully all over again.

I eyed her warily, unsure of what she expected from me. For that matter, what anyone expected from me. I had no idea who I was anymore. Dr. Marshall's last words blared through my head. "You are Mia Klein. There is no Leah." The statement was like a tidal wave that wiped out my entire world. I blinked and a line of tears tracked down my cheeks, blurring my vision.

Mom stood up and grabbed a handful of tissues. I expected her to hand them to me but she reached over and gently mopped the tears from my cheeks. "I'm so sorry, sweetie," she murmured, stroking my hair. Reflexively, I jerked away. Her eyes clouded over.

"I'm sorry," I croaked.

Her eyes brimmed with unshed tears. "Never apologize, Mia." I flinched at the name, but she missed it as she reached for the plastic pitcher sitting on a tray opposite the bed.

"Thank you," I said, accepting a cup of water gratefully. I took a long swig before placing it on the table.

"It's my pleasure, honey." A tear escaped her overflowing eyes.

"Are you sad?" I asked. I had Dr. Marshall's version of the

truth, but I had to hear it from Mom. I needed proof that this was all real.

She shifted forward in her seat and wiped away her tears as she smiled. "No, baby. I'm just really happy. I never thought I would see you again. When I think about what that monster did to you—" Her voice broke off as a man entered the room—Dad. He was older than I remembered. They both were. Of course they were. It had been a long time. His hair had slightly grayed and he had more wrinkles around his eyes. The easy smile I fondly remembered from years ago was absent. His face was distant and guarded.

"Hello, Mia. How you feeling?" he asked formally, stepping around Mom's chair. I flinched again at the name, only this time it hadn't gone unnoticed. Mom and Dad exchanged a look of uncertainty.

Snakes of dread withered in my stomach.

They knew.

I was fractured.

I closed my eyes, wishing I could block out the world. Sleep would have been welcomed. My new reality was as difficult as the one I had just escaped from.

My eyes opened again with Dad staring down at me. He did not reach out and I was relieved. His granitelike expression was more difficult to read.

"I'm okay," I lied. I wasn't hurting on the outside, but between Dr. Marshall's bombshell and Mom's tears and piercing words about Mother, my insides were a tangled mess. "Can you tell me what happened?" I asked.

Mom shook her head but Dad stopped her by placing a hand on her shoulder. "She deserves to hear it from us. It's all over the TV and besides, she's already been questioned by Detective Newton." He talked over me like I wasn't there but I caught the gist of his words. Mother was in trouble—had she been caught?

"Mia can't handle this after what happened this afternoon." Mom's voice rose an octave higher. "We shouldn't be pushing her."

"She has a right to know," Dad clipped out. The tension in the room became thick and uncomfortable.

Mom protested again but I interrupted her. "I have to know." She sank deeper into her chair as if my words had deflated her.

Dad began again in a flat tone, filling me in on what they knew about my abduction. On a bright sunny day in August of 2007, Judy Lawson had taken me from our front lawn when I was six years old. Mom and Dad hadn't given up on me like I was led to believe. According to Dad they had done everything in their power to find me. They worked with the FBI and even hired private investigators when the authorities eventually gave up the search.

Ironically, Mother's house—Judy's house—as it turned out was less than four miles from our house. Considering how long I remained locked in the basement, it may as well have been oceans apart. On the day that I escaped, an off-duty sheriff's deputy, who lived two houses from Judy, was outside watching his kids ride their bikes they had received that morning for Christmas when I burst from Judy's house and ran out to the middle of the street. He was the one who called the ambulance when he saw my scars and fresh bruises. Judy tried to get away in the confusion but he apprehended her before she could escape.

I sat in mute shock as all the details were laid out for me. Halfway through Dad's recollection Mom reached for my hand to comfort me. I had to fight the urge to pull away, not wanting to hurt her. I knew she was happy to have me back but I didn't know her. I didn't know either of them.

Mom squeezed my hand. "Are you up to some company?" she asked once Dad had finished. "Jacob has been eager to come see you, but we wanted to talk to you first. I don't think wild horses will keep him away any longer," she added.

Jacob?

Jacob was here?

I'd been afraid to ask about him. Fearing he was no more real than Leah. "Yes, of course I want to see him."

Dad left my side and opened the door. Jacob walked in hesitantly. He wasn't what I had been picturing. He was bigger and broader in the shoulders than Dad, and his hair was long. It hung almost to his collar and looked windblown. As he moved toward my bed, I couldn't help scooting back apprehensively. This was not my Jacob. The person standing in front of me was virtually a stranger. I searched his face for the boyish features I remembered from so long ago. Ten years of erased memories had me starting from scratch. There was nothing I remembered about his hardened face until he stretched into a slow smile. And then I saw it. The way his mouth quirked. It was faint, but familiar.

"How's it going, Mia?" he asked, reaching up to ruffle my hair like he had done when we were younger, another gesture I remembered.

The corners of my mouth stretched into a tentative smile. "Jacob," I breathed, surprising everyone by laughing with delight when he gave me a crushing hug. I could hear Mom chastising him to be easy with me, but I burrowed into his embrace. I couldn't remember the last time I'd been hugged with so much compassion. It felt like home.

He pulled away at Mom's urging. "Sorry. Did I hurt you?" he asked with concern, plunking down on the foot of my bed.

Dad and Mom exchanged a look, but neither made him get up. I was glad. Jacob, I knew. Jacob was a part of a different life.

"You didn't hurt me. I forgot what a hug like that felt like," I said, not giving much thought to my words. Only when I saw Dad flinch and Mom look away did I second-guess myself. Even Jacob looked visibly shaken. "I'm sorry. I won't talk about Moth—Judy, if you don't want me to," I said quietly.

Mom rushed to my side. Her eyes were bright with unshed tears again, but she maintained her composure. I was relieved. "Sweetie, we want you to be able to talk to us. You can tell us anything. The good and the bad." She gulped hard on the last word before throwing her arms around me. Her hug was gentler than Jacob's, but felt just as loving. My initial reaction was to stiffen, but she held on and after a moment I relaxed into her. Her embrace was so familiar that my own eyes felt damp. Just the scent of her had my mind suddenly recalling images long forgotten. Burrowing my nose into her neck, I tried to distinguish the smell. It was the outdoors. And then I remembered. Mom liked to plant flowers in the garden. That was the scent I remembered, the grass, the soil, playing in the sunshine. The sunshine that wasn't my enemy. Judy had taken this from me.

19

"**HOW ARE** you feeling today?" Dr. Marshall greeted me the next morning.

"Okay," I lied, watching as she claimed her seat from the day before.

I eyed her apprehensively. That was everyone's favorite question. Last night I had been able to push our disastrous first session to the back of my mind with the distraction of my family's visit. Now with the bright sunlight streaming through the window, there was no escaping her previous visit that had unraveled in my head.

"It was a tough session. I'm sorry I caused you pain. That was the last thing I wanted to do. Do you still trust me?"

I hesitated for a moment before shrugging. Did I trust her? I didn't know. Did I trust anyone? I wasn't sure about a lot of things, but I knew that none of it was her fault.

"Do you have any questions for me?" she probed gently.

Her question wasn't funny, but a hysterical laugh churned in my stomach, begging for a release. I held it back. She already thought I was crazy enough. No reason to give her more ammunition. I had about a million questions for her, but I had no idea where to begin. Everything I believed to be true was rapidly unraveling.

Dr. Marshall sat patiently while I tried to work through the conflicting demons in my head.

After a few minutes, I was able to contain the maniacal laugh before it could surface. "How could I make up a sister?" I asked. "Am I crazy?" The words came out in a rush on top of one another.

"*Crazy* is a word I don't like to use. Is your brain a little confused? Yes. But that's why I'm here. Together we're going to figure things out. Okay?"

"Okay."

"Good. Look at us making a step in the right direction," she teased, smiling at me. "As for your first question, that's a bit more complicated. Our brains are our most important organ. They control everything we do and everything that we are, and yet they are very fragile. A simple bump on the head can cause the brain to swell and completely stop functioning. In spite of that, the brain is a magnificent organ. It is designed to protect not just itself, but the body it resides in. When a person is put through a trauma that is severe enough, the brain has a way of shutting down certain aspects. It also provides a way to escape a situation. As we begin to learn more about your time with Judy Lawson, we will hopefully find a connection that will lead us to your sister, who more than likely saved you. I do not want you to resent the Mia you created. It was through her that you are most likely here with us today."

I mulled over her words. It was a lot to digest and I was still having a hard time grasping the idea that I had made up a whole person.

"Do you have more questions?"

I nodded, pulling my bottom lip in between my teeth. I was terrified of my next question and wasn't sure how to even ask it.

Dr. Marshall didn't push. She sat back in the chair with her legs crossed, patiently waiting for me to form my thought.

"Who is Leah?" I asked the question so timidly I was surprised she could hear me.

Judging by her expression, I could tell my question had thrown her off guard. This time it was her turn to search for the right words. I wasn't as patient though. My fingers fidgeted nervously in my lap and my right foot tapped the bed rail over and over again.

I was beginning to think she wouldn't answer until she finally opened her mouth to speak. "Leah was Judy Lawson's daughter. She died by drowning while playing in a friend's pool six months before Judy took you. The details are sketchy, but it appears that Judy took Leah's death hard, understandably. She took six months off after Leah's death and had just returned to work at your pediatrician's office. That is where she first saw you."

I digested her words, absently massaging the dull ache in

my head. It wasn't the steady painful pounding from the day before, but a reminder of how difficult the truth was to process.

"Is that why Judy kept me locked away?" Her name still felt foreign on my tongue. I had called her Mother for ten years. It felt like a betrayal to call her anything else. "Was she afraid I would die like her Leah?"

"Perhaps, but understand there is more to her psychological state of mind than we will likely ever know. I'm sure in the beginning she didn't want you to be found. The FBI and local authorities were combing the surrounding areas for you. Locking you in the basement meant that you wouldn't be found. As for the rest of the time, I can't tell you. According to some of the notes I have reviewed from her arrest, it would seem Judy truly believes that you are her Leah."

I picked at the blanket covering my legs, feeling uneasy. Everyone wanted to paint Judy as the bad person, but they didn't know everything. I had made it difficult at times while she cared for me. "I *was* her Leah," I admitted, feeling embarrassed that I was still confused.

"Mia, you did nothing wrong. You were dragged into a terrible situation and you learned to adjust the only way you could. You had no choice but to become Leah. That's something you have to understand. You were the victim in all of this. Do you understand?"

Victim? Somehow it just didn't feel right.

"But I—" I had a thought in mind, but cut it off before any further words could escape.

Dr. Marshall watched me carefully, as if she already knew what I was hiding. I shifted uncomfortably on my mattress. "Nothing you tell me will change the fact that you were the victim. I'm here to help you understand that none of this is your fault. I know it's going to be hard and at times more than you can handle, but I hope you will learn to trust me with all your secrets."

I nodded though I couldn't imagine confiding everything to her. There were things I had tried hard to bury. I shifted the conversation in a different but equally complicated direction. "Do I have to answer to Mia?" My voice shook slightly.

"Are you afraid to use that name?"

I shook my head. My fingers continued to pull at the strings on the knit blanket covering my lap. "It doesn't feel right. That name belongs to someone else."

"Yes, it does. It belongs to a part of you. You clung to that name, trying to maintain a part of your old life. Mia was your hope."

If Mia was my hope, then what was Leah? Without looking up, I wound the string around my finger, making the tip blood red.

"Would you like me to call you Leah?" she asked, watching me as I slowly unwound the string so that the blood flowed back into my index finger.

It sounded like another trick question. If I answered honestly, she would probably scribble on her notepad that I was too far gone, mentally unstable, and hopelessly incapable of accepting reality. I felt like I knew what Dr. Marshall and even my parents wanted to hear from me, but I couldn't bring myself to give it to them. In the short amount of time I had been in the hospital, everything had been dropped on me at once—details about Judy, seeing my family again, the truth about Mia. Each new detail was like a bomb exploding in my face.

As I pondered Dr. Marshall's question, I found myself aching for my room in the basement, the familiar surroundings. I had dreamed about getting outside that room for so long that I never contemplated what I would lose if I actually made it. How could I have known that Leah would be snuffed out the moment I opened that door? Grief like I had never felt before clawed its way up from my stomach.

Everyone believed it was a miracle that I was found, but would they feel the same in my shoes? In one instant Mia no longer existed and Leah was also gone. I was an empty shell.

My honest answer? I missed Leah. I missed my life. I missed Mother. I was nothing.

20

MY WRIST was free. I touched the discolored skin where the IV needle had been. It was tender. I poked it harder, causing a sting of pain to radiate up my wrist. It felt normal and oddly comforting.

Over and over again I rubbed, poked, and squeezed my wrist, reclaiming a small part of myself that had been taken the day I was found. It was insignificant, but at least something.

Eventually my wrist became numb from all my probing. I reluctantly released it and picked up the television remote. Over the past few days I had gotten into the habit of leaving the television on constantly. When I had visitors, which seemed to be all the time, I would reluctantly turn the volume down, but refused to turn the television off. One of the nurses tried shutting it off a few nights ago after I'd fallen asleep, but I woke up instantly. She smiled when I switched it back on.

I was growing tired of the sympathetic smiles from everyone. Like they were telling me they felt bad, but didn't know what to say. Anyone that spoke to me wore sympathy like a badge. For years the one thing I craved most, other than sunshine, was human interaction, different people to talk to, opportunities to make friends, but I never imagined everyone would pity me. I hated it.

The television served as a distraction, so I could watch people who had no idea who I was. The characters on the screen didn't care about me, as long as I kept the channels away from the news stations. They couldn't seem to go five minutes without another mention of me. Every aspect of the last ten years of my life was under a microscope. Pictures of my basement room had been released to the news media. In the harsh lights of television it looked so much worse than I remembered. My empty bookshelves looked barren. They hadn't always been that way. There was a time when I had a nice collection of books lining the shelves. Nowhere in the news story did they mention how books had helped me survive, provided an escape. It felt like a false representation of what my life had really been like. Those books had helped me keep Mia alive in my head.

I flipped the channels abruptly when they flashed the picture of my bed, stopping on a cartoon with bright images of characters singing cheerful songs every few minutes. I didn't have much experience with cartoons, but I could see the appeal, especially if you were a kid. The songs were supposed to make you want to dance, to feel happy. I wanted them to make me happy. I could flutter around the room singing with the forest animals. Anything to avoid thinking about the images on the news channels. I could explain my empty bookshelves, but my bed with the soiled sheets and metal chain was a different story. It was shameful and everyone had seen it. From that point forward I avoided the news stations at all costs. Holding the remote was a small luxury that made me feel powerful. Unlike my time with Judy, I could watch what I wanted, when I wanted.

I'd been too busy pinching and squeezing my wrist to fully digest what the absence of the IV in my arm meant. I could leave the bed and walk out of my room if I chose. No one said I had to stay. The point was pressed over and over again that I was no longer a captive. In the two weeks I had been at the hospital I was too weak to do much more than use the bathroom, eat, and sleep. The only time I ventured out of my room was when an orderly wheeled me to some test or procedure.

I had only recently graduated to sitting in a chair in my room. It was a vast improvement when Dr. Marshall came in for our sessions. I felt better sitting in the chair. Less vulnerable.

I slid my legs over the side of the bed, feeling a little shaky as I stood up. It only took a few seconds to feel sturdy enough to walk. My body was slowly growing stronger from the food that was constantly pushed on me. My weight was carefully monitored and according to the nurses, I was bulking up nicely.

Judy's last punishment had withered me away to an all-time low. My ribs and collarbone stuck out to the point where I almost resembled a skeleton. I had overheard the doctor telling Mom and Dad that I wouldn't be released until my weight showed vast improvements. Mom took his words to heart and started bringing me food from the outside that I had never eaten before. Last night we all sat around my bed eating my very first pizza that I could remember. It only took one gooey bite with the melted cheese and sauce running down my chin for me to declare it my favorite food.

I slipped on the new terry cloth robe Mom had brought me over my cotton pajamas, which were also new. Everything around me was new. Considering how soft they both were against my skin, I felt kind of weird for missing my old clothes, but I did sometimes.

Before leaving my room, I stopped in my bathroom to relieve my bladder. I avoided looking in the mirror as I washed my hands, following the same thorough regimen that had been pressed upon me for years. I squirted extra soap on my hands, scrubbing them a second time. Freedom from the room was within my reach, but I was stalling. I should have been excited, ecstatic even. Instead I was terrified at what lay beyond the door. My hand reached for the soap nozzle a third time, but I forced myself to step away from the sink and leave the bathroom.

The hallway was busy when I finally worked up the nerve

to pull my door open. I stood in the doorway filled with uncertainty, wondering if someone would stop me. It would only take one step to leave the doorway, but everything outside the confines of the room was unknown territory. Scanning the hallways for an authority figure that might object, I tentatively stepped across the threshold, waiting for an order to be barked at me.

No one even looked my way.

With sweaty hands I took one more step away from the door. I was now in the hallway, and yet still no acknowledgment. Peering to the left, which was normally the direction I was taken for testing, I abruptly turned right, stepping slowly but steadily as I passed other rooms. I couldn't help peeking inside the rooms as I passed, curious about the other patients and the ailments that brought them here. Most of the rooms held two beds, making me wonder why my room had my bed alone. I was thankful, but curious nonetheless. It would have felt awkward to share with someone anyway.

I continued to shuffle down the hall, making a left turn when I hit a junction. I didn't know where I was headed, but it was the furthest I had walked in years. My legs were starting to burn from exertion, but I ignored them and pressed on.

A nurse pushing an IV stand approached. I stiffened, expecting her to ask me where I needed to be, but she merely flashed a smile as she passed.

Picking up my pace before she could change her mind, I made a right turn and spotted a sign I didn't even know I was looking for. Smiling, I followed the directions, making another right turn where the hallway opened up into a huge reception area banked with a wall of windows and two sets of double doors.

I expected strange looks from the various people scattered about since I was decked out in a robe and pajamas, but again, no one seemed to care. I paused at the doors. Thinking about what was beyond them made my heart jump erratically in my chest. My hands trembled as I reached for the door handle. I glanced back over my shoulder at the safety of the hallway I had just come from. If I turned around I could be back in my bed within a few minutes with my television remote in hand. I could pull the blankets up to my chin and hide.

I closed my eyes and took a deep breath. I'd been hiding long enough. It was time to be brave, to face the world. Exhaling with determination, I pushed on the handle—only the door didn't budge. Disappointment coursed through me. I had been denied once again. Sudden tears filled my eyes. I felt like an emotional roller coaster, going from fear and wanting to hide back in my room to acute disappointment and genuine heartache. All because a door wouldn't open. It felt symbolic. I could literally see the outside, brilliant sunshine, perfect green grass, and yet once again it was just beyond my grasp. It wasn't fair. I was forever destined to be locked away.

My disappointment turned to anger as I pounded my fist on the door.

"It sticks sometimes," a raspy voice said behind me. An elderly, wrinkled hand reached past me and pushed hard on the door. It made a grinding noise, but popped open.

"Thank you," I squeaked as the older man walked around me and held the door open. I stood paralyzed, unsure of what to say or do next. Human interaction wasn't my strong suit. Most of what I had to say to strangers was parroted from what I had seen on television. I envied the characters in the shows and the ease they displayed while interacting with others like it was nothing. I realized it was all make-believe. I just hoped to be able to one day feel that comfortable.

"You coming?" The older gentleman gave me an odd look and I realized I'd screwed up another interaction by standing there gaping at him.

"Oh, yes, thank you again," I said, walking through the open door. I tried to smile to show him I was normal and capable of acting like a real person.

"It's my pleasure, young lady," he acknowledged, returning my smile before shuffling off.

My shoulders sagged as I watched him walk away. I wasn't ready for this. I couldn't smile at people and hold conversations. The process somehow got screwed up in my head. I reached back for the door, ready to admit defeat.

"Was that you banging on the door?"

"What?" I asked, spinning around toward a bench off the sidewalk behind me.

"I can't believe an old man totally out-Hulked you."

A younger guy, relatively close to my age, sat at the bench that was positioned near the entrance, but with full access to the sun.

I looked around to see who he was talking to, but could only assume his comment was meant for me because no one else was within close proximity. "Excuse me?" I asked, not understanding his meaning. I stepped closer to him and the bench, unable to resist the pull of the sun's warm rays. "Are you talking to me?"

"Do you see anyone else around?"

"Well, no," I answered. Although his tone was playful, his bluntness confused me. My pulse began to quicken. What was I supposed to say next? I was about to screw this up just like I had with the old man. I looked back at the doors, wishing I were behind them.

"Neither do I," the boy said, cackling loudly as he held up the walking stick I had missed.

"Oh, so you're blin—I mean, you can't see," I said, stumbling over my words.

He laughed harder. "Sorry. I didn't mean to freak you out. Sometimes I just can't resist a little blind humor. Here, as a peace offering, I'll share my Reese's Peanut Butter Cups," he offered, holding up an orange package.

I hesitated. I wasn't exactly sure what they were, but I had the feeling they were some kind of chocolate candy.

"Come on. I won't bite," he said, wiggling the package out at me. "You know you want to."

I flushed at his teasing. I knew he had to be poking fun at me, but it was hard to tell with his eyes hidden behind dark glasses.

He wagged the package at me again. "They're really good. Everyone that's cool does it."

A smile tugged at the corners of my mouth while my legs

made the decision for me. They had reached the extent of their output and were practically screaming at me to sit. I sat cautiously on the bench next to him, leaving as much space open between us as possible. The sun was bright and hot. I could feel it radiating against my skin. For a brief moment I wondered if everyone had been wrong. Maybe I was allergic. It only took a second to decide it didn't matter. Sitting outside felt too good to care. I closed my eyes and tilted my head back, letting the sun wash over me.

"Feels good, huh?"

I jerked my head toward him. How did he know I was enjoying the sunlight? Was he just pretending to be blind? I felt stupid for falling for his ploy. I was a dumb girl who had no idea how to tell when someone was messing with me.

"It's not nice to screw with people," I said, making a move to stand up, but my legs clearly weren't ready.

"By offering to share my peanut butter cups?" he asked.

I sighed. Instead of talking to Dr. Marshall about my stupid name, I should have asked her how to do this. How to make sense with people. "By pretending you can't see."

He snickered before answering. "I can't."

"Then how could you tell I was enjoying the sun or that I couldn't open the door? And why are you laughing?" I asked defensively.

He shot me a wry smile. "Well, I'm blind, not deaf. You sighed real big when you sat down. As for the door, you were the one pounding on it. That was easy to determine after you thanked the old man when he held the door open. Being blind doesn't mean I'm not aware of what goes on around me." His friendly tone was gone. I'd offended him.

"I'm sorry. I'm not really good at any of this," I muttered, hoping he'd be aggravated enough to leave me in self-loathing.

He didn't leave though. Instead he offered the candy package to me again. "Here, you can have the last one. Good at what, by the way?"

"That's okay. I don't want to take your last one. I'm not sure I even like them."

"You've never had a Reese's?" he asked incredulously.

"No."

"Holy alien nuts. Are you the one messing with me now? Playing with a blind kid's emotions?"

Alien nuts? What was that supposed to mean? "Uh, no. I'm serious."

He shook the package at me. "You definitely have to eat one now. Wait, you're not one of those freaks who can't stand chocolate, are you?"

"No," I answered, accepting the candy package that was practically shoved in my face. I tore the orange wrapper, revealing a round piece of chocolate. The scent of chocolate and peanut butter wafted into my nose. I brought the candy up to my mouth, taking a small, tentative bite. My teeth sank down into the chocolate that was softer than I had been expecting.

"Wait, you're not allergic to peanut butter, are you?"

I shook my head, forgetting he couldn't see me. "No," I said, chewing on the candy that tasted heavenly. It melted deliciously on my tongue except for a small part that I pulled from my mouth, blushing when I realized it was paper. Turning the remaining chocolate over, I saw that it was sitting on a small piece of brown paper. Pulling it off, I popped the rest of the candy into my mouth before it could melt.

"Judging by that sigh, I'd say you're a Reese's fan. I'm Gunner by the way," he said, holding his hand out.

I wiped a little melted chocolate off my fingers before holding out my hand. "Le—I mean, Mia," I said, letting go of another piece of the old me. I could almost feel it dying as I said my given name.

He twisted on the bench to face me. "Are you sure about that?" he asked, tapping his fingers on his leg.

I shrugged, forgetting again that he couldn't see me. Gah, I was so bad at this. "So they tell me," I muttered.

"Ah. I know who you are. You're practically a celebrity here," he said, nodding his head as he connected the dots.

Well, that didn't take long. Bring on the pity party.

"Do you like to play checkers?" he asked abruptly.

"Um, checkers? I've never played."

He slapped his hand loudly on his jean-covered thigh, startling me enough to make me jump. "It's settled then. We have to go play," he said, hopping to his feet and grabbing his walking stick. "Shall we?" he asked, holding out his hand.

I looked at his hand warily for a moment. Over the past couple weeks Mom had reached for my hand almost constantly whenever she was with me. I liked the feeling of warmth when her fingers wrapped around mine, but I didn't know how I felt about holding someone's hand who I really didn't know. I sat gnawing on my bottom lip, contemplating what to do. Gunner waited patiently while I worked through my inner turmoil. It only took me a few moments to accept his offered hand. I didn't want to offend him. Despite our rocky start I enjoyed talking to him. It felt normal.

GUNNER'S HAND dwarfed mine, but it felt nice. Once I was standing, he tucked my arm around his. "You don't mind, do you? I hate using my stick in crowded places. Just don't let me run into anything." He laughed.

It took me a moment to adjust to his close proximity. It was one thing when Jacob surprised me with his spontaneous hug, but I wasn't related to Gunner. I had no idea if this was okay. Sure, I'd read plenty of books over the years about boys and girls interacting, but it was all new to me.

Gunner urged us forward toward the glass doors. "I'll show you a cheating method." He felt along the wall for a large button with a blue outline of a wheelchair engraved on it. "Push here," he said.

I pressed the button and the doors opened on their own. I shook my head at how stupid I must have looked earlier.

"Magic, right?" Gunner laughed, walking forward again. He kept his pace slow, which I was grateful for. My legs had gotten a little rest while we were sitting down, but they still shook slightly with each step. I hated feeling so weak.

Walking through the halls with Gunner was a different experience than my previous venture. He seemed more comfortable being on display than I was. Despite being blind he was keenly aware of his surroundings.

Gunner talked the entire time we walked. It seemed like he knew everything there was to know about the hospital. I wanted to ask him how long he'd been here but decided maybe that was too personal considering we had just met. As we approached the hallway where my room was located we ran into an elderly janitor blocking our way as he mopped the floor.

"Excuse us," I said. A smile spread across my face.

The janitor turned with a smile that slowly slipped from his face.

My own smile slipped away. Great, more pity. Was there anyone in this hospital who didn't know who I was? Gripping Gunner's hand, I mumbled that he should be careful not to slip as we made our way over the wet section of the floor.

"Don't let me fall," Gunner said. "The last thing I want to do is bust my ass in front of a girl I just met."

I snorted, shocking us both.

"Did you just snort?"

"No," I said, blushing brightly.

The custodian wasn't the only one who acknowledged us as we walked down the hall. Nurses, orderlies, doctors, and even other patients all waved as we walked by. I was amazed that Gunner could tell where we were just by the sounds around us. I had firsthand experience with how certain senses could become heightened after the loss of another sense, but I'm not sure even after all my time in the dark that I could have been as good as he was.

Gunner's room was in the same wing as mine. By the time we reached his room, the last of my energy was spent. I sank down into one of the chairs at the small round table in his room before my legs could give out.

"You okay?" he asked, sitting in the chair opposite mine.

I nodded and then smacked myself in the forehead. "I'm fine."

"Other than hitting yourself?" he asked, smirking at me. "Are you ready for me to smoke you at checkers?"

My cheeks warmed again and I was glad he couldn't see it. I had blushed more in the last hour than I think I ever had. "Um, I've never played, so that shouldn't be hard."

He didn't tease me after that comment. I kind of wished he hadn't figured out who I was. It was nice, even for a brief moment, to have a conversation with someone who didn't know all the sordid details of my past. At least I knew he couldn't see the images they showed on the news.

As he explained the rules of the game I wondered how he could tell the difference between the pieces until I noticed that the red pieces had a crown etched on them while the black pieces had a sword. The rules were simple enough and before I knew it I was playing my first-ever game of checkers.

"So, did I convert you into a Reese's fan?" he asked, jumping three of my pieces and setting them to the side. He used his hands to feel around the board after each one of my moves. I looked at the board incredulously, wondering how I'd made such a bad move that allowed him to jump me so many times.

"It was delicious. I didn't know chocolate and peanut butter tasted so good together."

"They're definitely my favorite. Wait until you try them in ice cream."

I shifted in my seat, fiddling with one of my pieces on the board. "I've never had ice cream either, or maybe I have and I just don't remember it," I said, sighing. There was so much I didn't know. How was I ever going to function as a regular person?

Gunner didn't comment at how weird that was. His eyes didn't fill with tears like Mom's had when I accidentally let something slip. He also didn't press me about how it made me feel like Dr. Marshall would have. Gunner just nodded like it was perfectly normal.

We spent an hour together, stumbling through two games of checkers, which I lost horrifically, and a conversation that ran into multiple stumbling blocks. Gunner gave me a crash course on music by playing songs he had stored on his phone. I scooted closer, amazed at the number of songs the phone held. If I had one I would never need a cassette player ever again.

We were just starting our third game of checkers when Mom swept into the room looking stressed out and panicked.

"Mia," she gasped, pulling me in tightly for a hug. "You

weren't in your room." Her voice struggled coming out of her throat.

"Uh, is that not okay?" I asked, bracing myself for a punishment. I kept my eyes averted from Gunner. Whatever was about to happen, I wished he weren't around to hear it.

Mom sniffled, pulling back from our hug. "Of course you can leave your room," she said, flashing me a watery smile. "I was just worried when I didn't find you there, that's all."

Gunner sat in his chair, looking expectantly in the direction of Mom's voice. I blushed again, forgetting that introductions were socially expected.

"Mom, this is my friend, Gunner. Gunner, this is Mom," I said, feeling awkward that I had goofed the introduction by not using her name.

"Pleasure," Gunner answered. "Don't worry, by the way. The worst thing that happened here was that your daughter got her butt kicked at checkers. Oh, and we discovered she's addicted to Reese's cups," he continued, smiling.

I could see it on Mom's face the instant she realized Gunner was blind. I recognized the look. It was the same pitiful expression I'd received countless times myself in the last few days. I thought about how much it must have sucked for him to put up with it constantly until I reminded myself he couldn't see. He had the perfect shield.

If Gunner could sense how Mom was looking at him he gave no indication. I envied his ease. Even without sight he didn't have an ounce of my social awkwardness. I could only hope that one day I would be able to fit in.

"Yes, well, we really need to get going," Mom answered, nodding toward the door like we were trying to keep my exit a secret from the poor blind kid. "You have an appointment with the nutritionist in fifteen minutes."

I reluctantly rose to my feet. "See you later, I guess," I said to Gunner. I wasn't sure if I should reach out to shake his hand.

"Definitely. We'll pick up the game another time," Gunner told me, flashing another one of his wide grins. "Hey, tell the nutritionist the only thing you want to eat is peanut butter cups. It'll be funny to mess with her."

The corners of my mouth rose into a smile and a warm feeling spread throughout my chest. It took me a moment to recognize the foreign emotion. I was happy. It wasn't the short bouts of pleasure I would get when I knew I had done something to please Judy. This was legitimate happiness. Gunner genuinely seemed to like me. For a small slice of time he made me forget that I was a circus sideshow attraction.

"Did you eat breakfast?" Mom asked, tucking my arm through hers as we strolled down the hall.

I nodded, feeling the ease of a few minutes prior leaking away. Things were harder with my family. Every time I opened my mouth I felt like I was spouting something that would make one of them flinch or clench their fists in anger. It was easier to keep my mouth closed.

"I talked to your doctors this morning and they all came to the agreement that you can be released next week," Mom chattered on. "Your weight is still an issue, but our meeting with the nutritionist should get us headed in the right direction. The rest of your injuries are healing as well and soon all this will be a distant memory," she added in a voice that sounded forcefully cheerful. I caught her glancing at my neck briefly as she steered me into my room.

My fingers moved to my neck. I knew I wouldn't feel the bruises, but the faint yellow discoloration was a reminder of what had happened. The marks were a flashing sign of Judy's anger and one of the reasons I couldn't look in the mirror. They were the first thing everyone seemed to look at upon meeting me, but painted a picture they didn't understand. Everyone assumed Judy's attack on me was unprovoked, but they had no idea about the part I had played in it. Dr. Marshall kept insisting I was the victim. I wondered what she would say if she knew the truth. Would she still think I was the victim if she knew all the times I'd been a bad girl?

True to his promise, Gunner came to my room after my family left later that evening. He was carrying the checkers game in one hand and his walking stick in the other. "Up for another game?" he asked, standing in my doorway.

"Yes," I answered happily. His timing was impeccable. My visit with my family had been trying and left me on edge.

Gunner made his way effortlessly to my bed. He was able to navigate my room like it was his own. I was tempted to ask him how long he'd been blind, but felt it would be rude. I had already alienated my share of people this evening. There was no reason to push my luck.

"How'd your appointment with the nutritionist go? Did

you tell her about the peanut butter cups?" he asked, climbing up on the foot of my bed and folding his walking stick.

I folded my legs to give him room and pulled the wheeled table between us for the checkerboard. "It was fine, except that the joke didn't go as planned. Everyone walks around on eggshells so much with me that when I told her all I wanted to eat was peanut butter cups she didn't know what to say. It's like no one wants to take the chance of upsetting me. When I told her I was kidding, she didn't laugh. She weighed me and then gave my mom a high-calorie diet for me to follow."

He chuckled, opening the checkers box. "You could definitely use that to your advantage."

"Really?" I asked, setting up my pieces.

"Oh yeah. Tell your mom you want a pony or something crazy like that."

We laughed together. I loved how well Gunner and I were getting along. I had been so afraid that I would never be able to make friends.

"And as far as the high-calorie diet, you're seriously lucky there. Every girl I've ever known complains about their waistlines. I once dated a girl who literally lived off celery and five cheese cubes a day. I once offered her a single bite of my cheeseburger and you would have thought I pushed her into a vat of chocolate. Needless to say, we weren't right for each other."

I digested his words, but my knowledge on the subject was limited. Judy always kept me on a strict diet, but clearly that was for her own purposes. I couldn't imagine deliberately depriving yourself of something if you had a choice.

"How did you two even get together?" I asked, hoping I wasn't getting too personal.

"I don't know. I think I was her charity case for the semester," he said, grinning.

My tongue felt like it was glued to the roof of my mouth. Did people do that? Unsure of how to answer, I scooted back into my shell.

Gunner wouldn't allow me to retreat though. He moved to a different subject before I could even begin to feel awkward.

"Well, it's good you're not watching your weight. I've arranged for a little surprise. It should be here any minute."

"You got me a s-s-surprise?" I stuttered out. For me, surprises only came twice a year, once for Christmas and once for my birthday, and only if I was good. My voice shook with emotion.

"Sure. It's no big deal though," he said. "I just sent a nurse on a little errand. Ah. I think I hear her footsteps now."

I quirked my head to the side, trying to see what he was talking about. Only when someone stopped in my doorway did I finally hear the clicking of her shoes on the hard flooring. I spotted a woman who looked noticeably older than Mom. Her hair was completely gray and pulled up into a tight knot on her head. She had a wide smile on her face and seemed to be full of energy judging by how quickly she was moving.

"I got your order, but you better eat quickly before they melt." She sat the small brown bag on the table and then turned on her heel to leave. "I gotta go check on Mr. Schultz.

He's demanding my attention. Don't make yourself sick now."

Gunner didn't seem concerned as he handed me a cold container.

I pried the lid off my container and dug my plastic spoon into the ice cream. Even though he couldn't see me, I noticed that Gunner paused while I brought a spoonful of the ice cream up to my lips.

I was unprepared for the taste sensation that exploded in my mouth. Ice cream lived up to its name. It was rich and creamy and literally melted in my mouth. Maybe now I had a new favorite treat.

"Oh, wow," I proclaimed, shoving another spoonful in my mouth.

Gunner laughed, digging into his own container. "It's Chocolate Lovers'. It's one of my weaknesses. I guarantee if you eat enough it'll put some pounds on you."

I would have agreed with him but I was too busy shoveling spoonfuls of ice cream into my mouth.

"Stick with me, kid, and I'll have you trying so many new things your head'll spin." He grinned at me, taking an oversize bite of his ice cream. "Hey, did I get any on me?" he asked, looking at me as melted ice cream drizzled from the corners of his mouth and down his chin.

I couldn't help but smile as a warm feeling of joy coursed through my veins. I liked Gunner. A lot. "Gross." I laughed, trying to keep my own bite of ice cream from running out of my mouth.

"What? You're the one who dripped on your shirt," Gunner said, pointing toward my arm.

"Where?" I asked, turning my arm over to inspect my sleeve. "I don't see anything."

"Right there," he answered just as a glob of ice cream landed on my chest. I looked up to see Gunner holding an empty spoon. "Oops, did I do that?" he asked with a devilish grin on his face.

I felt more shocked than anything and unsure of how to react. Mother used to punish me severely if I ever spilled food. Not that Gunner would have known that. It wasn't his fault that she was so strict. I watched as he dug into his ice cream container again, holding up a large spoonful as it melted down his arm. "You better not," I said, idly threatening him.

"Yeah? What are you gonna do?" He tossed the ice cream at me again and it landed in a small pile on my lap. We both launched into a fit of laughter and I joined him as we began pelting each other with spoonfuls of ice cream until the containers were empty. We made an absolute mess of my room, but I didn't care. I had never had so much fun in my life. Not that I had ever had any friends, but Gunner was already the coolest person I had ever met.

The following day he showed up in my room with his hands full, trying to juggle his walking stick and whatever it was he was carrying. He searched for the edge of the door with his foot and covertly closed it behind him as he entered.

I held my breath and stood apprehensively from my bed. Since I arrived at the hospital, I insisted on keeping the door open at least a crack at all times. Having it closed reminded me too much of the basement prison I had escaped from. My eyes locked on the door. I was torn and fighting back the shriek that burned in my throat, but the last thing I wanted to do was drive my new friend away.

"What's up? I've got another surprise for you, but figured you'd prefer the door closed for this," Gunner said intuitively.

Curiosity got the better of me as my eyes moved reluctantly from the closed door.

"Okay, so actually, I'm the one who prefers the door closed," he said wryly when I didn't respond. He dropped his walking stick to the side and placed the items in his hands on the small, round table. "What we're about to do may not be fit for the eyes of others."

"Really?" I squeaked out like a mouse, wondering what exactly he had in mind.

"Trust me," he said, fiddling with the stuff on the table.

I watched curiously from my chair as he placed his cell phone into what looked like a small cassette player. Within a few seconds my room was filled with a steady, methodic beat. I smiled. I hated to break it to Gunner, but we had covered music the day before.

He stood in the empty space in the middle of the room and began jerking spastically with his arms and legs like he was having a seizure. For a moment I almost panicked and considered reaching for the call button on the side of my bed. Gunner's spastic motions stopped and he began twirling slowly with his arms outstretched. Giggling slightly, I realized how stupid I was because he was just dancing, although it wasn't like anything I had ever seen on television.

"Do I hear you laughing at my moves?" Gunner asked, gasping slightly as a fine sheen of sweat dotted his forehead. I shook my head without answering. I had no idea how to break it to him that whatever I had just witnessed didn't look like dancing.

I clamped my hand over my mouth to stifle a chuckle, but it was too late. Laughter escaped between my fingers and filled the room. "I don't think that was dancing," I spit out between giggles.

"I'm hurt," he gasped, clutching his chest. "I've got mad skills, girl."

"You definitely looked mad."

"Wow. Big talk. Let's see you do better."

I shook my head. "I can't," I answered. I may have laughed at him, but truthfully, I had no earthly idea how to dance.

"Sure you can. That's the beauty of dancing. Anyone can do it. Some bad, some good, but it doesn't matter," he teased, holding out a hand. "It's all about letting the music talk to your body."

I dug my heels into the floor. "Gunner, I can't," I whispered.

He stepped toward me, closing the distance between us. "You can do this, Mia. I know it."

"What do you mean? How do you know?"

"The way you responded yesterday. I know a fellow music lover when I'm around one. It talks to your soul. Now it's time to let it talk to your body," he said, pulling me to my feet. "And at least you know I won't laugh at you," he said, pointing to his dark glasses.

"I'm sorry I laughed at you," I said as a new song swelled through my room.

"I'm not. You have the prettiest laugh I've ever heard. Even if it was at my expense. Now, stop stalling."

He released my hand and stepped back, leaving me in the middle of the room. For a moment I felt vulnerable, but slowly my body began to respond to the subtle beat of the music. My feet stepped back and forth and my arms swung from side to side as my body swayed along. I know it was silly, but I closed my eyes so I wouldn't have to see Gunner looking like he was watching me. With my eyes closed I felt free as the music took over my body.

I danced through one song and then another and another one after that. Eventually, I opened my eyes and Gunner joined me. We held hands, dancing together with abandon—dancing until we had nothing left to give.

22

"DO KIDS our age really act like that?" I asked Jacob, who was watching the television show I'd turned on.

We were both lying on my bed while Mom sat on one of the chairs crocheting. I had been in the hospital officially three weeks. My new life was slowly beginning to shape into a routine. I woke up, had my daily session with Dr. Marshall, and then spent the rest of the morning with Mom. After she and I ate lunch, Gunner would usually find me and he and I would spend the rest of the day together while Mom ran errands and got out of the hospital for a little while. Evenings were spent with my family as we continued trying to get to know one another.

Jacob laughed. "Hell no. Sorry, Mom," he added when she looked up sternly from her crocheting. "School is boring compared to all the drama on this show. Plus, *none* of the chicks at school are anywhere near as hot. Everyone on this show is a freaking model."

Mom chastised him again, but I was too busy gnawing on my lip to respond. A part of me was relieved that school wouldn't be as confusing as it appeared on the show. Jacob's declaration still didn't help the anxiety I felt about starting school. Mom had announced earlier after my daily session with Dr. Marshall that she had stopped at the school and finished my enrollment. I spent two days taking proficiency tests that would determine exactly what I knew. I got the impression that everyone was skeptical about what kind of education I could have received while locked in a basement for ten years. It made sense, I guess. As far as they were concerned, Judy was a monster who treated me like a prisoner. They had no way of knowing what an emphasis she put on education. The proficiency tests Mom had me take for school were all easy in comparison. If I knew they would lead to me being thrown into school so soon, I would have dragged my feet in taking them or flunked them on purpose.

Now it appeared I was set to start as soon as I got settled at home. Mom's news created butterflies the size of dragons in my stomach.

I wanted to ask Jacob more questions but didn't want them to know I was worried. They both already hovered over me enough. It was as if they were afraid I was going to break at any moment. I didn't want to give them yet another thing to worry about with me. Over the last few weeks, it had become obvious Dad was having issues being around me.

Nobody would say it, but each meal seemed more strained than the one before.

Finally, three nights ago, he gave up the charade and hadn't shown up since. Mom and Jacob seemed to have a harder time accepting it than me. I understood, probably better than they did. I made Dad uncomfortable. Mom and Jacob continued to make up excuses for him. When Jacob arrived alone, carrying yet another pizza for our dinner, they both tried hard to reassure me that Dad was stuck at work, but I had read the annoyance in Jacob's eyes. He opened his mouth to say something, but Mom shook her head before flashing a smile my way. I could have told them it didn't matter. I might be having issues adjusting to life on the outside, but I wasn't dumb. They didn't have to hide the truth from me.

"I wouldn't be nervous, sis. School's a piece of cake," Jacob said during a commercial break.

"Oh, I'm not," I lied.

"Good. You'll have no problem fitting in. All my friends can't wait to meet you. Plus, even your old friend, Amber, found me during lunch today to ask about you."

My head snapped up so abruptly at his words that it startled him. Amber? Had I heard him right? Amber wasn't my friend. She was Mia's friend. According to Dr. Marshall, she was a figment of my imagination. "Amber?" I asked, gripping the edge of the bed.

"She was a little girl you used to play with. Her family moved into the house at the end of our street two months before you were taken. You two were inseparable," Mom said.

I couldn't believe it. Amber was a part of my world.

"How did you sleep last night?" Dr. Marshall asked the next morning as we settled in for my session. She reached into her briefcase to extract her notepad.

"Good," I lied, folding my legs under me.

She looked up from her briefcase. "Mia?" It wasn't a question so much as a gentle scolding. We both knew I was lying. After three weeks of daily sessions she already knew me better than anyone else.

I picked at the skin on my thumb. All my cuticles were dry and cracking. Even though it hurt, I couldn't resist picking at them. "I miss my dreams," I admitted quietly.

"Your dreams about Mia?"

I nodded.

She scribbled on her notepad. "Are you remembering the dreams better now?"

I shrugged. It was too hard to explain. Mia had been a part of my life for so long. I never questioned how it was that I could see her. I should have. Dr. Marshall could spout out her clinical mumbo jumbo about brains protecting themselves, but how did I create something that didn't even exist? That concept was still hard for me to grasp.

"Mia's best friend is real. She was my friend before Judy—well, you know . . ." My voice trailed off.

She nodded.

I sighed, hating when I felt I was missing something crucial.

"That makes sense. Of course you would want to keep

some familiarity in your means of escape. Giving her to Mia was almost like a gift."

"She was a great friend to Mia," I mushed, not caring if I sounded crazy.

"I bet she was. I'm glad she was there for you."

I opened my mouth to argue that she wasn't there for me, but that's exactly what Amber was there for. It was hard to sort through all the mess. A familiar flutter of panic began to beat in my chest. I could feel my pulse begin to race and my palms became damp.

"How's your friend Gunner doing?" she asked, changing the subject. Dr. Marshall was good at that. It was as if she instinctively knew how hard to push before retreating, and lately Gunner seemed to be her favorite go-to topic.

I took a deep breath, trying to calm my nerves and the rapid fluttering in my chest. I reached for my glass and took a drink. I wasn't thirsty, but I needed a buffer as I switched gears.

Dr. Marshall waited patiently. She never pushed me to hurry. We both knew that I just needed a minute.

"He's good," I finally answered when my near panic attack was under control.

"Is he still introducing you to new things?" she asked, looking at the iPhone in my lap that Mom had given me the day Gunner and I had met. The iPhone was already loaded with over three hundred songs Jacob had sorted into what he called "playlists," but I referred to them as cassettes, much to his amusement. Gunner and I had spent hours going through all the songs, picking our favorites. Gunner's tastes were different from mine. He liked the louder songs that vibrated your body when they were turned up. I went for the softer ballads that told a story. We both agreed that neither of us liked pop music all that much. Gunner claimed it all sounded the same. For me, pop music was just too cheerful.

I couldn't help the goofy smile that crossed my face as I continued to discuss Gunner. "Yesterday he made me try sushi," I said, scrunching up my nose.

She eyed me inquisitively for a moment before asking her next question. "I'm taking it you didn't like it?"

It was a logical question, but I had the distinct feeling she wanted to ask me something different. Call it intuition. Maybe in her eyes it was too soon for me to get close to a guy. "I almost threw up," I answered honestly. "I didn't believe him when he said people actually eat it. He's a prankster, you know."

She laughed. "Not only do we eat it, but we also pay good money for it."

"Gross, you eat raw fish?"

"It's an acquired taste."

I shuddered. It would never be an acquired taste for me. "Clearly, but I'll take a cheeseburger and fries any day."

"That's where he made his mistake. He should have given you the sushi first. It's not fair to give you a juicy burger and fries and then expect you to like sushi," she said, winking at me. "Do you two have plans for today?"

I nodded, barely able to contain my excitement. Gunner had promised something special since I was being released the next day. He knew how nervous I was about leaving and he promised to make me forget about my fear of what lay beyond the hospital walls. It was a tall order considering the anxiety I was experiencing. I was scared to leave what had come to feel like a sanctuary. Thanks to Gunner's influence, I was able to talk to everyone in the hospital with more ease. They greeted me like an old friend, especially after I had learned most of their names.

"Gunner says it's a surprise."

"Sounds like he's becoming a very good friend."

I gnawed on the side of my thumb. "He is. I'm going to miss him."

She tapped her pen on her notepad. It was a tic that I wasn't even sure she was aware of. "I'm sure you will at first, but you're going to make lots of new friends. Your mom says you'll be starting school next week. How does that make you feel?"

The piece of skin I was tugging at with my teeth came free, leaving a small trickle of blood. "Fine," I lied.

She eyed me knowingly. "Mia."

I huffed. It was annoying that she knew me so well. "I'm scared. Why can't I stay here for a little while longer? I don't think I'm ready."

"Mia, this," she said, sweeping her hands around the room, "this is a small fraction of what you're going to experience. I know the world feels like a scary place at the moment and I can't even imagine what you must be feeling. You barely got a chance to live before you were ripped away. We haven't even begun to scratch the surface of what you went through, but I also know you're still harboring feelings of guilt. You're a brave young lady, Mia, and I know without a shadow of a doubt that you're going to find your footing. I will be here to help you through this transition as will your family. You won't be alone."

I pondered her words, turning them over and over again in my mind. It all sounded so easy when she put it that way, and yet the idea of walking out of the building the next day was overwhelmingly frightening.

My session with Dr. Marshall ended when Mom showed up with lunch. Dr. Marshall went over my schedule and the anxiety medicine and sleeping pills she was prescribing for me. "I want you to call me if you start to panic and the anxiety pills don't work." She handed Mom two slips of paper. "I'll prescribe something stronger if this one doesn't work." She and Mom looked at me sternly.

It was no secret that I kept things bottled up. I didn't like to complain. Gunner had teased me the day before, saying I was an anomaly in a world of whiners who sought out attention. I rolled my eyes, which was a brand-new gesture I was perfecting. Along with exposing me to new things, Gunner was also schooling me on how to fit in. The irony of the situation wasn't lost on me. I'd once read a quote about the "blind leading the blind." It couldn't have fit us more perfectly.

My thoughts were pulled back to the conversation between Dr. Marshall and Mom when I heard my name mentioned. "Remember, baby steps," Dr. Marshall instructed me. "No one is expecting you to fit right in."

I nodded numbly, trying to keep my concern from reaching full-on freak-out mode.

Dr. Marshall surprised me by giving me a tight hug before she left. In the seventeen sessions we'd seen each other, she had yet to touch me. Her hug was unexpected, but I couldn't resist returning it tightly. Hugging was still so new to me that each one felt different from the last. This one felt like a promise of hope and strength. It was as if she were trying to pass on the emotional weapons I would need to survive.

Mom and I ate a quiet lunch after Dr. Marshall left. "Tomorrow, once we get you settled in at home, I thought we could do some shopping." Mom grabbed a chip out of her bag with two fingers.

My bite of sandwich stuck in my throat. I took a long swig of Coke, which was another Gunner influence.

He was so funny, pretending like he was having a heart attack when I told him I had never had a soda before. Without a word, he snatched his wallet off the table and grabbed my hand. The next thing I knew we were standing in front of a soda machine and he was handing me dollars to feed into it. He wasn't satisfied until we had one of every kind. Getting the cold cans to his room turned out to be a feat. I'd ended up dropping one, which promptly exploded, earning me a frown from a nurse who paged for custodial. Undeterred, Gunner dragged me back to the vending machine to replace the exploded drink. After finally making it back to his room, he promptly set up what he referred to as a taste test. I liked most of the drinks I tried, but in the end, Coke was the winner. Since then I had been guzzling it like water.

"So, would you like that?" Mom asked.

I couldn't even form a sentence. Instead, I nodded like a puppet. Somewhere in my deepest dreams, shopping was another item on my list of things I yearned for but never expected to do. I'd read about shopping in books and seen it on TV, but that was the extent of my experience with it.

"I figured you could use some new school clothes. You can't very well wear your robe and pajamas every day." She was teasing. I had learned to tell the difference. "Your room could also use an update. I was going to go without you, but figured you might like picking out your own things."

My eyes became misty, but I wasn't sad and I wasn't hurt. My eyes were wet from joy. "Thank you." I reached out tentatively to touch the back of her hand. It was the first time I had initiated contact between us.

Mom's eyes matched mine, tears spilling down her cheeks as our fingers laced together. Maybe everything would work out.

My gesture seemed to bust the invisible wall that had been firmly wedged between us. Our conversation became easier. We didn't have to work so hard to keep it going. Whether we meant to our not, we avoided talking about the last ten years. Instead, we talked about my new room and our upcoming shopping spree.

I was still buzzing with excitement when I met Gunner that afternoon. I went on like a chatterbox, dominating the conversation as he guided me away from our wing of the hospital. Only when he started laughing did I realize I'd barely given him an opportunity to talk. "Oops." I blushed deeply, grateful that he couldn't see the ten different shades of red on my face.

He patted my hand that was tucked through his arm. "I like it. You finally sound like a normal teen."

"What do I normally sound like?"

He didn't even hesitate before answering. "An adult with the weight of the world on their shoulders. And that's when I can actually get you to talk. You have a beautiful voice. I'm happy to hear it filled with such happiness."

My cheeks heated up again, but for a different reason. He told me I had a beautiful voice. I didn't even know that was a thing.

Gunner guided me off the elevator, directing us toward a sign for the stairs. "Um, where are we going?" I finally thought to ask as he had me pull the heavy door open. It didn't escape my attention that a week ago I would have struggled with it.

His grip on my arm tightened as his feet navigated the stairs. I held on to the railing in case he stumbled. "It's a surprise."

I grinned. I liked his surprises.

We traveled up two flights of stairs that surprisingly left Gunner more winded than I was. I wrapped my hand around his arm, helping him up the remaining step. It made me want to break our pact and ask him why he was at the hospital, but I resisted. We had decided while getting to know each other that we wouldn't ask the hard questions. He didn't ask anything about my past and I didn't question why he was in the hospital. Over the last week I noticed I was visibly getting stronger while Gunner's health seemed to be declining. My hope was that he would decide on his own to tell me the truth.

As we reached the final step we came upon a final sign that read ROOF ACCESS. Gunner recovered quickly, urging me toward the door. Unsure what to expect, I pushed the door open with my shoulder and was blinded instantly by brilliant sunlight. Squinting in the bright light, I cautiously led Gunner out the door.

It took my eyes a few minutes to adjust, but once they did I couldn't help feeling awed by the sight. I turned in slow circles, trying to take everything in. Gunner and I had ventured outside several times to hang out on the bench where we'd first met. We called it our spot. The problem was it was dwarfed by the buildings and trees and parking lots around it. Here on the roof though there was nothing but openness. The hospital was taller than the other buildings around it so the view was completely unobstructed for miles in every direction.

I stood in the middle of the roof with my arms spread out. The wind was stronger than it was on the ground. It blew through my hair, whipping it around my face, and pulled and tugged at my body. I tilted my head back so the sun could soak my face with its bright rays. This is what freedom felt like. I wished I could bottle the feeling. I would carry it with me forever.

Gunner had done this for me. Somehow he had figured out how to show me the world without actually stepping foot into it. It was my opportunity to try the world on for size before I was forced to jump in. He had given me the best gift I had ever received.

23

TWO FOLDING chairs and a small insulated bag sat off to the side of the door. Inside the bag were a couple of Cokes and two Reese's cups. I didn't ask how he had managed to pull that off. Gunner had a way of getting others to help him without question. He'd even thought to bring binoculars so I could see the houses miles away. Together we stayed on the roof until the sun began to set.

"Thank you for all of this," I said warmly. Gunner turned his face toward me at my words. "You've made these last couple of weeks bearable," I admitted. "You made me feel like less of a freak." The words were stilted and came out in an uneven cadence.

Gunner sighed dramatically. "Well, it's been tough, but if I'm going to give Mother Teresa a run for her money, I need to be kind to all."

"Even the freaks," I added.

He chucked a rolled piece of his candy wrapper at me. Even though he was blind he was able to throw it with pinpoint accuracy as it bounced off my head. "Don't be a jerk. It's rude to call my friend a freak. Besides, it should be me thanking you. It's been amazing to share in all of your firsts. You made me feel like I could see again."

"Did you call me a jerk?" I asked, tossing my own wrapper at him. Ironically it missed him by a mile.

He smiled bluntly. "I call it like I see it. You're no freak, Mia." He reached for my hand and gave it a squeeze. "You don't know this, but I was a little pissed at the world when I was forced to check into this luxury spa again. Then you showed up and gave me something else to focus on. You made me remember a crucial thing I'd forgotten."

My heart tripped at his words. This was the closest we had come to discussing why he was here. "And what is that?" I asked.

He wrapped his fingers around mine, tracing his thumb over the top of my hand. "Appreciation. To stop cursing at fate and be thankful for everything I've been given. I was so pissed over the cards I'd been dealt and then I met you. Timid Mia who wasn't even sure what name to claim. Mia who had endured more struggle than most people would ever know."

His statement made me uncomfortable. I tugged at my hand, not liking where the conversation was headed. Gunner held on tightly for a moment before releasing me. "Don't run away, Mia. I've waited all week to tell you this. You're so much stronger than you give yourself credit for. I know you don't think so. I can practically feel your self-doubts radiating off you. In a world filled with people who cry over the most insignificant, trivial things, there's you. You don't have to tell me what you went through. You're entitled to that small measure of privacy. I want you to know though that I think you are the bravest person I've ever met and you've helped me more than I could ever help you."

I opened my mouth to argue. He was crazy. He'd done so much for me over the last week. Didn't he see that?

Before I could utter the words he continued speaking. "Mia, the truth is my head is playing host to a pesky tumor. I've been dealing with it for years, but it's now decided to try to take over. I was so scared before. I put on an act, pretended to be brave. A cheerful front was easier than wearing my fear like a badge. I was terrified of an afterlife or a lack thereof. Whatever the case may be. But I'm not afraid of dying anymore. You gave me that."

His words were like a knife to the heart. I even looked down at my chest expecting to see crimson gushing like a fountain. My wound was buried deep inside, hidden from the naked eye. No one could tell that I was hemorrhaging pain. I'd obviously known that Gunner was sick. Why else would he be in a hospital. I guess I just hoped that like me, he was here to get better.

My eyes welled up. I blinked furiously, willing the moisture to stay where it belonged. "I don't want you to die." My voice was a trembling mess. "Can't they fix you?"

Gunner reached for my hand again now that he knew I

wasn't going to bolt. "They're going to try. It's risky though. Tumors are tricky and they're not sure they can get all the tentacles that are wrapped around my brain." He was trying to make light of the situation for my benefit, but I could hear and feel his fear.

I was stunned into silence. He was sick. Really sick. It wasn't fair. We had just become friends. I didn't want to lose him.

"Don't worry. I'll still be able to beat you at checkers for a while."

I nodded even though I was well aware of the fact that he couldn't see me.

We were both somber as we headed inside when the nighttime chill bullied us from the roof. It took us twice as long to make it down the stairs. Gunner didn't have the energy he had earlier in the day. I now saw what I'd been so unwilling to admit before. I insisted that he put his arm around me, so I could bear the brunt of his weight.

When we reached the bottom of the stairs, I opened the door and grabbed a wheelchair that was parked in the hallway. Gunner didn't even protest as I guided him to sit down. It was just another clear sign that something was wrong. He quietly reached for my hand as I pushed his wheelchair down the hallway.

Gunner insisted that we go to my room first. "I want to say good-bye to you in private," he said wryly, fiddling with the walking stick in his lap.

"Okay," I agreed. I could tell that my impending release

was as hard on him as it was for me. I willed myself to hold it together. He deserved for me to be the strong one this time. It was the least I could do for him.

I pulled up a chair and sat across from him so our knees touched. "This isn't good-bye, Gunner. I'm going to visit you after my sessions with Dr. Marshall."

He shook his head. "Mia, I don't want you to come see me until after my surgery. You'll be busy starting your new life. I don't want you chained to my bed."

His words were like a sharp jab to my gut. He had no idea what an accurate metaphor he had used.

"I'm not going to abandon you. I know what it feels like to be alone and there's no reason why you should have to experience that."

He leaned forward, resting his hand on my knees. "I'm not trying to be a martyr. I'll have plenty of people with me. But you've had your share of loss. I'd rather we treat our time together like going to camp, you know? We can talk on the phone and text."

I had no idea what he was talking about but I couldn't help smiling sadly. "I never went to camp."

"Picture lousy food, smelly cabins, and adults forcing you into sing-alongs. Actually, they're cool," he joked. "Anyway, the important part about camp is the week you invest in trying to get the girl you like to notice you. If you play your cards right, you get that girl to kiss you. That's the goal."

A month ago I would have laughed at the thought that I would be sitting across from a guy who was making it pretty clear he wanted to kiss me. I thought life outside my prison was a dream that would never be fulfilled. That I would die without ever feeling someone else's touch.

"Mia, are you ready for another first?" Gunner whispered, moving his hand to my cheek. I leaned in, closing the distance between us without even thinking about it.

I nodded my head. This time it didn't matter that he couldn't see me. He could feel the movement beneath his palm. Gunner removed his glasses, keeping his eyes closed as he erased the remaining distance between us. My stomach began fluttering, making my entire body quiver. I closed my own eyes as Gunner's lips settled gently against mine. Goose bumps formed on my arms as he deepened the kiss. His lips were softer than they looked, forming perfectly with mine. He pulled away slowly, leaving me in a momentary trance. My lips tingled as I raised my fingertips to my mouth. My first kiss had lasted only moments, but it was something I would never forget.

"Good-bye, Mia." Before I could fully register his words, Gunner stood up with his walking stick to leave the room.

My fingertips were still on my lips when he paused in the doorway. "Be brave, Mia. No matter what happens. Be brave."

THE NEXT morning I zipped up my bag and looked around my room one last time. It looked barren without all the cards and flowers I had received over the past three weeks. The majority came from people I had never even met who had seen my story on the news. The cards were stored in the box that Jacob had already carried to the car. All the flowers were tossed or given away to other patients. The army of stuffed animals was crammed into a big trash bag so Jacob could carry them down on his next trip.

Mom signed her name on the last of the forms she'd been given for my release. "You ready, sweetie?"

I nodded, swallowing the lump in my throat.

"Are you nervous?"

I nodded again, which wasn't a lie although the lump in

my throat had nothing to do with my fear of leaving. Even though we'd said our good-byes the night before, I'd still expected Gunner to come by before I left. I debated taking matters into my own hands but I wanted to honor his wishes. Like our pact, I felt I had to keep my promise.

Jacob arrived and shouldered my duffel bag and the large bag of stuffed animals. "Are we ready to get this party on the road?" he said, winking at me.

"Mia?" Mom reached for my hand. I hesitated for a moment before meeting her halfway and grasping her hand firmly in mine.

We left my room as a family—or part of a family since Dad didn't show up. I felt he hadn't adjusted to me being found. Maybe he was keeping his distance because he saw what Jacob and Mom were too stubborn to see. Maybe he saw what I saw. Did he see that I didn't belong? Deep down did he realize that the daughter whom he lost so many years ago was forever gone? No matter how hard Mom wanted me to be her Mia there was always going to be a part of Leah inside of me. A big part.

The hospital staff called out their good-byes as we made our way down the hall. I waved at all of them and accepted hugs from several people. I was getting good at the whole hugging thing.

I couldn't resist peeking in Gunner's room as we passed, but it was empty and dark. I pivoted my eyes straight ahead and focused on the next step in my life like Dr. Marshall had instructed.

Jacob waited with me in front of the hospital while Mom retrieved the car. I fidgeted in the wheelchair that the hospital insisted I use. It was a silly policy. I was quite capable of walking on my own. Wasn't that the whole point? I was finally strong enough to leave.

Jacob placed the bag of stuffed animals on the ground in front of my chair and plunked down on the bench next to me. "Mia, there's something I think you should know before we get home," he said, looking down at his hands. "Mom and Dad wanted to wait, but I feel you have the right to know. You've been kept in the dark enough to last a lifetime." He paused, taking a deep breath. I didn't know where he was going, but the look in his eyes gave me the impression I wasn't going to like it. "Mia, Dad doesn't live at home with us anymore. He hasn't lived there for a very long time."

His admission was like a quick punch in the gut. My stomach reacted by churning the eggs I'd eaten for breakfast uncomfortably in my belly. I cast my eyes down to my fingers, which were already looking for an outlet. They scratched at the cuticle at my thumb, trying to pull skin free. "How long?"

Jacob watched my frantic digging but didn't try to stop me. "He moved out exactly a year after you were taken. He said he couldn't handle it anymore. Mom was still too torn up about your disappearance to fight him on it. I think he broke the last part of her heart that day. He's a chump."

My fingers freed a small tag of skin and I pulled at it with my nails until a bead of blood rose to the surface. The pain was minuscule compared to the way my heart was pinching.

My fault. Of course it was my fault. I felt I should apologize to Jacob, but the words were trapped in the void in my chest. It was a no-win situation. If I wouldn't have been found my family would still be in shreds. Lost or found, all of this would always land on me.

My family was broken.

I broke it.

Mom pulled up before we could say anything else, bouncing cheerfully out of the car. It was different from what I had been expecting. I'd vaguely remembered our car being blue or maybe black. This one was silver and smaller than the car I remembered. Jacob opened the trunk and stowed my bag and stuffed animals next to the box he'd carried down earlier.

I opened one of the back doors and climbed in.

"Fasten your seat belt," Mom said, yanking on a strap near the back of my seat. She handed it to me and I buckled it into place. Memories flooded my mind. It had been ten years since I'd ridden in a vehicle like this, but I remembered Mom being adamant about seat belts. It was an insignificant memory, but felt like a big deal to me.

Jacob climbed into the front passenger seat. He looked back at me as I tried to smile. The bombshell he dropped on me still had me reeling, but he'd been right, I needed to know.

Mom slowly pulled away from the overhang covering the front entrance. I couldn't resist twisting around in my seat to get one last look. The seat belt bit into my side, but I didn't care. My eyes swept over the building that had become my haven. As our car rounded the driveway, a waving orderly off to the side of the building caught my attention just before Mom made a right turn out of the parking lot. My hand covered my mouth when I spotted Gunner holding up a massive sign with two words plainly printed on it.

BE BRAVE.

Nothing more, nothing less. It was his way of saying goodbye. I knew he couldn't see me but I kissed my fingers and pressed them against the window.

The drive home passed in a blur as I took in my surroundings. It was disorienting watching the different landscape. I didn't remember there being so many buildings or cars before. My fingers were almost white from gripping the seat in a death grip anytime another car got too close to us. I could feel the first stirrings of a panic attack approaching and I patted my pocket. The bottle of pills rattled reassuringly. I didn't pull them out yet; I would only take one when I absolutely needed it.

I knew we were home the moment Mom pulled into our driveway. The familiarity of the house was etched deeply in my mind. Everything down to the white shutters and red door were the same. It was astonishing. I unlocked my seat belt and slowly climbed from the vehicle as memories assaulted me. I remembered this house. I dreamed about this house for ten years. This house had belonged to a person who didn't exist. Now it belonged to a mountain of memories that were crushing me. Memories of me playing on this very lawn moments before Judy had snatched me from the life I had known.

"Honey, I have something to tell you before we go in," Mom called out to me.

I tried to focus on her words but all I can see is me playing with my doll Daisy. Judy smiling down at me and taking my hand. Why did I go with her?

"Mom, I already told her," Jacob said, walking up the path with my bags in hand.

I looked at them both, confused, trying to stop the flood of pictures from the past in my head.

Mom looked strained. "Jake, I told you I would do it. She deserved to hear about your father from me."

My brain strained to keep up with the chaos. It felt like a million gallons of water being dumped on me at once. It was a building taller than the hospital landing on top of me, obliterating me once and for all. My surroundings began to spin. Darkness took over and the last thing I heard before hitting the ground was Mom calling out my name in panic.

I woke to the low sound of Jacob's and Mom's voices. I opened my eyes, feeling disoriented. The blue sky had been replaced with a smooth white ceiling that slanted up into a tall peak. "They released her too early." They were talking quietly, but I could still make out Mom's words. "We should take her back to the hospital."

"I'm okay." I sat up slowly and swung my legs around so I could sit up on the couch.

Mom rushed to my side and knelt in front of me. Tears were streaming down her face. "Honey, I'm so sorry I didn't tell you about your father sooner. It was unfair to keep it from you. I think we should go back to the hospital."

I flushed in embarrassment, wishing my father was the source of my problem. That would have been a more rational explanation for my behavior. I could have corrected Mom but I couldn't take the chance of telling her the truth. What if they considered this a setback and decided a mental hospital was more fitting? I wasn't sick enough to go back to the regular hospital. "I guess I was a little overwhelmed. Hearing about Dad and seeing the house again. I felt an attack coming on when I was in the car. I should have taken a pill like Dr. Marshall told me to. I'm sorry I worried you but I don't want to go back to the hospital." It was a bald-faced lie. I wanted to go back to the hospital with every fiber of my being. It would be so easy. I could see Gunner again and everything would be the same. Gunner's sign flashed in my head. BE BRAVE. They were simple words but held so much meaning.

Mom eyed me skeptically. "Are you sure, sweetie? I hate that you were that upset."

I pasted a smile on my face. It felt heavy, but it was all I could muster. "I'm fine. I promise." I climbed to my feet to show her that I was at least capable of standing.

Jacob threw his arm around my shoulder. "She looks fine to me," he said, ruffling my hair. "Come on. I'll show you your room." He guided me to the familiar staircase. I could have told him he didn't need to. I knew every inch of the house. Mia may not have existed, but she kept my memories alive for me. Jacob and I climbed the steps together with Mom trailing behind. I couldn't resist running my hand along the banister as we climbed. I loved this banister. Its rich, smooth wood shined beneath my palm.

Mine was the second room at the top of the stairs. Jacob stopped in front of the door, letting me push it open. Unlike the rest of the house, the room was not what I had pictured. It looked nothing like the teenage room I'd made up for Mia, nor was it the room I remembered from my childhood. One word described it. *Bleak*. It was empty of any kind of decoration or belongings. A bed almost twice the size of the one I had slept on for the past ten years sat nestled between two nightstand tables. A long dresser sat across from the bed with a matching desk under the window. It was all very plain.

Mom walked into the room and stood beside me, placing her hand on my shoulder. "All of your childhood things are packed away. We can go through them whenever you're ready, but I figured we would start from scratch if you're still up for a massive shopping trip."

I pushed the feelings of bleakness from my mind. Rotating slowly in a circle, I examined each wall. It was a blank slate. For the first time in my life I saw real possibility, an opportunity to express my own tastes, whatever they were. "Yes, please."

Jacob coughed behind us. "Well, that's my cue to hit the road. I love you, but there's no way I want to get roped into one of Mom's epic shopping trips. You've shirked the duty long enough. It's time to pay your dues."

I could hear Mom's sharp intake of breath behind me. "Jacob," she chastised.

A snort of laughter left me. Maybe it was a tasteless joke, but it felt so right in that moment. It felt normal.

Jacob gasped, doing an almost dead-on impression of Mom. I reacted immediately. My body shook uncontrollably from laughter to the point where my side ached.

"See, just lightening the mood, Ma. If this party became

any more somber, I'd have to start whistling a funeral march," Jacob said as Mom slapped his arm.

Five hours later, I could see why he had ducked out. Shopping with Mom was not for the faint of heart. It was like running a marathon. That being said, I couldn't remember a time when I'd had so much fun. It was surreal to think that everything we purchased was for me. I tried protesting at one point, feeling Mom was going overboard, but she wouldn't have it. "I have ten birthdays and Christmases to make up for. Don't burst my bubble," she said, dipping a tortilla chip into our dish of salsa. We stopped to recharge and fuel up at a cute little Mexican restaurant Mom had suggested.

Eating out at a restaurant was a new experience for me. The small establishment was buzzing with crowded lunchtime activity. I found myself too preoccupied with looking around at the sights and eavesdropping on conversations at other tables to eat much. It was another everyday ritual that most people took for granted that I had only read about in books. Now that I was experiencing it, the words and flowing paragraphs I had read could no longer give the experience full justification.

I no sooner sucked down my first Coke when our waitress instinctively returned with a brand-new glass, filled to the brim. My old glass was swept away like it was no big deal. After using the same exact dishes, day after day for years, it felt a bit unsettling although I couldn't show it.

I turned my attention back to our table, finding Mom watching me adoringly. I had already come to recognize the misty look in her eyes. She took a sip from her drink before speaking. "I've dreamed about this moment for the last ten years," she said. "I missed you terribly, Mia. I'm so sorry I missed so much of your life. It breaks my heart that I wasn't there to soothe you when you needed me most."

I looked down, rubbing my finger over the wood grain pattern on the table. "I thought you guys didn't love me anymore. Judy told me you gave me away because I was sick."

She released a half-sob and reached for my hand. "Sweetie, the only sick one was her. I'm sorry she made you believe that. I could kill her for what she did to you."

I jerked my head up, horrified by the thought. Surely she didn't mean that. My teeth bit down on the soft flesh inside my mouth until I could taste blood. It was soothing.

Mom misread my reaction and squeezed my hand tightly. "I'm sorry, honey. I know you don't like to talk about *her*. I just want you to know that monster will pay for what she did to you."

Monster? I shook my head. Judy wasn't a monster. The monster lurked inside her. It wasn't Judy's fault that my actions had provoked the monster time and time again. I opened my mouth to defend her but abruptly slammed it shut. I didn't want Mom to know about all the bad things I had done. I wasn't ready for her to look at me with disgust or hate like Judy had. I was determined to be the good daughter this time. To step into the role my Mia had created. I could be perfect.

After lunch, Mom's last surprise was to drag me into a

bookstore where she insisted that I pick out anything I wanted. I stood in the middle of the store, completely overwhelmed. I had read hundreds and hundreds of books in my life, but that number seemed insignificant while standing in a bookstore boasting a selection of millions of titles. It took a while to find the section of books I preferred and even longer to choose anything. Truthfully, I wanted everything I laid my hands on, but disciplined myself to only a few until, at Mom's urging, my stack had grown to twenty titles. I spent over an hour mulling over my stack, adding a few titles, only to put them back again when I would stumble upon another title I thought I wanted more. Mom sat patiently, never once rushing me along. Finally, I managed to whittle my stack down to the books I wanted most. Mom followed behind me to the register, but I didn't notice until she plunked down her own stack on the counter that she had grabbed all the books I showed interest in, but had discarded to keep my stack under control. I tried to protest again, but she only smiled as she handed over her credit card that had to be worn out from use.

IT TOOK six trips to carry in all my new belongings. The only thing that stopped Mom from continuing to shop was that we had run out of room in her car. As it was, some of what we purchased still had to be delivered, like the matching bookshelves and an oversize chair I had picked out that would be perfect for reading. Two of the bags in the car held all the brand-new books that would soon fill my shelves.

Jacob grunted, carrying the heavier bags up to my room. "Did you guys leave anything in the store?" he teased, placing the bags on my dresser.

I grinned sheepishly. "I tried to say no but—"

Jacob held up his hands to interrupt me. "Believe me, I understand. If you remember, I tried to warn you. I used to hate going back-to-school shopping with her. She'd drag me to one department store after another and make me try on hundreds of shirts and jeans, but only actually pick out a couple before dragging me to the next store to start the process all over again." He sank down on the foot of my bed, shaking his head. "And don't even get me started on the horror of shoe shopping." He shuddered dramatically for effect.

I laughed at his description, but truthfully I had enjoyed shoe shopping almost as much as I had book shopping. The pair of shoes Mom brought to the hospital for me was the first pair I had ever owned that weren't slippers. Since I never left my basement room, Judy never provided anything more. I accidentally let that fact slip to Mom who then took the revelation as a challenge. I now had eight pair of shoes that were all mine. When I would ever wear them all was of no concern to Mom. She assured me that a wide selection of shoes was essential.

"Let's go get the rest of your bags and then I thought later I'd take you out with some of my friends, if you're not too tired," Jacob said, pulling me up from the bed.

I gaped at him. "You want me to meet your friends tonight?"

"Sure. You start classes on Monday, so Mom and I thought it might be easier to meet a few people beforehand. Don't worry, they're all cool. They just want to meet you. I'll be with you the whole time."

I twisted my hands nervously. Reluctantly, I agreed although I had serious anxiety about embarrassing Jacob in front of his friends.

He ruffled my hair. "Trust me. I got your back."

His words meant a lot, but I was still nervous about starting school on Monday. It made sense that meeting some people ahead of time would make it easier. I was just terrified that no one would like me.

I was able to forget my apprehensions when Mom and I began setting up my room. She let me dictate everything, saying it was my room after all. We hung up some of my new clothes in my closet and neatly folded the rest before storing them in my dresser drawers. My books were stacked on my dresser until my bookshelves arrived, but I already had them in the order I wanted to read them.

Mom helped me dress out my bed in a new deep purple comforter with matching skirt, sheets, and pillowcases. I picked it because of how soft it was to the touch. The lamps added to my side tables and throw pillows in accenting lighter shades of purple tossed at the head of the bed completed the look. We took a step back, admiring our work. With those small touches, the room was transformed.

Originally I had balked when Mom insisted on buying the half-dozen throw pillows that graced the top of my bed. Just like the shoes, I thought she was being overly extravagant. The twin bed I slept on for the last ten years had exactly one thin pillow with a white case that always smelled harshly of bleach. Judy was methodical about washing my bedding once a week.

Mom left my room once everything was put away. She claimed she was in dire need of a soak in the tub, but I had the impression she was giving me a little space to absorb my new surroundings. I didn't realize how much I needed the privacy until I was left alone. I sagged onto my bed, running my hands over my soft comforter. It felt surreal. Less than a month ago I had been chained to my bed, convinced I was going to die. Now I was here. It could have been a dream. I dug my fingernails into my palm, wondering if I would suddenly wake up at the sound of Judy's footsteps coming down the stairs.

When that didn't work I scanned my room, looking for something else I could use to test my theory. My eyes paused at the pair of scissors sitting on my nightstand table. We had used them to cut all the tags off my stuff. Reaching across my bed, I grabbed the scissors and pushed the tip into my palm. The metal dug into my hand with delicious pain. It felt good. They were too dull to draw blood. Opening the blades, I ran the sharpened edge along my palm, pressing hard until a line of blood appeared. I swiped at the thin trail of blood with my thumb. As I lay back against my mountain of pillows, I smiled, accepting that it was real. I thought the confirmation would provide some sort of comfort, but truthfully, I still had a feeling of dread in my stomach, longing for the simple life I'd lost.

I grabbed my new cell phone off my bedside table. I had no idea how to work the hundreds of different things it could supposedly do. I tried to talk Mom into returning the phone when she showed up at the hospital with it, but she was adamant about me having one. "I need to know that you're safe," she had implored. Then once I met Gunner, I was glad to have the phone because at least we had exchanged numbers before I left the hospital.

The other thing I had come to appreciate was the countless amount of music I had at my disposal. I stuck my earbuds in and clicked on one of the songs Gunner preferred. Peace settled through me as the music throbbed into my eardrums. It almost felt like he was with me.

I'd been gone from the hospital for only one day, but I already missed Gunner. I felt a bit needy, but I couldn't resist typing out a simple text to him. My finger hovered over the send button for a minute before I abruptly deleted the text. He told me he would call me.

The sounds of pots and pans clanging in the kitchen grabbed my attention so I headed downstairs where Mom roped me into giving her a hand. Helping to prepare dinner was another first for me. Gunner would have been proud. The way Mom bustled around the kitchen was awkward initially. I stood near the counter, unsure of what I should be doing. Mom must have sensed how I was feeling. She slowed down and showed me around the kitchen before setting me at the counter to make a salad.

It took her a few minutes to show me how to cut the vegetables, but I quickly got the hang of it. She buzzed around the kitchen, preparing spaghetti and meatballs, keeping up a steady stream of conversation at the same time. She asked me questions I could answer without venturing into the *bad zone*. I took my time, keeping my answers neutral.

Jacob hung around in the kitchen sampling everything

Mom and I were making. I laughed when she chastised him for stealing another meatball. I had missed this kind of interaction while hidden away in my basement. This was what being a family felt like. It was so perfect that my chest actually ached. How could I not feel comfortable here? Everything was going to be okay. The only thing missing was Dad. I wanted to ask about him, to get some kind of idea why he left, but it would have ruined the moment. That was a subject that could be visited at a later time. For now, this was all I could ever think to ask for.

"Jacob, carry the dishes to the table, and if you steal another meatball on your way, I'm going to whack you," Mom threatened, brandishing a wooden spoon.

A grin spread across my face until I spotted Mom looking horrified. All the activity in the kitchen seemed to stop. Jacob was suddenly too busy studying the floor to make eye contact, and Mom acted as if she had committed a crime. At first I wondered what I had missed, but then I could feel a rush of warmth creeping up my neck, making its way to my cheeks. I could feel it coating my skin like an extra layer of clothing. The mood in the room instantly became somber. I swallowed hard, wanting to tell them it was okay. I wasn't made of glass. I would not shatter from mere words. I guess I hadn't proven that I was stronger than that.

This was my fault. It always came back to me and what happened. I was beginning to think we would never be able to get past it. For the briefest of moments I missed my basement room so acutely I could barely breathe. Life was easier there, more compartmentalized. At least there I was only disappointing Judy. Here I was disappointing Mom and Jacob. The thought gutted me. I didn't want to disappoint them.

Dinner was a quiet affair. Jacob tried several times to recapture the levity from earlier, but an ominous atmosphere cloaked the room. Mom kept her eyes on her plate, picking at her food. A rock settled in the pit of my stomach. I should apologize.

After finally making it through the charade of dinner, Jacob and I began clearing the dishes, but Mom shooed us from the table. "You two go have fun." She gave Jacob a quick hug before turning to me with outstretched arms. I didn't mean to flinch. Really, I didn't. I knew she wasn't going to hit me, but instinctively, I jumped. I could see the hurt radiating in her eyes. "Be careful," she choked out. I leaned in to allow her to hug me, but it was awkward. I had managed to keep myself as fragile as glass in their eyes.

Jacob and I remained quiet as we piled into his car. He turned up the radio and backed out of the driveway in one motion. "Well, that was awkward," he chuckled.

I was too busy gnawing on the side of my nail to answer.

"You know none of this is your fault, right? We—well, more accurately, *Mom*, is having a hard time adjusting. She doesn't want to hurt you any more than you already have been. It's not always going to be this awkward." He patted my knee. "So stop trying to chew your thumb off. It's going to be cool."

I pulled my thumb from my mouth self-consciously and

stuck it under my leg to resist the temptation. "I'm not going to break," I muttered.

"I know. If you were that fragile you wouldn't be here. I've seen the pictures."

I blanched, remembering the humiliating experience of being photographed in front of a room of people. After an extensive interview with Detective Newton at the hospital, a female police officer with a kind face and gentle demeanor arrived, stating that she needed to document my injuries. Mom remained on the side of the room, watching stoically as a nurse helped lift my clothing to reveal ten years of bumps, bruises, and scars. Mom and I never talked about my injuries after that day. Knowing that Jacob had seen the pictures made the spaghetti dinner we had eaten churn painfully in my stomach. Those pictures would last forever as proof of every bad thing I had ever done.

I couldn't look at him. As much as I tried to resist, my hand refused to stay under my leg. By the time Jacob pulled up in front of an unfamiliar two-story brick house, I had drawn blood from my tender thumb.

"You ready?" he asked.

I shrugged. I had no clue if I was ready. I wasn't sure I even knew what ready meant anymore. One thing seemed certain, it couldn't be much worse than our disastrous family dinner or the car ride over.

How wrong I was, like times a million.

Jacob strolled in through the door without even knocking and led me toward the back of the house where I could hear a steady drone of voices. The closer we got, the louder it became. The noise was comforting. I hoped maybe no one would notice our arrival. It was a nice thought, but I couldn't have been more wrong. The moment we stepped out the back door to the patio, the drone of voices switched off as abruptly as a light switch. The patio was easily as big as the inside of the house, with a pool and outdoor eating area. It was dark outside so the outdoor lighting strung around the perimeter was turned on. Thirty-plus pairs of eyes pivoted toward us, all dead set on me. I shot Jacob a look of panic and scooted behind his shoulder.

"Guys, this is my sister, Mia. I'm sure some of you remember her," Jacob introduced me. He nudged me out in the middle of a large cluster of unfamiliar faces. I hated the feeling of being on display.

A few people smiled tentatively, but the majority of them stared at me in morbid curiosity. I'd seen the same look my first few days at the hospital. I was more of a story than a person, something fascinating to gawk at. Then Gunner took me under his wing. I'd give anything to have him with me at the party.

"How about a drink?" Jacob asked, leading me toward a cooler that sat near the edge of the pool. With that everyone returned to their conversations and virtually ignored me. I sagged with relief.

Jacob handed me an ice-cold Coke. "Come on, I'll introduce you to some of my friends."

I cradled the soda, thankful to have something to occupy

my hands. "Can we wait awhile?" I asked, popping the tab on the can.

Concern colored Jacob's face.

I smiled meekly to show him that everything was okay.

My smile must have been convincing enough because he hesitantly agreed. "Sure. I guess it's a little overwhelming."

I nodded, grateful that he understood.

Jacob leaned in, whispering names into my ear so I would know who everyone was from a distance. I would never remember all of their names but I appreciated the effort. Finally, a group of guys standing at the opposite corner of the patio called him over.

"Go. I'll be fine," I said, encouraging him with a shove of my shoulder. I was eager to have a moment to myself.

He looked torn. "Seriously, it's okay, Jacob. I'll just stay here and observe everything."

"I didn't bring you here to abandon you. Are you sure you don't want to come with me?"

I shook my head. "I'd rather stay here."

"Mia, if you're uncomfortable I can take you home."

"No, I'm fine," I lied, trying to appease him.

I could tell he still had his doubts so I gave him another little shove toward his friends.

"All right," he grudgingly agreed. "I'll be back in a few minutes."

I nodded, taking a sip of my Coke. With Jacob gone, I scooted away from our spot in the open, moving toward the shadows on the other side of a small changing room. I felt instant relief under the camouflage of darkness. Observing everyone would be much easier without worrying whether they could see me.

A few minutes passed and Jacob hadn't returned like he promised, but I couldn't blame him. From my vantage point, I could see him laughing and talking animatedly with a group of five guys. I couldn't hear what they were saying, but I envied the ease of their interaction.

Several minutes later, I was still standing in the shadows with my soda finished. I twirled the empty can in my hand, wishing I was brave enough to get another. A couple of girls stopped along the wall adjacent to where I stood. They began a conversation, unaware of my close proximity. They spoke with such confidence and self-assurance. I felt slightly intimidated so I backed farther into the shadows to make sure they wouldn't see me. Both girls were dressed nearly identically in long, bright, strapless dresses that flowed around their ankles. Their hair was shiny light blond with streaks of vibrant purple at the temples. I wondered if they dressed alike on purpose. They could have been related. It made me think of Mia. If she were real, I think we would have dressed alike.

I debated stepping forward to join their conversation. After all, the whole reason Jacob had brought me to the party was to meet people before I started school on Monday.

I took a half step forward, pausing when I caught their hushed conversation.

"I heard she was, like, tied to the bed, covered in her own crap," one of them said.

"Yuck. TMI, Patricia. My dad says the woman who took her was a real whack job. After going through something like that does anyone really think Mia will ever be normal? I'm surprised she can even hang out in public, you know?"

I cemented myself to the wall, unable to retreat or to confront them. I stood there listening to a conversation that everyone at the party was likely having about me. Deep down I had been expecting it.

"Truth. Did you see her when they got here? She looked like she wanted to cry. It's obvious she's one step from the loony bin already. I totally feel bad for her," Patricia said.

The other girl nodded her head in agreement.

"I don't even know how she can go to school. I'd be so humiliated. I once saw this movie where this little girl was, like, forced to raise herself in the woods, and when they finally found her she couldn't even function and stuff. She was like a wild animal."

"That sucks. I don't even know what to say to her. I mean, do we, like, congratulate her for being rescued or whatever?"

They both chuckled slightly at the idea.

"Don't ask me. To tell you the truth, I'm not sure it's any more fair for us than it is for her. I mean, should we be subjected to that kind of crazy?"

I couldn't take anymore. Forcing my feet to move, I scooted along the side of the wall, keeping the shadows in front of me to remain hidden. I didn't want to expose them to my "kind of crazy" a second longer. I was so intent on putting distance between us that I wasn't paying attention to where I placed my feet. The ground disappeared beneath my right foot, making me lose my balance.

I tumbled sideways into the pool. The water rushed over my head and my only thought was that I had no idea how to swim. Water pulled at my clothes, dragging me away from the surface and down to the bottom of the pool. I pawed at the water for a moment, but went nowhere. All noise from the party evaporated, replaced by blissful silence. I could hear the pounding of my heart. I stopped pawing at the water. It was peaceful beneath the surface. Nothing harmful could reach me under the water. There were no judging looks, no misguided condescension, but, best of all, I wasn't disappointing anyone. I never wanted to leave. I stopped fighting as I allowed the water to pull me farther down toward the bottom of the pool where I found the darkness I craved. It was glad to see me.

A SET of strong arms that felt like steel bands encircled my waist, dragging me away from the darkness. I wanted to fight back, to make them leave me alone. Their grasp was relentless though, tugging me toward the light and away from my safe place. My head broke the surface as Jacob waded into the water, taking me from the arms of whoever had rescued me.

"Mia, are you okay?" Jacob said with panic as he tugged me to the edge of the pool. My rescuer followed behind us, helping me to the steps. "You could have drowned. Why were you so close to the pool?" he asked, pausing in his tirade.

I was too exhausted to answer and already missed the silence of the bottom of the pool. My legs scraped against the steps and I tried to get myself to a standing position. It took several attempts. My limbs felt like they were made of concrete and I realized it was my wet jeans. "I'm okay," I said, keeping my eyes down. I could hear everyone snickering and didn't need to see them doing it too. I had already proved how crazy I was.

A towel was thrown over my shoulders when my feet hit the deck. I wasn't even aware my teeth were chattering until Jacob tucked the towel under my chin.

"Man, I owe you big-time," Jacob said, holding a fist out to a guy who was soaking wet like I was.

They knocked knuckles together. "Not a problem. Three summers of lifeguarding. You okay, Mia?"

"I'm fine," I answered unconvincingly through chattering teeth.

Jacob slung another towel across my shoulders. "I better take you home. Mom will have my dumbass head on a pike if you get sick." He propelled me toward the door after throwing another thank-you at my rescuer. I kept my eyes averted away from everyone else as we left. They could continue their party and say whatever they wanted about me after I was gone. The freak was leaving the building.

"You sure you're okay?" Jacob asked, kicking up the heat in the car even though it was mild outside. My teeth were still chattering.

"Yes. I'm sorry I ruined your party."

Jacob shot me a sideways glance. "You didn't ruin my party. I'm the doucheking who left you alone. I promised Mom I'd take care of you." He thumped the steering wheel in frustration.

I wasn't exactly in a position to contradict anything he said. I didn't want to seem fragile, but it was hard to stick up for myself after being pulled unwillingly from a pool. Weary from what felt like an endless day, I rested my head against the window. The streetlights broke up the dark, whizzing by the window as we passed them. My eyes felt heavy, like I could have fallen asleep.

Mom was sitting in the living room crocheting when Jacob and I staggered in ten minutes after leaving the party. Her look of surprise at our early arrival turned to concern when she saw me dripping water all over the hardwood floors. "Mia, what happened?" she asked, jumping to her feet. The question was meant for me, but she looked to Jacob, demanding an answer.

"I fe-l-l in the pool," I answered, trying to talk around my knocking teeth.

"She should get in a hot shower. She's been shivering like that since she came out of the water," Jacob said. He was as wet as I was, but didn't seem to be fazed.

Mom clucked her tongue. "You should too. She can take a bath in my tub, so you can shower in your bathroom. After that I want an explanation."

Jacob nodded, dripping water as he walked away. Mom shuttled me up to her bathroom. She bustled around, turning the water on full blast in a large oval-shaped tub. The only thing I had in my basement bathroom was a walk-in shower stall. Not that Judy would have ever let me use a tub anyway. She believed they were unhygienic. If she saw me now she would freak. Glancing at the stall on the other side of the tub, I wondered if I should insist on showering instead.

Mom was, of course, oblivious to my dilemma. I watched as she picked up a bottle of scented soap and dumped a generous amount into the tub. Big frothy bubbles popped up on the surface, hiding the water underneath. Only when the bubbles were threatening to escape over the edge of the tub did she twist the water off.

"I'll get you some dry clothes while you settle in," she said, smiling at me before heading out of the bathroom. She closed the door, leaving me to face my demons alone. I glanced again at the shower stall, taking a half-step toward it before changing my mind. Shaking my head to clear my thoughts, I stripped out of my sopping wet clothes and stepped into the steaming, deep bathtub. Hot water lapped over my knees. I sank down, letting it wrap me like a cocoon as the water came close to overflowing over the side of the tub. The bubbles tickled my nose, making me smile for the first time that evening.

I leaned back and closed my eyes, tempted to lower my face under the water, but part of me was afraid I wouldn't come up again. What happened in the pool was tugging at my thoughts. It was frightening to think about how easy it had been to stay underwater, to give up. It was a part of me I didn't want to acknowledge. There were so many times in the past I could have given up before my escape. I'd always been so intent on surviving another day, to get to something more. My mind used to trick me into believing that everything would be better if I ever made it outside my room. Now I realized my mind had been lying to me.

A soft knock on the door broke through my thoughts.

I sat up, making sure the bubbles were still covering me.

Mom pushed the door open. "I brought your pajamas," she said, setting them on the bench seat under the window. "Is the water warm enough?"

I nodded. "It's perfect. Thank you for letting me use your bathroom."

"Honey, what's mine is yours. Anytime you want to take a bath or escape Jacob's mess, it's yours. So, other than your pool mishap, how did the party go?"

I reached out a finger and popped one of the bubbles without making eye contact. "It was good," I lied. I didn't see the point in telling her what I had overheard. She would only tell me not to listen or something to that effect. The fact was there was nothing she could do to change everyone's opinions of me.

"That's good. Hopefully school on Monday will be a little easier. I know it's going to be an adjustment, but they're excited you'll be attending."

I nodded because I knew that's what was expected of me. Inside, I was screaming. If anything, tonight proved how ill-equipped I was to interact with regular society, let alone my own peers. School would be my own personal hell. I wished I were still at the bottom of the pool.

● ● ●

Sunday was a mixture of terror and nausea. It was on the tip of my tongue all day to beg Mom to let me stay home. To tell her exactly what happened at the party. I wasn't ready for anything more than staying at home. Rather than beg Mom I broke my vow and texted Gunner.

Can't do this, I pecked out slowly. It took me more time than it should have and countless mistakes to finally get the short message typed out. Typing on a glass screen felt weird and my fingers weren't fond of it.

Do what? His reply came instantly, which helped ease the knot in my stomach.

School. I'm not ready.

You've got this, Mia. You're stronger than you think.

I miss you.

No, you don't. This place is a drag. I miss you too though. Have a Reese's. That'll cheer you up.

His words made me laugh.

Despite my misgivings, texting Gunner helped, although Monday still arrived long before I was ready.

• • •

Jacob was already gone by the time Mom and I left the house.

"You nervous?" she asked as we backed out of the driveway.

What a question. I wondered if my slightly green complexion had tipped her off. Nodding my head, I gave up any pretense of being ready for what lay ahead. I had more important things to worry about anyway, like keeping the contents of my breakfast in my stomach.

"You're going to be fine, honey." Mom said, patting my hand at a stop sign. "Before you know it you'll have a slew of friends and it'll be me begging you to stay at home with your old mom."

I nodded, peering out the window. I didn't believe her, but

if it gave her some measure of comfort then I was all for pretending.

I don't know what I was expecting as Mom turned into the school parking lot. "Ready?" she asked, pulling into a visitor's parking space. I was relieved to see that it at least looked like the schools I had seen on television or read about in books. That was a small bit of comfort.

"Let's go," I said, quaking inside with fear.

She patted my hand again and opened her car door. "It's going to be fine."

She could keep saying the words but it wouldn't make them true. I climbed from the vehicle, hiking my new bag up on my shoulder as I warily eyed the building in front of me. Dr. Marshall would say this was an important step in reclaiming my identity. Gunner would have made it bearable. The problem was neither one would be with me.

Mom guided me into the building and opened the door to a bright office that was chaotic with morning activity. Students stood in clusters at the front desk barking out demands. Most seemed to have grievances about tardies or problems with teachers. Their issues were foreign to me, but I was thankful that they were all too wrapped up in their troubles to give me a glance.

Mom signed in at a clipboard sitting atop the counter. The woman behind the desk instructed us to take a seat until Ms. Newman, my counselor, could see us. Sitting down, I felt even more inconspicuous as I observed the comings and goings of the students around me. Most of them, like the group of girls standing in a huddle to our left, were treating the office like it was a meeting spot. Their chatter was loud and punctured by even louder squeals. They were hushed more than once, but it was obvious by their giggles they didn't take reprimands seriously. They finally dispersed and headed out when a loud bell rang throughout the building. The office quickly emptied except for the line of students still waiting to get their schedules fixed.

A short woman with a wide smile and bright eyes walked out from an office behind the counter. "Mrs. Klein, Mia? Hi, I'm Ms. Newman." She held out her hand for me to shake. "Mrs. Klein, it's so good to see you again." The sincerity in her voice was a pleasant surprise. "Why don't you follow me to my office so we can chat a little before I release Mia into the jungle?" She smiled and winked to let me know she was joking. I returned her smile though her words made the churning in my stomach even worse.

Ms. Newman's office matched her personality. It was bright and cheerful and overflowed with splashes of color. Motivational posters lined the walls, and ceramic animals with goofy faces sat atop almost every available space in the room. The office was almost too stimulating, but I liked it.

"I printed up your schedule, Mia, and went over your limited transcripts. Your case is unusual since you weren't previously enrolled in any kind of school. Despite that, we were pleasantly surprised with the scores you received on the series of tests we provided you. They show you to be even slightly more advanced than a typical rising senior. We decided, however, that being around other students your own age would be an easier transition so we've placed you in our junior classes." She nodded at Mom for confirmation, who nodded in return. "Judging by your scores, you might find some of your classes repetitive, and we don't want you to get bored, so if that becomes an issue we will reevaluate things, okay?" She paused, looking at me.

I didn't know what she was expecting from me. I understood everything she had said, but if there was a choice there for me, I didn't see it. They had no idea where to stick me. That was the point. The girls at the party had been right. "Okay," I answered, giving them what they wanted.

Clearly it worked because she beamed at me. "Excellent. I want you to know that I have an open door policy. I am here to help make this transition as easy on you as I can. We all want you to be successful at Dewy High. Do you have any questions for me?" she asked, handing me my schedule.

I shook my head, fiddling with the strap on my bag. I actually had about a million questions, but I didn't want to look dumb. The most pressing thing was the schedule I clutched in my hand.

"All right then," Ms. Newman said. "I'm going to give you a pass that you can take to Claudia at the front desk. She'll make sure you get a student aide to walk you to your first-period class. Welcome to Dewy High, Mia," she said, reaching out her hand.

Mom stood up and I realized that signaled the end of our meeting. "Thank you for all your help," Mom said, shaking Ms. Newman's hand.

My handshake was less enthusiastic. "Thank you," I mumbled, studying my schedule to try and make sense of it.

"My pleasure. Don't forget about my open door policy, Mia," she called out as we left her office.

Mom and I stopped to see Claudia, who was currently on the phone. "I guess I should head out," Mom said, looking as unsure as I felt. "I'll pick you up out front after school, okay?" She gave me a quick hug. I had to fight the urge to cling to her and beg her not to leave me. I opened my mouth to ask if I could wait a few more days. Would it really hurt anything? I realized though that a few days weren't going to help anything. Hiding out was an option I didn't have.

27

I **WATCHED** as Mom walked out of the office, leaving me behind and all alone. My heart was thundering so hard in my chest it actually hurt.

"Can I help you?" Claudia asked, hanging up the phone.

I gulped hard, trying to swallow back my fear. "Ms. Newman said to give you this," I said, holding out the small piece of paper with shaky fingers.

Claudia looked over the pass for a moment. She pulled out of a sheet of paper and filled out the top section. "Give this to each of your teachers and bring it back to me at the end of the day. Here's a map of the school and your locker number. You'll need to bring a lock from home." She handed me the small stack of papers and returned to her computer, dismissing me without another word.

Standing there gaping at her, I wanted to ask about the student aide Ms. Newman had mentioned, but Claudia had already helped the next student in line. Backing away from the counter, I clutched the stack of papers tightly in my hand. What was I supposed to do now? Panic seized me as I studied the schedule and the map. I had no idea which way to go. A guy wearing a jacket with a lion etched on the back bumped into me. I opened my mouth to mumble an apology, but the words refused to come out.

Making my way to the door, I pried it open and hugged the wall once I was clear of the office. Air wheezed out of me in painful gasps. An invisible hand inside my chest squeezed my lungs painfully. I slammed my eyes closed, groping for the pills Dr. Marshall had prescribed. I could feel the panic attack creeping in like a stalker.

"Mia?" a voice called out as my hand closed around the bottle in my pocket.

My eyes popped open as my lungs continued to torture me. "Yes," I whispered, staring back at a girl who beamed as she watched me curiously.

"I'm Heather. I'm supposed to show you to your first-period class," she said, showing me all her teeth as she smiled brightly.

Trying to regain control of my erratic breathing, I took a deep breath and exhaled. "I'm Mia," I answered lamely, re-membering that she obviously already knew my name since she had said it. I waited for the inevitable to happen when she would recognize me. At any moment I expected her smile to drop and she would freak out over being paired with the school nutcase.

The inevitable never happened. Heather seemed to be as nice as she appeared. "Who do you have first period?" she asked, pausing to take a look at my schedule.

My hand was damp with sweat, turning the schedule into a wrinkled, slightly smudged mess. "Uh, looks like Mr. Knight," I answered, smoothing out the paper against my leg.

"Mr. Knight? Lucky. I hear he's good, but that's an AP class. You must have a serious Einstein brain. I tried to get in last semester, but they denied me. Big loser, huh?" She held up her finger and thumb in the shape of an L against her forehead. "Have you taken AP classes before?" I gaped at her. Her quick-fire questions had me feeling loopy.

She giggled at my expression. "Sorry. I know I talk superfast. My dad says if my brain was as fast as my mouth, I'd have no problem getting into Mr. Knight's class. So, did you just move here?" she asked, switching gears.

"Uh, not exactly." I had no idea how to answer her question. I assumed everyone would automatically know who I was and would be too busy staring or trying to get away from me to ask me questions.

"Really, where'd you go to school last year? Please tell me you weren't an Eagle. They're a bunch of assholes."

Once again, she rendered me speechless. I wasn't sure what she meant by *eagle*, but calling a bird an asshole didn't make sense. I sorted through her questions, trying to pick the easiest one to answer. I settled instead for something that would get her from point A to point B quickest.

"I'm Jacob Klein's sister, if you know him."

To anyone else her reaction probably would have been considered comical by the way her mouth formed a wide O before snapping closed. I kept my head up, waiting for judgment day to begin.

In spite of what I thought would happen, Heather seemed to be more impressed than morbidly curious. "Oh, wow. You're like a celebrity. I can't believe I was such a ditz. Your picture was only on all the news stations, like every day. Sheesh, they even did a special announcement here at school when you were found. I'm not usually such an airhead." Her words once again came at me as a rush of letters thrown my way, but this time I had no problem putting them in order.

I let out a small breath of relief. If Heather felt disgusted being next to me she was doing an awfully good job at hiding it. "That's okay," I said. "The picture they used on the news was a bad one."

The picture was taken by someone who had snuck into my room and started snapping shots before Mom could kick him out. My hair was plastered to my head from sleeping and my face looked as pale as white sheets. It was disconcerting to say the least. That picture though was used by every news station for their stories about me.

"I bet you're sick of questions," Heather said as we stepped away from the office.

I shrugged. "Sorta. I'm more worried about what everyone is saying behind my back," I admitted.

"Please, anyone with half a brain is thinking you're the

bravest person ever. Anyone who says otherwise is probably functioning with a quarter of that."

I smiled. Maybe things wouldn't be as bad as I feared. There might actually be people at the school who would treat me like anyone else. I thought calling me brave was over the top, but I also didn't want anyone to think I was a prime candidate for a straitjacket.

"I bet this is completely freaking you out. Dewy High can be a cesspool of cliques and drama sometimes, but you'll get used to it. Are you freaking out? I know I would be."

I couldn't help laughing at her words. "Freaking out" was one way to put it. "I am freaking a little," I admitted, downplaying it a bit. "I'm not even sure how I'm supposed to figure all this out," I said, holding up my schedule, which was still foreign to me.

"Your schedule? That's easy," she said, pausing in the hallway. "Here, let me see it." She held out her hand for my sweaty, crumpled schedule. "Okay, so these are your classes," she said, pointing to the first column. "This is the room number, and this is your lunch period. Hey, you can eat with me and my friends if you want," she said excitedly.

Joyful thoughts danced in my head from her invitation. Lunch was an obstacle I wouldn't even let myself think about.

"Mr. Knight's class is room 112, and the numbers run in sequence from there. One hundreds are on this floor and the two hundreds are level two. The cafeteria is down that hall. Easy, right?" Heather chattered along, barely stopping for air as she pointed to the left. "Oh, and the gymnasium is down that way, but I see you lucked out and didn't get stuck with gym anyway. I'm totally jealous. My dad is, like, an exercise nut. He insists I take PE every semester. I think he's afraid I'm going to get fat, but please. I bet I burn most of my calories for the day making runs for the office. You should see if you can become an aide next year and we can totally hang out."

We'd known each other for all of five minutes and Heather was talking to me like we were old friends. She was definitely cool. "Sounds easy enough," I answered when I could get a word in.

"Okay, I better head back to the office before Claudia sends out a posse. She's always saying that I screw around too much on my runs. Please. I'm just more helpful than all her other aides. Mr. Knight's class is right there. Do you want me to go in with you? I can do that. I probably should have offered that from the beginning."

Before I could even think about answering, she was already striding toward the classroom door. She opened it like she seemed to do everything else—in a rush. The door banged into the wall, scaring everyone inside, but Heather didn't seem to notice as she flounced into the room without a care in the world. I envied her confidence.

"Good morning, Mr. Knight, this is your new student," Heather announced. I flushed when all eyes in the room pivoted to me.

"Ah, yes, you must be Mia. I've been expecting you. It's a pleasure to have you," Mr. Knight said, holding out his hand. "I received your test scores on Friday and I'm not going to lie, they blew me away," he said, completely ignoring Heather who gasped at his words and was rendered silent for the first time since I met her. "You know your history," Mr. Knight continued, shaking my hand vigorously.

I could feel my skin warming again. "Thank you," I whispered, trying not to look at the class who was studying me even more intently after his statement.

"I better head back to the office," Heather said, whirling around wistfully. "Mia, I'll meet you outside the cafeteria at lunchtime," she said, exiting the room much like she had entered it.

"Mia, you can sit in the empty desk next to Connor," Mr. Knight instructed me. "Connor, raise your hand, please."

I nodded, making my way anxiously down the row so I could sit as soon as possible. Mr. Knight continued with the lecture he'd obviously been in the middle of when Heather and I showed up. It took me a few minutes to calm down enough to take in my surroundings. Some of my fear evaporated. I was sitting in an honest-to-goodness classroom and I was still alive. It was every bit as I imagined it would be, complete with overflowing bookshelves and a towering stack of papers on the edge of Mr. Knight's desk.

The desk I'd been assigned to was in the second row, three seats back, so I had a view of almost the entire room without having to crane my neck. The room was less crowded than I expected with fourteen students by my count, including me. Other than that, it lived up to all my expectations. No one was looking at me, which I was immensely grateful for.

Mr. Knight talked until the bell rang. I noticed that every-one in the class was busily scribbling notes to keep up with him. Feeling like I was doing something wrong, I opened up my own notebook, but didn't know what I should write down. He was discussing the first stages of the Civil War in great detail, but I already knew everything he was covering. I'd pre-viously written a sixteen-page report on the Civil War and used every resource Judy dragged home from the library for me. The subject had sparked some interest in me so I de-voured anything I could get my hands on.

Mr. Knight had a soothing voice, and a nice way of ex-plaining it that made the subject even more interesting, so it was easy to listen to him.

Everyone scrambled to their feet in a rush when the bell rang. I grabbed my bag and peered at my schedule in a panic. My next class was room 122, so at least I was still on the right floor.

"Mia, a word," Mr. Knight called after me before I could follow the crowd out of the room.

I paused at the door, wondering if I'd done something wrong. Maybe I was supposed to take notes after all.

"Well, what did you think?" he asked.

His question caught me off guard. When it came to school, no one had really asked me what I thought. Judy was certainly never interested in my opinions.

"I liked it. You have a great way of explaining a tough, de-tailed subject."

"I noticed you didn't take notes."

I shifted my feet. "I sorta know everything you talked about," I answered, afraid he might get upset.

He barked out a loud laugh, making me flinch. "That's what I figured. I hope I didn't bore you."

"Oh no. It was nice to hear your explanation," I answered honestly. "It was more entertaining than just reading about it."

"I'm glad to hear that. Feel free to add to the discussion tomorrow. I would love to hear your insights. You better head to class now before you're late," he said as students starting filing into his class.

"Okay," I answered, hurrying off. I didn't see myself ever feeling comfortable enough to talk out loud, but I liked Mr. Knight a lot. If all my teachers were as cool, maybe school would be survivable. Between Heather and AP American History, I was feeling faintly better.

I found my second-period class a minute before the bell rang. The room was fuller than AP History and everyone seemed to be looking at the same thing—me. I pretended I didn't notice when three girls in the back leaned in together and started whispering while never taking their eyes off me.

I stood at the front of the room, shifting from one foot to the next and wishing I could disappear to avoid the staring. It would help if the teacher would show up. Wasn't the whole point of going to school to actually have an adult figure in charge? The second bell rang and I contemplated backing discreetly out of the room, thinking maybe I had the wrong class.

The noise level swelled. Whispering became outright talking. I was clearly the topic of discussion, but no one was even trying to hide it. I needed to leave. I could not stand here on display in front of everyone. Before my feet could get on the same page as my brain the classroom door swung open and a harried-looking younger man entered the room.

He looked like he had either slept in his clothes or pulled them out of the hamper. His hair was disheveled and standing on end and his face was covered in stubble, making him look unkempt. "I'm Mr. Cruz. Your teacher, Ms. Gritzki, is out sick today," he said, running a hand over his hair, making it stick up even more. "Apparently, it's now acceptable to call in at the last minute." He tossed his briefcase on the desk. "Young lady, take your seat," he instructed.

"Uh, this is my first day," I stuttered out.

"Wonderful," he sighed, snatching the slip of paper from my hand and scrawling his signature on it. "Sit there," he barked, pointing to an empty chair to the far right of the room that was isolated from the rest of the desks.

Embarrassment flooded my cheeks. Clutching my pass in my hand, I made my way to the desk, keeping my eyes on the floor in front of me. All the confidence I had gained during first period was long gone. I sank down in my seat, letting my hair fall across my face.

"I'm not feeling the whole teaching gig today so entertain yourselves," Mr. Cruz proclaimed, sitting in Ms. Gritzki's chair. He plopped his feet up on the desk, obviously not caring that his shoes were sitting on a stack of papers. "Just keep it down. I have a headache," he said, pulling a cell phone out of his pocket.

His words were all the encouragement everyone needed. Desks scraped across the floor as they were pushed together and the talking became a steady hum in the room. Discreetly peeking out through my hair, I saw that almost everyone in the room had pulled out cell phones, except the girls in the back who were still watching me. I turned back to face the front of the room and let my hair fall down in place.

Unlike first period, which seemed to fly by, second period felt like it was moving backward. I sat at my desk, watching the minute hand on the clock slowly tick around. I could make out snippets of conversation around me, hearing my name mentioned more than once. It was more of what I had experienced in the hospital. I hated that they knew all the sordid details. Most came from the trio in the back who managed to talk about me the entire period. It was official. Even after Heather and Mr. Knight, I hated school.

The bell to end the period saved me just short of jumping from the window. I surged gratefully to my feet, ready to escape the oppressiveness of the room. I was in the process of retrieving my bag from the floor when I was shoved hard from behind. Caught off balance, I stumbled forward, catching myself hard on the desk to my left.

"Oops, sorry," I said instinctively. Years of living with Judy had trained me to always apologize even when I wasn't at fault. One of the girls giggled when she reached her friends who all shot me the same look before heading out the door.

Yay. High school was so much fun.

Sighing, I rubbed my side which probably had an

indentation from the corner of the desk. Mr. Cruz was too wrapped up in his cell phone to care.

Third and fourth periods were marginally better. At least both teachers were present, but the whispering from my classmates continued. By the time the bell rang for lunch, I had resigned myself to the fact that Dewy High School was one of the seven realms of hell.

Thankfully, Heather kept her promise and met me outside the cafeteria so I wouldn't have to walk in by myself. The space was loud and far too chaotic to garner any attention over our entrance. I breathed easier as I followed Heather to her table.

She kept up a steady stream of talking like before. All I had to do was nod my head in response to keep her going. She shifted conversations rapidly, but I found it oddly distracting in a good way. I was grateful she was at least treating me like a person and not a spectacle.

"Katie and Molly, this is my new friend, Mia." She finally came up for air to introduce me to the two other girls at the table.

"Hi," Katie said, looking down shyly at her plate.

"Hey," I answered.

Molly's response was slower to come. "Mia," she said leisurely. I could see she made the connection. "So, you're her, huh?" I waited for more of what I had been hearing all day in classes, even braced myself to leave the table when she made it clear she didn't want me there. Nothing happened though. Molly gave me a smile and returned back to her book.

At least it wasn't a snub. My hands released their death grip on the edge of the table and the knot between my shoulders began to unravel. I opened my lunch bag and pulled out my sandwich, nibbling on the corner of it while Heather gave me more of an overview of Dewy High. She seemed to know everyone, or at least it seemed that way when she would point them out. I found it funny that she didn't call them by their given names, but rather nicknames she had made up. "It's only for people who get on my nerves," she said, justifying her actions. Molly and Katie didn't say much for the most part except to interject an opinion on someone she was talking about. Katie was quieter and answered in one-word syllables the majority of the time. Molly wasn't shy like Katie, but she also kept her words to a minimum. She was the exact opposite of Heather. She only spoke enough to get her point across. All three turned out to be pretty cool and not just because they seemed to accept me without qualms.

The bell ending lunch sounded way before I was ready for it. I didn't want to go back into another new class. The idea of being on display for three more periods was as appealing as being dipped in chocolate and fed to ants. Molly saved the day when she asked about my schedule and announced I shared my next two classes with her.

"I'm sure you can sit by me in Mrs. Blaine's class. She's pretty cool," Molly said, walking briskly down the hall.

"Thank you," I puffed, trying to keep up with her.

We were the first two students to arrive in Mrs. Blaine's room, which made the transition much easier. After she signed my slip Molly and I found two empty desks together. I realized I'd been doing things wrong all day. Getting to class early provided me a vantage point where I could observe the arrival of everyone else without being the one on display. By the time the other students arrived and filled the room no one noticed me.

Molly got us to sixth period in the same manner and with the same results, making me wish I shared all my classes with her. It was a breath of fresh air compared to my earlier class periods. We parted ways after chemistry and I hurried to my last class of the day, anxious to test my theory.

I had a better lay of the land and was able to find the room relatively easily, even without Molly as my guide. I wasn't the first one to arrive, but there were only a handful of students seated when I hurried through the door. Most of them were too busy talking to pay attention to me, but I did notice while getting my paper signed that one girl in particular was studying me intently as I found my desk.

I shifted in my seat, untucking my hair from behind my ears to shield my face. I only wished it were longer. Maybe then the girl staring would leave me alone. I pulled my notebook and pen out and began doodling on the page. At least I looked busy. Out of the corner of my eye, I saw the girl rise from her seat and head my way. I scribbled a meaningless note on my notebook, so she wouldn't know that I saw her coming.

"Are you Mia?" she asked.

I sucked in a deep breath, bracing myself for what she

might ask next. I bit my lip in frustration. Why couldn't people leave me in peace? "Yes—I am," I answered, jerking my head up with the intention of telling her off.

"I'm Amber," she said, smiling sheepishly.

I nearly fell out of my chair. Amber, my real-life childhood friend, who had also somehow found a way to live in a world that didn't exist. Mia's best friend was standing directly in front of me. And she looked nothing like she was supposed to.

28

"**SO YOU** met Amber?" Dr. Marshall asked after I filled her in on my first day of school.

I nodded, folding my hands in my lap and settling back on the cushioned seat. This was my first appointment in her actual office. It felt different from the sessions we had in my hospital room. More formal. "She was different."

"Different from what you were expecting?"

I nodded again.

"I imagine she was. The Amber you know was manifested in your head. That Amber could have been purple if that's how your brain would have decided to paint her. Don't forget, Jacob was different too," she said, noticing the look on my face.

"I know," I said, climbing to my feet. I was too antsy to sit still. I'd been sitting all day. I wandered around her office, taking in her multiple framed certificates and plaques. The wall was an impressive résumé. I found it reassuring. Dr. Marshall at least appeared to know her stuff. If anyone could fix the *crazy* in my head, it was her. "It's just that everything is so different and hard," I admitted, moving back to my seat. "It was awkward. We really had nothing to say to each other. I guess it's hard to come up with conversations of relevance after ten years."

She nodded. "I know it feels that way. I'll be the first to acknowledge that life is not easy on a normal basis. Unfortunately, your circumstances are far from normal. You've been thrown into a society that is completely new to you. Some people are going to be cruel. They won't understand what you went through, but that's the nature of life. It's not your job to make them understand either, but if you don't, you'll have to wait for their ignorance to catch up with everyone else."

"They think I'm a freak," I said, louder than I intended.

"Mia, you're not a freak."

I shrugged, sinking back down on my seat. "Maybe I am. I feel like a freak."

"Mia, you're a young lady who has gone through a horrific experience. It's going to take you time to find your place. No one is expecting you to come out of the gate running. You have to acclimate yourself to the culture around you. The young people at your school will get to know you quickly. People fear what they don't know. When they get to know you they'll discover the amazing young lady that you are. Don't let your past define you. Judy deprived you of social growth and development. It's now time to shake off her oppressiveness once and for all."

I fidgeted uncomfortably in my seat. Dr. Marshall wouldn't be saying all these good things about me if she knew the whole story. Everyone was so quick to paint Judy as the bad person, but what about me? What about the bad things I had done? If they knew all the details they wouldn't be so quick to crucify her. If I was as brave as everyone claimed I was, I would tell them the truth and accept my punishment just like I had with Judy.

I answered all Dr. Marshall's questions about school dutifully. She kept spitting out the same advice, telling me I needed to be patient. I didn't believe her. School was nothing like I always imagined it would be. I built it up as a sanctuary of sorts, but it resembled nothing close to that.

My session ended with Dr. Marshall giving me a homework assignment. She wanted me to smile at those who were talking about me. Smile? Maybe she was the crazy one. It was an impossible task. I nodded like a puppet, but there was no way I was going to be able to smile at anyone.

Leaving her office, I pulled my cell phone from my bag and typed out a text message for Mom.

Her reply came back almost immediately, stating that she would pick me up in twenty minutes. Obviously, she didn't have the same issues with texting that I did.

I decided to wander from the wing where Dr. Marshall's

office was located to the part of the hospital I had spent almost a month in. Walking down the familiar halls was comforting. I missed this place. Nurses who remembered me smiled as I made my way to my old wing. I was breaking a promise, but I couldn't help myself. I knew I promised Gunner I would stay away. It was the one thing he had asked from me, but I couldn't bring myself not to check on him. My feet propelled me down the hall like an invisible hand was pushing me from behind.

"Mia, how are you doing?" Pamela, my favorite nurse, asked, hugging me tightly.

"Good. I miss this place though."

She rolled her eyes. "You jest. No one should ever miss this place. What are you doing here?"

"I had an appointment with Dr. Marshall and decided I would visit G—" I cut myself off. What if Gunner had informed everyone that he didn't want to see me? He'd been adamant about his request and might have anticipated that I wouldn't honor it. "Everyone," I finished, correcting myself.

"I'm glad you did, sweetie. It's so good to see you," she said, giving me another hug before continuing back down the hall. I spoke to a few other nurses along the way, making quick time to get to the real reason I had come.

The hallway outside Gunner's room was empty, but I still paused at the partially open door. Hopefully he wouldn't be too mad. Before I could chicken out, I pushed the door open only to be disappointed when he wasn't there. Some of his belongings were scattered about, including a partially opened package of Reese's Peanut Butter Cups. I smiled, wondering if he would suspect it was me if I took the last piece of candy. If anyone would appreciate the joke, it would be Gunner. I thought about waiting around to surprise him, but my phone chimed in my bag. It was Mom and she was waiting outside Dr. Marshall's office. The surprise would have to wait until my next session. I just hoped Pamela and some of the other nurses wouldn't tip Gunner off that I had come to visit. Maybe when I got home I would work up the nerve to try calling him, even though I would prefer if he made the first move and called me.

I made my way past Dr. Marshall's office, finding Mom sitting outside in her car. Concern laced her features as she took in my expression. "How was your session?" she asked.

"Good," I answered, looking out the window, trying to push aside my disappointment over missing Gunner. It would have been good to talk to him although I couldn't help feeling like missing him was a sign.

"Did she ask about school?" Mom probed.

I nodded as she sighed. As soon as Mom picked me up from school earlier she had peppered me with questions about my day. Not sure how to express my feelings without hurting her, I took a page from my new friend Katie's verbal hand-book and answered in one-syllable words. I could tell Mom was disappointed that I wouldn't open up to her, but better she was disappointed than hurt.

Mom finally gave up and I felt a pinch of regret. I wanted to tell her everything. To spill all the sordid details, but I couldn't risk the consequences. She would either hate me or just want to ship me away. It wasn't worth it. Eventually, she would stop asking.

Jacob was climbing from his car with pizzas in hand when Mom pulled into our driveway ten minutes later. The passenger side of his car opened and a familiar figure stepped out. I'd barely talked to him a few nights prior and really didn't even thank him appropriately for pulling me out of the pool.

"Hey, Kevin. How's your mom liking her new job?" Mom greeted him as we all entered the house together.

"She's in heaven. Dad says she could be picking up litter on the side of the road and she'd still be happy to be out of the house."

"After six years of taking care of triplets, I can't say I blame her. Are the younger kids enjoying school?"

"They are. They might be driving their teacher into early retirement, but they love it."

Mom laughed again. "They are a bit rambunctious."

Kevin grinned at Mom as she turned on the kitchen lights. "You can say it. They're Tasmanian devils. Sorry, we haven't met officially. I'm Kevin," he said, addressing me.

"Mia," I answered, sliding my hand into his. His hand was easily twice the size of mine. It reminded me of Gunner's. It felt rougher though, covered in calluses and dry cracks. "Thanks for the other night, by the way."

"No problem. I consider it a perk of being a lifeguard to save pretty girls." He winked at me.

I blushed as Jacob punched him in the arm. "Dude, you didn't seriously just hit on my sister. I'll take you out at the knees," Jacob said, cracking his knuckles menacingly.

"You wish, bro," Kevin laughed, winking at me again. "We both know I'd wipe the floor with you." He flexed his bicep for emphasis. Jacob took a swipe at him and the next thing I knew they were rolling around on the floor. At first it looked like they really were fighting. I wasn't sure what to do, maybe yell out to Mom for help.

She walked into the room, interrupting them. "Boys, dinner." She moved to my side and linked her arm through mine. "And you know there's no roughhousing in here," she added. She gave me a squeeze of reassurance. "Boys," she said, shaking her head.

I glanced back at Jacob and Kevin who were already on their feet talking about some game that was on television the night before. There was no anger in their voices and all signs of their scuffle were gone. The fist-sized knot in my throat unraveled. I didn't understand what had just transpired, but obviously they weren't really mad at one another.

"So, Mia, what did you think of Dewy High?" Jacob asked, passing out cans of Coke from the fridge.

I sat down at the table, accepting the plate Mom handed to me, searching for the right answer. "Um, it was okay," I finally said when all three of them turned to look at me.

Kevin snorted, but tried to cover it up as a cough when my eyes met his. He winked at me again. Why did he keep doing that? Did he know it distracted me?

"Uh-oh," Jacob said, taking two slices of pizza from one of the boxes.

"What?" I asked.

"*Okay* is a telltale way of saying it sucked."

Mom pulled out the chair next to me and sat down. "Did something happen, Mia?" she asked, looking concerned.

This is what I wanted to avoid. I didn't want her to think she always needed to worry about me, but with all three of them staring at me expectantly I had no choice but to answer. "Not really," I replied, picking a pepperoni off my slice of pizza.

"Was it your classes?"

I shook my head. "No, those are okay. Pretty easy, actually. It's everyone else," I said miserably. I only wished Kevin hadn't been there to hear me complain. Some things were better left between family members.

"Were they jerks?" Mom asked in a high-pitched voice.

Jacob snorted. "Momma bear engage," he said, elbowing Kevin. "Tell me who it was. Kevin and I will have a little talk with them."

"I don't know their names and it's too many anyway. Everyone knows who I am. They think I'm messed up."

Mom clucked her tongue angrily next to me. "You're not messed up, sweetie," she reassured me. I looked up in time to see her and Jacob exchange a look. I was about to ask what the look meant, but Mom's phone rang first.

"Hello, Blake," she said, rising from the table as she answered the phone. She moved into another room for privacy.

This time there was no mistaking Jacob's aggravation as he grabbed one of the pizza boxes and his soda. He nodded his head to gesture Kevin to follow him.

Kevin shot me an apologetic look, grabbing his own soda.

I sat at the table by myself, systematically picking apart the pepperonis I'd removed from my slice of pizza. Straining my ears, I could hear snippets of Mom's conversation with Dad. He must have asked how I was adjusting. Mom's answer was muffled, but I thought she told him I was fine. Adjusting well. I wondered why he didn't come see me himself. Did he hate me? Was I the reason he'd left? I was like a wrecking ball, destroying everything in my path.

Suddenly, I was no longer hungry. My stomach felt a bit uneasy. I tossed my plate into the trash and climbed the stairs to my room. A strange sense of déjà vu followed me as I made my way up the steps. I could hear the guys talking and laughing as I passed Jacob's room. They sounded so happy and carefree. I wished I felt comfortable enough to go in with them. Instead, I headed to my room and closed the door, shutting the world out.

THE NEXT day passed in much the same fashion with the exception that I was able to find my classes without any help. I kept my head down the majority of the time, wishing everyone would stop looking at me. The whispering had turned into outright taunts anytime a teacher wasn't around. Lunch period with my new friends was the only time I felt I wasn't on display.

I practically jumped from my seat after seventh period when the final bell rang. Racing from the building to get to Jacob's car, I clutched my books against my chest as a weak attempt to shield myself from all the staring and finger-pointing. A bag over my head would have been more effective. I read a book once where the main character had to make it through hazing week to get into a fraternity. That's what I felt like here, but times a hundred.

I could hardly catch my breath by the time I made it to Jacob's car. In my haste to leave so quickly I hadn't considered that at least inside the building I was slightly more protected. Without the watchful eyes of the teachers, the students were free to glare and jeer and downright cackle any way they wanted. Indecision filled my head, crawling down my spine with a chill. I could run, maybe wait for Jacob closer to the building, but that too was like running directly into the storm. Reaching up to massage my aching head, I felt beads of sweat forming, ready to trickle down my face.

"Hey, you ready?" Jacob asked, jingling his keys in his hand.

He didn't ask how my day went. I was pretty sure my face said it all as we climbed into his car. Maybe he sensed it had been much the same as the day before, if not worse.

"How about some ice cream?" he asked, starting the car.

I nodded, smiling weakly as I wiped the sweat from my forehead.

He opened his mouth to comment, but reached over instead and turned on the radio.

That was fine with me. I peered out the window, grateful that he wasn't pressing me for details about my day. Jacob seemed to get it. Maybe he had heard his fair share of snide whispering just like I had and already knew everything. Whatever havoc my arrival may have caused in his life, I felt terrible for it.

As Jacob pulled away, a group of girls standing against their car all shot me a look. They didn't point or shout, but clearly I was the object of their fascination. I averted my eyes.

I was on my time now. They could make their nasty comments during school hours.

If Jacob noticed them he didn't let on as he turned out of the parking lot. He was strangely quiet, but I didn't question it. I was lost in my own world. Just being away from school was a huge weight lifted from my shoulders.

It took a while to reach the ice cream parlor, but the moment Jacob pulled into the parking lot a fuzzy memory tugged at my subconscious. The building shaped like a giant ice cream cone.

"I know this place," I said, taking in the faded sign and weathered parking lot with cracks and small potholes scattered about.

"We used to come here every Saturday before you were taken. It was Mom's weekly treat when we were good." Jacob's voice was laced in a mild hint of sorrow.

"I remember," I said in awe. "I always got chocolate and vanilla swirl, but you only liked the chocolate." The memory wrapped around me like a warm blanket. I grasped it tightly, afraid it would leave before it could fully take root.

Jacob nodded. His eyes glistened brightly with moisture. "We stopped going after . . ."

My own eyes welled up. "Every moment in our lives is now categorized as either *before* or *after*. Is it wrong that I'm starting to hate the significance of both words?"

"Not at all. I know exactly what you mean. We'll make this our *now*," Jacob said.

I nodded, opening my car door.

Our *now* consisted of Jacob and me sitting on the bench in front of the small ice cream stand, licking our cones before they could melt down our wrists. Jacob was back to his normal chatty self but avoided talking about school, which I was eternally grateful for. Instead, we talked about everything else, like the books I'd read and loved and television shows he had watched over the years that I missed. We stayed on the bench talking for nearly three hours. It was the perfect distraction.

The sun was beginning to lower on the horizon when we arrived home with a bag of greasy burgers and fries we'd picked up on the way. Jacob had called ahead to tell Mom so she wouldn't start cooking. Dinner felt awkward and stiff from the moment we sat down. Jacob told Mom where we had gone after school and she became melancholy from the news. She excused herself to use the bathroom and when she returned her eyes and nose were red. My chest began to ache and I looked down at the burger I no longer wanted. Everything was so damn hard. Whatever I did seemed to have painful repercussions. Finally giving up the pretense of eating, I excused myself from the table, anxious to escape the gloom that seemed to have saturated every fiber of the house.

Mom and Jacob continued to talk as I raced upstairs. Their voices changed from a low murmur to nearly shouting. Jacob was clearly upset over something. Leaning against my bedroom door, I massaged the fissure that had opened up in my chest. It was as if a hook had been inserted with the sole purpose of tearing and ripping my heart to shreds. I should have thought about taking one of the pills Dr. Marshall prescribed, but it wasn't medication I needed to feel better. I wanted something familiar, something I could relate to. Twisting the lock on the doorknob, I climbed on my bed and reached under my pillow, pulling out a small box of supplies that I had gathered the night before. I pushed up my sleeve, uncovering a hidden white bandage wrapped around my forearm. It had soaked through slightly with blood and puss. Unwrapping the bandage pulled away pieces of scab combined with the fine hairs on my arm. I sighed deeply, taking comfort in the stinging sensation that followed. What remained were the raw, oozing remnants of a burn that looked as agonizing as it felt. I closed my eyes, embracing the pain that felt like a warm blanket on a cold night. I reached into the box and pulled out a lighter I'd found stashed in Mom's junk drawer in the kitchen. Flicking the dial, I moved the lighter back and forth, mesmerized by the way the small flame appeared to dance at my control. I lowered the lighter to a spot on my arm, just below the already damaged, oozing wound.

White-hot gratification coursed through my skin. My flesh seared as my arm began to shake, but I held firm until the pain eclipsed what I felt in my heart. I clicked off the lighter, admiring the burn that was severe, and yet soothing at the same time. My hand shook as I pulled out the tube of burn cream I had snagged from the medicine cabinet. The ointment burned nearly as much as the flame had, but I dabbed it on my sore gingerly, feeling content as I rewrapped my arm. I couldn't imagine this would go over well with

Mom or Dr. Marshall, which is why I kept the burns small and hidden.

I fell asleep with my head resting against the mound of pillows that felt too comfortable beneath my head. Too extravagant. I would never admit it to anyone but I sorely missed my small thin pillow that always smelled of bleach. It had always served its purpose. Not once in all the time I'd been away did I ever give any thought to the thinness of that pillow. Life was so much simpler. I didn't want to return to my prison. I just missed certain aspects. Judy. I missed her, as morbid as that sounded. After everything she had done to me. The lies. The beatings. Beneath years of mental and physical torment she had been the only thing I'd ever known. I felt like Judas for even thinking about her. What would people think of me? Mom would be crushed if she knew.

My conflicting thoughts carried into my dreams, pulling and tugging at me.

Judy was standing over me in my small, narrow bed, screeching at me to get up. I jumped from my bed, afraid of being punished by the leather strap she held in her hand. A tugging on my arm brought my attention to a second person in my prison. A person who shouldn't have been there. A person who had never showed up despite the million tears I'd shed. Mom was suddenly in my prison. She held my arm in a death grip, making it ache painfully as she attempted to drag me away. Judy's face contorted in anger, changing from pale to a deep purple shade almost instantly. She raised the leather strap high in the air, bringing it down sharply.

I jerked awake before the strap could rip away a layer of skin. The pillows beneath my head were damp with sweat. Gasping, I tried to dislodge the scream that was still stuck in my throat. The arm Mom had gripped in my dream ached painfully beneath the bandage I'd applied earlier.

It was just a dream.

A nightmare.

My gasps eventually subsided, leaving behind a throat as dry as the Sahara. Climbing from my bed, I left the mound of pillows and the last remnants of the nightmare behind as I headed out of my room. On quiet feet, I felt my way down the dark hallway. I was the master of moving around without detection. A muffled sound caused me to pause before I could descend the stairs. I turned to look behind me. Jacob's door was firmly closed without a trace of light. Mom's door though was open a crack and partially lit. The sound came again. This time I could make out a half sob. Indecision rooted me in place. It was obvious Mom was crying. I felt a stirring in my gut. It took me a moment to rationalize what the stirring was. Sadness. I felt sad that something had upset her enough to make her weep in her room well into the night.

Without conscious thought my feet moved down the hallway. I paused outside her door, wondering how'd I gotten there. The sobs were louder standing outside her room. They were gut-wrenching, tearing at my very soul. How could I comfort her? We barely even knew each other. Knowing this did not stop me from peeking carefully into the room.

Mom sat in the center of her bed with her head bowed.

Pictures were strewn across her comforter as if they had rained down around her. In the dim light I could make out some of the images of a much younger me. A younger me that I didn't even remember. She was surrounded by memories that were no longer me.

Swallowing hard to dislodge the cantaloupe-sized lump that had formed in my throat, I started to back away when I saw what she held in her arms. Air escaped my lungs in a whooshing sound that would have been heard if not for her sobbing.

Her body was curled around the object I dreamed about, thought about, missed for an eternity. Nestled in her arms was the thing that had started it all.

Daisy, my old doll.

30

MY NEW friends were the only thing that made school tolerable. They had accepted me into their circle in spite of the
fact that we seemed to be on display every single day. I had
hoped that everyone's morbid fascination with me would
have worn off by now, but the stares and finger-pointing and
whispering still followed me everywhere I went. I hated that
it was disrupting my friends' lives also.

"Fuck that," Heather said, reacting to another of my
apologies. "It should be them apologizing. No offense,
Mia, but all it'll take is some new drama to start around
here and you'll be old news. Besides, next year when we're
seniors we'll be running the show. I'm thinking about
running for student council. Maybe you should run for office
too."

I blanched at her words. I'd rather swan dive off Niagara Falls in the middle of winter. "No, thank you," I said, shifting on the concrete bench to get more comfortable.

The mild weather outside enticed us to escape the fishbowl atmosphere of the cafeteria for the small area behind the building. The students called the space "The Quad," though it really wasn't anything more than a concrete slab roughly the size of a basketball court. By most standards it was bleak— no trees or grass. Just a handful of picnic tables that were quickly claimed.

Normally The Quad was untouchable, but Heather had staked out a table earlier when I expressed a desire for a break from the constant stares. The Quad was far from empty but it was better than the cafeteria.

"Speaking of drama. Did you see Cara John freaking out on Felix again? Talk about a couple that is a walking reality show. And what about her new highlights? Train wreck," Molly said, speaking out of the corner of her mouth.

"Nice, Molls. I'm trying to cheer Mia up and you're acting like everyone else."

"Just keeping it real. How about when you become president, you ban bad hair. That'll cheer everybody up."

"Mia, just be yourself. Eventually everyone will realize you're no different from anyone else," Katie said quietly, setting her book down to look at me.

"Well, you know that and I know that, and our future president here knows that, but until the novelty of Mia's kidnapping dies down, she's different to everyone here at school who has seen her face plastered all over the TV screens," Molly proclaimed.

I fidgeted uncomfortably. My new friends had been careful to avoid talking about my kidnapping during the short time we had known each other. It wasn't that I was keeping my past from them. Considering how much the news had reported my story, everyone knew more about my life than I was comfortable with anyway. It just felt nice not to talk about the heavy stuff. I got enough of that from Dr. Marshall. I pondered Molly's words, weighing them in my head. It made sense. How long would it take for people to forget though? That was the question.

"I agree. It's their loss," Heather said, stealing one of my chips. "Besides, I'm selfish. I like having you all to ourselves. Case in point." She pointed to a guy staring at me as he passed us on his way back into the building. "Why don't you take a picture, it lasts longer," she called out after him.

"Heather," I choked out, not sure if I should laugh or cry. "Now they're really going to talk about me." I groaned, dropping my head into my hands.

My friends burst into snorts of laughter. I couldn't help joining in after a minute. How could I stay mad at them? Our conversation moved to lighter topics after that, much to my relief.

My classes were mostly repetitive of everything I'd already learned on my own. How ironic that as much as everyone preached about all the wrong Judy had done, my education had been stellar by comparison. Even Mr. Knight's class had become tedious. All the teachers seemed preoccupied with spring break that was approaching fast. I began to wonder why I was even there.

Things at home were equally strained. Most times it was still tense and awkward. We were all trying to pretend to be a normal family, but something felt slightly off. Nobody wanted to say what that something was, but I knew it was me. I was the squeaky wheel on a once-functional bicycle. To make matters worse, I hadn't heard from Gunner again. I tried texting him, but he never answered back. I had the nagging feeling he was giving me the brush-off.

My sessions with Dr. Marshall weren't much better. We had hit a stalemate on what I was willing to share with her. She pushed me to open up more about my childhood and the punishments I'd received. She tried to convince me that the road to recovery would only be forged when I began to let go of all the secrets I was holding deep inside. She poked and prodded, but the more she tried to get the truth out of me, the more I stubbornly resisted. By the end of my second month home, I could tell she was becoming frustrated.

"Tell me about your friends at school," she asked after I deflected her line of questioning about my early years with Judy yet again.

"Molly and Heather?" I asked, looking up from the patterns I was tracing on my leg with my fingernail.

"And the quiet one. What was her name again?"

"Katie," I said, wondering why she had brought them up again. I tried talking about my friends a lot the first few weeks, but at the time Dr. Marshall seemed more interested in digging into my childhood with gusto. It was a clever strategy on her part to bring them up again, but I wasn't stupid. She just wanted to distract me and get me talking about Judy's punishments. If she wanted to continue the tug-of-war, so be it.

"Tell me more about them. You eat lunch together every day?"

I scraped my nail across my skin, liking the way it puckered. "Yes, and share a couple classes too. It's not like anyone else wants to sit with me. Everyone else is too busy watching me like a circus show. I thought you said they'd get over it."

She drummed her fingers on her desk. "Why do you think that is?"

"I don't know. You're the specialist, right? You tell me," I said sarcastically. It felt good to unload. If she knew so much, why hadn't she given me the secret formula to get all the bitches at school to stop giving me a hard time?

She scribbled something on her notepad, but didn't rise to the bait. "Do you and your friends ever attempt to invite anyone else to eat with you? Is it possible some of the other kids feel excluded?"

I snorted. "You're kidding, right? The way other kids treat me is our fault? Besides, why would my friends exclude anyone? They welcomed me with open arms."

"Yes, but the four of you might be unintentionally discouraging interaction."

I shook my head at her mid-sentence. The other kids had

no problem interacting with me throughout the day with their snide comments and finger-pointing. My friends just didn't take any crap. That was the difference at lunch. "It's just easier with us four," I finally answered in frustration.

"Why do you think that is?"

I groaned. I hated this line of questioning. It was as if Dr. Marshall was searching for a certain answer and instead of asking me directly, she took the long way to get there. It was like we were tiptoeing around the issue. "I don't know. Maybe they hate everyone else too," I answered.

"Why?"

Of course, why—why—why, that was all she ever asked. I should save us the step and say it for her. "Because everyone else is a bunch of assholes and my friends probably already know that," I said, raising my voice.

At least there was no point in Dr. Marshall asking "why" again. I had already given her a hundred examples of what my classmates had done. Clearly, they were assholes.

My session ended before we could delve into the subject any further. I couldn't help noticing that she looked troubled as I stood up and gathered my stuff. It was unsettling to see her eyebrows drawn together and the small frown on her face. I debated asking her if she was okay, but our relationship didn't stretch that far. As a matter of fact, I knew next to nothing about Dr. Marshall except for the small bits I'd gleaned from walking around her office. Obviously, she was extremely intelligent. The countless certificates and accolades that lined her walls testified to that. She wasn't one to collect knickknacks though, which made it hard to figure out what she liked. She only had one framed picture in her office and it was of her and an elderly woman who looked like an older version of her. I had tried to ask on another occasion if she was married or had children, but she always deftly side-stepped my questions. I figured it had something to do with the whole patient/doctor confidentiality thing.

I tossed a wave over my shoulder, telling her I'd see her again on Friday. Jacob was waiting outside to pick me up since Mom worked late on Wednesdays. "How was your session?" he asked when I climbed into his car.

"Same. I sit there while she tries to shrink my brain." I grinned at him while I buckled my seat belt.

He laughed. "Nice. You're getting good at that."

Jacob and Kevin had made it their mission to teach me the finer points of humor. Admittedly, I was a bit of a stiff for a while. Now I practiced all my jokes on them. Most were lame, but I was catching on. Humor was an odd concept for me. I wasn't exactly exposed to many funny things for ten years. I'd found humor in books on occasion, but firsthand experience was something different.

"Thanks," I grinned, turning the radio up when I heard a song I liked. Music was definitely one of my favorite parts of my new life. I couldn't get enough of it. "Where's Kevin?" I asked when my song ended and I turned the radio back down to a conversation level.

"Working. The water park's getting busy now because of different counties starting spring break. Just one more week and we'll get to chill at the beach on our break too."

I smiled broadly. Shortly after I was released from the hospital, Mom had taken me to the beach, but a cold front had kept me from getting the real beach experience. To make up for it, Mom had reserved a condo on the beach for the entire week we'd be on spring break. A week away from school, and the beach as an added bonus. I was beyond excited.

"I can't wait."

"Me either, kid. It's been ages since we've been on a vacation."

"I don't even remember going on one. Did we go on vacation before?"

Jacob looked sideways at me before answering. "We went on our best ones before, you know? You don't remember the Disney Cruise to the Bahamas?"

I shook my head, searching for the memory. Cruise ships were huge. How could I forget I'd been on one? I closed my eyes, trying to recall anything to help me remember. "Nope," I answered. "How old was I?"

"Four or five, I think. You seriously don't remember? You got sick the first night on the ship and puked everywhere. I think Mom was tempted to throw you overboard. The staff felt so bad for you they gave you a big stuffed Goofy. I was totally jealous."

"Ha, you're so funny." His words though triggered something in my subconscious and a memory I had long forgotten slowly unraveled. The more I thought about it, the more I did remember throwing up all over the stairwell. And the Goofy stuffed animal. I remember it was almost as tall as I was. I dragged it everywhere I went, insisting that he get his own seat during dinner. More memories flooded my mind. I could recall the waterslide that flowed into a pool in the shape of Mickey Mouse's head. The memories were faint, but at least they were there. "I do remember it. Didn't you lose your swimsuit on the slide?" I asked, laughing.

He groaned. "Of course you'd remember that part."

I grinned. "What other trips did we take?"

"We went to Yellowstone once, but we were both too little to remember much there. Mom has a whole photo album of pictures if you want to look at them."

I scratched a fingernail across my leg. I had avoided all our family albums since coming home. Mom tried to get me to look at them, thinking a glimpse into my childhood before Judy intervened would help jog my memories, but I couldn't bring myself to see the images of a past that was taken from me. "What trips did you take after?" I asked, ignoring Jacob's suggestion.

He gripped the steering wheel hard for a moment before answering. "We really only went on one and it was pretty much a disaster. Mom refused to leave the state, so we went to some local resort. I don't even remember the name. Mom and Dad spent the whole time fighting while I tried to ignore them by pretending I was digging a hole to China in the sand. I wanted to escape their endless fighting once and for all. Dad moved out as soon as we got home so I guess I got my wish," he said, smiling dryly.

"What were they fighting over?" Like I had to ask. Me. It was always me.

Jacob didn't answer right away. He pulled into our driveway, but neither of us climbed from the car. "Dad wanted us to take a real vacation. He was pissed though that Mom refused to leave the state. She was convinced that the moment we left we would get the call that you had been found. She never wanted to be more than one tank of gas away. Dad told her she needed to let you go, but she refused. He moved out as soon as we got home and checked out of our lives almost completely. He tries to make lame-ass, halfhearted attempts during the holidays, but it never feels genuine. He will always be a total asshole in my book. Your time in the hospital was the most I'd seen him in the last five years, so don't go blaming yourself."

I nodded. Since being home I had come to understand Mom's complete devotion to Jacob and me. At times it felt overbearing, but I could also appreciate that she was terrified of losing me again. "I'm sorry you were left to handle the fallout."

"I'm sorry you were left to suffer," he said, squeezing my hand.

"It wasn't that bad," I answered. "I missed you, Jacob. More than you'll ever know."

"I missed you too, sis. You don't have to cover for what that woman did though. We all know she deserves to rot in hell." His words were angry, dripping with hate. "I hope they lock her away for the rest of her life and she gets what she deserves in prison." He pounded on the steering wheel for emphasis.

I avoided his words by climbing out of the car. I knew he hated Judy. He'd made no secret of it. Mom hated her. The whole world seemed to hate her. I guess I should hate her too. I wanted to ask about her, but knew that wouldn't go over well. I couldn't help wondering where she was at the moment. I knew she was in jail but I had no idea where. Was she sleeping on a cot much like the one I slept on for the last ten years? Did she think of me? Was she sorry? I wondered what I would say to her if I were ever given the chance. Honestly, I wasn't sure I had the nerve to face her.

I WOKE up on the first day of spring feeling slightly lethargic. You would think I'd have been excited. After all, it was the last day of school before spring break and soon my family and I would be at the beach. I just needed to power through one more day in hell.

"Hey, sweetie, you okay?" Mom asked when I dragged myself into the kitchen for breakfast. "You look peaked."

I shrugged, popping two slices of bread into the toaster.

"I think when we return from the beach we'll schedule an appointment with your counselor at school," she said, taking a sip of her coffee.

"Why?" I asked dully, wishing we didn't have to talk about school so early in the morning.

She smiled, setting her cup in the sink and placing an arm

across my shoulders. "Dr. Marshall and I were talking, and we think maybe you should do some of your classes from home."

"Really?"

"I looked into it and you'll still have to go to the campus for three classes a day in order to fulfill the state requirements, but the remaining four classes you can do at home. That way you'll still get some interaction with other students, but maybe then you'll have a chance to adjust to things easier."

It sounded perfect to me. I mean, not going at all would have been ideal, but I would take whatever I could get. I threw my arms around her impulsively and gave her a tight hug. "Thank you, thank you."

"I'm taking it you told her," Jacob said, walking into the kitchen.

"You knew?" I shoved on his shoulder for keeping it from me.

"Maybe now you'll stop moping around."

"I don't mope." I protested even though I knew he was right. Finding an excuse to show enthusiasm for school had become a chore. If not for my few friends, it would have been unbearable. I'm sure a break was just what I needed. Eventually, I would become old news and could blend in like any other kid.

"You know, we could have tried making some kind of arrangement so you could have eaten lunch with me and Kevin," Jacob offered.

"Are you kidding? Lunch is the only thing that's keeping me sane, thanks to Molly, Heather, and Katie. As a matter of fact, that's all I'll miss about that place. Besides, it's not like they were about to rearrange the whole school just to make things easier for me."

Mom and Jacob exchanged a look. "What?" I asked as my eyes darted between the two of them. "Do you think I'm wrong for wanting to accept Mom's offer? You just don't know what it's like there sometimes. It's not like I'm quitting school altogether," I said in a huff.

Mom stepped in and placed a hand on each of my shoulders, looking me in the eyes. "No one is saying you're wrong, honey. We all just want what is best for you." She pulled me in for a hug, squeezing tightly. "You two better get going now. You don't want to be late." She turned and walked into the living room as Jacob and I collected our bags.

We pulled into the school and Jacob took his usual space in the student parking lot. If he ever noticed the way people stared at me he gave no indication, but there they were, on cue. All I could think about was Mom's news. I could sneak in and do three classes a day. Then everyone would have to find someone else to whisper about. I just didn't get why the fascination had lasted so long. I was the most boring person ever. If anything they were more focused on me now, eight weeks later, than they had been when I first arrived. *Freak* and *crazy* were thrown around so often I began to wonder if I should just save everyone the trouble and change my name.

Jacob and I parted ways as soon as we walked through the doors since our first-period classes were on completely different ends of the building. The morning passed with few comments and incidents. I'd learned a few weeks prior that hugging the wall while I walked made me a harder target to knock into or to uproot anything I might be holding in my arms. Teenagers sucked.

Heather and my crew were waiting for me at our usual table when I arrived for lunch. They were alone, of course, which would have driven Dr. Marshall crazy. She could say what she wanted, but I liked that it was just the four of us. It was one of the only times I got any peace at school.

Heather was already chattering Molly's and Katie's ears off, nothing out of the ordinary there. She waved as I sat down without even pausing in her story. Heather didn't have an off switch. Normally I didn't care. Her chatter buffered the other cafeteria noise.

I let her talk until she paused to take a drink of her Coke before I interrupted with my own news. "This is my last lunch with you guys," I said, taking a bite of my sandwich.

"What?" Heather asked, nearly choking on her drink.

"After spring break I'm switching to part-time, which means lunches at home. You guys will just have to come over to my house to hang out," I said.

I waited for them to agree. After all, that's what friends did—support one another. At least, that's what I thought. All three stared at me though like I was speaking a foreign language.

"Unless you guys don't want to come over," I said uncomfortably. Maybe we weren't as close as I thought. I wanted the floor to open up and suck me in.

"Talking to yourself again?" a snide voice asked behind me.

I nearly groaned out loud. As if things hadn't become awkward enough. Why couldn't they just leave us alone? I tried to ignore the voice behind me, wishing that Heather would suddenly start chattering again. Anything to fill the silence, but she and the others sat oddly still.

"I'm talking to you, freak," the voice said again, filled with amusement. Her name was Monica. She and her friends had been bullying me from day one. Up until then I had chosen not to acknowledge them, but she had never been this bold.

I gripped the table tightly before turning around to confront her. I was sick of the pointing, sick of the teasing, I was sick of all of it. One measly day. That was all I needed from them, but they were determined to be assholes to the bitter end. "Can't you just leave me and my friends alone?" I demanded, rising to my feet.

Monica looked taken back. Good. I was sick of letting everyone walk all over me. Glancing around, I noticed that we had gained the attention of the entire cafeteria. That was also good. Dr. Marshall had been after me for weeks to stick up for myself. This was my shot to show everyone I was done taking their crap.

"What friends?" Monica asked sarcastically, finally finding her voice.

Great, now she had insulted my friends. They did not deserve her crap any more than I did. I surged toward her, coming face-to-face. She recoiled slightly, just as I thought.

Feeling powerful, I stood in front of her, ready to defend my friends at all costs. "You know, just because we don't conform to your clique, doesn't mean we deserve your shit." I hated that my voice echoed through the cafeteria, sounding shaky.

Monica covered her mouth, shaking with laughter. "Oh, lord. You really are crazy," she said. "I thought maybe you were just pretending, to get more attention or something, but you totally believe they're real."

I rolled my eyes. She was such a bitch. I turned my eyes apologetically to my friends who looked as horrified as I felt. "Sorry," I mouthed to them before turning back to Monica who was now laughing manically. Maybe she was crazy. "Just leave us alone," I told her, turning back to my friends. She wasn't worth the effort.

"Hey, Mia, if your friends are really sitting here, would I be able to do this?" Monica asked, sweeping her arm out to take a cheap shot at Heather.

I couldn't believe her nerve. My anger got the best of me and I made a move to defend my friend—only, something wasn't right. Monica's arm had swung wide and should have connected with the side of Heather's face. But, it didn't. Her hand moved through Heather's head, like she was a ghost. I stood frozen, blinking my eyes to try and understand what I had seen. None of it made sense.

I could see Monica laughing again, but to my ears there was dead silence.

I turned toward Heather who looked at me remorsefully. She had nothing to say. It wasn't like her, not the Heather I had come to know. Molly and Katie wore the same gloomy expression on their faces. I reached out, not believing what I had seen, but Heather shook her head before the three of them abruptly disappeared, leaving nothing but an empty table behind. One solitary lunch remained—mine. All evidence of my friends had been erased.

Monica grabbed her side, laughing hysterically beside me. Tears of merriment danced in her eyes. My eyes swept across the cafeteria. Everyone else either laughed and pointed or wore cringing looks of pity. Not one face showed an ounce of compassion. I covered my ears, trying to block them out. They were nothing. I needed to get out. Whirling around in a circle, I searched frantically for an escape, but the crowd in the cafeteria closed in on me, sealing me in a tomb.

Their roaring filled my ears, echoing through my head. It was all I could hear. And their faces—nothing could hide their faces. Their features looked distorted and demonlike. A scream formed in my chest, clawing frantically up my throat and tearing it to shreds. I welcomed the release. It felt so good.

The bodies swarming me stepped backward and the laughter dissipated. They had gotten the proof they were waiting for. The crazy girl had finally lost her shit. My screams wailed across the cafeteria like a siren, piercing to everyone else but comforting to me. I could see the darkness creeping in, making me smile. The horrified onlookers no longer mattered. My one true friend had come to rescue me. I tumbled forward, thankful to be welcomed into its embrace.

PART THREE

I WOKE moments later, or days. I had no idea. All traces of the darkness were gone. I blinked into the bright light above my head, trying to make sense of where I was. My head felt heavy, my brain muddled. I lifted my arm to rub my eyes so I could see. My arm refused to move. I twisted my head to find that my wrist was bound to the bed.

A filling of dread engulfed me and I slammed my eyes closed, unable to bear the truth. Tears leaked out behind my closed eyelids, flowing down my cheeks. I was still in my basement. I had never left.

Grief unlike any I had ever felt blanketed me as sobs tore through my body. I knew I should muffle them. If Mother heard me she would be angry. I couldn't stop my crying. Ripping their way through me seemed to be the only option.

I could hear the sound of approaching footsteps. The urge to brace myself like I'd always done was there, but I could not find the will to care. I refused to open my eyes. Facing the truth would likely kill me this time.

A cool hand reached out and touched me. Instinctively, I jerked away. That hand would cause me pain.

"Mia, you're going to be okay." Wait. Where was the low, gravelly voice? This voice I knew. It wasn't real. It was another manifestation of my betraying head. "Are you in pain?" Her cool fingers touched my wrist as they fumbled with the cuff that held me to the bed. Her voice sounded so much like Dr. Marshall's it made a new fountain of tears flow down my cheeks.

A second later my wrist was free. No longer able to resist, I opened my eyes, hoping against disappointment. Dr. Marshall smiled down at me as she made her way to the other side of my bed, unfastening my right arm, which I wasn't even aware was bound also.

Peering around the room, I saw that I wasn't in my basement prison. I was clearly in some kind of hospital room. It wasn't all a dream. My brain was still muddled and felt like mush. I was confused.

"What happened?" I asked once she freed my right wrist. "What were these for?" I lifted one of the cuffs before letting it fall back down the side of the bed.

She scooted the only chair in the room close to my bed and sat down before she answered. "You suffered a breakdown," she said gently. "I had hoped to prevent it from happening."

"A breakdown?" I asked, trying to remember what had

happened. My memories were just at the edge of my mind, dancing away as I tried to reach for them. If I had a breakdown, did that mean I really was crazy?

"Mia, do you remember going to school on Friday?"

"I think so. I mean, I did go, right?" Friday was a great day from what I remember. It was the day Mom told me I would be changing my school schedule. I remembered how happy I'd been standing in the kitchen with her and Jacob and then we left for school, but for some reason, I couldn't remember anything after that. The memory was there. I could feel it taunting me, but it refused to come to the surface.

Dr. Marshall watched me carefully. "Mia, do you remember what happened in the cafeteria?"

I pulled myself to a sitting position, shaking my head, hoping that would help clear it.

"Mia, let's talk about your friends."

Her voice sounded like it came from the other side of a tunnel as my memories finally began tugging at the edges of my mind. Horrific memories. I tried pushing them away, but now they refused to stay hidden.

A familiar roaring filled my ears as the events of Friday unfolded in my mind, completely eclipsing everything else.

"Mia, breathe," Dr. Marshall said from the other side of the tunnel that separated us.

I willed myself to breathe. *In, out. In, out.* I slowly chanted in my head until the roaring subsided. "Will I ever be normal or am I always going to be crazy?" I finally whispered when I was able to breathe without hyperventilating.

"Mia, you are as *normal* as anyone. A person is not crazy.

They can be mentally unstable or they can have a sickness that makes them believe something that is not true."

"Which am I?" I asked, feeling more tears burning behind my eyes. Years without crying and now I couldn't keep them at bay.

She pondered my question for a moment before answering. "Mia, you're a beautiful soul who suffered a traumatic experience and because of that you see things that are not really there."

"I don't understand."

"I mean that due to the trauma you suffered while growing up, your mind creates hallucinations to help you handle the trauma."

I nodded my head. We'd already gone over this. That's where my Mia had come from. It didn't explain the others.

"Your mind has provided you a safety net to help when you enter an atmosphere you're ill-equipped to handle. This is not your fault, Mia. We pushed you when you weren't ready. Sending you to school too soon was a decision I deeply regret. I was so intent on probing into your time growing up with Judy that I neglected what was happening right in front of me. Heather and the other friends you created stepped in to do the job I should have done. She protected you when you needed a protector. Until our last session, I had no idea things had escalated to the point they had at school. By the time your mom and I talked it over, it seemed we had waited too long to intervene. We failed you. More importantly . . . I failed you. I'm sorry for that."

"How could they feel so real?" I asked, running a finger

along the metal bed rail. "How could I have whole conversations with someone who didn't even exist? I don't understand any of this." I sounded like a child.

"How does the mind do anything? The Mia you created helped save you from abuse and captivity. She gave you entrance to a world that you were being denied. Heather and the others did the same thing. They're all very protective over you. I suspected you weren't ready for school. I wasn't even sure you were quite ready for the outside world. Your body may have been physically ready, but your head was not. I felt at the time that spending time at home reestablishing your relationships with your family would better help with your recovery. I underestimated how overwhelming that would be for you. I should have waited to sign your discharge papers."

I shot her a questioning look, not understanding what she meant. "Why?" I asked.

"You had already exhibited signs that your brain had manifested other hallucinations while you were in the hospital. My hope was that being released from the hospital would distance you from them. Initially, it appeared I was right. The hallucinations had given you closure and had already taken steps to let you go."

Her words were confusing me. I didn't understand what she was trying to tell me. It was just me at the hospital. My Mia was already gone by then. She wasn't making any sense. The only person I knew was Gunner. I shook my head in denial.

Dr. Marshall actually looked pained as she waited for

me to figure out what she was trying to get me to understand. I shook my head again, refusing to give her what she wanted.

"Mia, tell me about Gunner," she finally said, giving me no out.

Gunner? What did he have to do with this? Why would she bring him up when we were talking about my broken head and its need to trick me? Gunner was special. He didn't belong in this conversation. The first stirrings of aggravation rose up in me.

"You remember how scared you were about all the *firsts* you'd be tackling?" She spoke softly, pushing me toward a door I didn't want opened. Not now, not ever. What she was saying was not possible. "You were scared about how you would handle all the things you didn't understand. Do you remember that?"

I refused to answer her, digging my fingers into my rib cage until they poked painfully between each one.

"Mia, Gunner was there to help you. He made all those *firsts* less intimidating. He gave you the confidence to believe you were ready to face the outside world."

"You're wrong," I said in a quivering voice. "Everyone loved Gunner."

"Everyone loved you, honey. Gunner's personality inside you gave you the confidence to talk to the people who terrified you. He gave you the push you needed. A push we all were grateful for."

I shook my head again. "No, this isn't right." A filmstrip of memories ran through my head. I could see myself stowing a candy bar wrapped in orange paper in the pocket of my robe, shuffling down the hall that first time, making my way to the doors that would lead outside, stepping outside and seeing Gunner for the first time. Now though, the bench was empty except for me, talking to someone who wasn't there. My mind recalled another memory of me climbing the stairs, holding my arm out like I'm helping someone up, but now all I could see was me alone.

I rubbed my eyes, trying to clear the truth away. I didn't want to see any of it. The memories wouldn't stop though. Next I stood against the wall outside the office at school. I'm breathing heavily in the memory, on the verge of a panic attack. I lifted my head as if someone had called out to me, but in this memory no one was there. Again I was alone, walking down the hall, talking to myself.

The last memory was the worst. I sat in the cafeteria talking to my three friends, but of course, they're not really there. It's just me alone at the table, talking to no one while everyone in the cafeteria looks on.

A flush of embarrassment rose to my cheeks as I grabbed my arm, wishing for the flame from my lighter. Everyone knew. Everyone except me. All those kids who judged me at school had been right. No wonder they came after me so relentlessly. I had been the freak since day one. Dr. Marshall may not use the word, but there was no denying that I was crazy. I longed for my basement prison, missing its safety. I would even take the punishments over all of this.

My heart ached for Gunner. How could he not exist? "Everyone liked him," I said defensively. I began crying harder, grieving for my loss. If only my tears could wash me out to sea, away from the harsh realities of truth. I hated the truth. I hated this life. Most of all I hated my brain. If I could scoop it out of my head, I would gladly do it. I'd stomp it into a pile of mush that could never be retrieved again.

A nurse came in to save me from drowning, carrying a life preserver in the form of a needle. As she found my vein, I would have thanked her if I weren't drowning in a million tears I had kept locked away for so many years. The medicine quickly took effect, sending Dr. Marshall and the ruthless truth fading into the background. I drifted to sleep, feeling more loss than I'd ever felt in my life.

33

LIFE INSIDE the Brookville Mental Facility was as different as night and day versus a regular hospital. There were more rules and schedules galore. Visitors weren't allowed to pop in whenever they wanted and patients weren't allowed to roam freely. I couldn't have cared less about any of the goings on inside the facility. There always seemed to be a group activity or session we were forced to attend. We were watched constantly and our every move was monitored by the watchful cameras stationed throughout the entire building. I ignored the cameras like everything else, refusing to interact with anyone who talked to me. I went where they told me, ate what was served in the small cafeteria, and accepted whatever pills were handed to me before lights-out. If this was my life, then this was what they would get.

Day after day I met with Dr. Marshall but I remained stoically silent. There was nothing left to say. I had nothing left to give. Accepting her revelations became more than I could handle. I found myself second-guessing everything and everyone around me. My days when I wasn't being forced to participate were spent sitting alone, keeping my room as dark as the nurses would allow. The faces of everyone that walked by my room felt like they were taunting me. They would glance at me as they passed, but were they real? I had no idea. I wasn't sure I cared anymore. My only solace came when I was given my daily dose of medication at which point my mind drifted into a state of nothingness. No threat of creating imaginary friends or first kisses with a boy who didn't exist.

Mom and Jacob tried to visit me the first couple of weeks, but I was too ashamed to see them. Like Dr. Marshall, they knew I was crazy and chose to keep it from me. They let me make a fool of myself, coddled me when I deserved the truth.

My next therapy session with Dr. Marshall consisted of my continued silence. For her part, she remained unaffected and did all the talking. She opened her laptop and pulled up cases similar to mine. Even though I refused to talk, my eyes devoured the words on the screen. It didn't escape my notice that many doctors believed my condition was a camouflage for deflecting other mental illnesses.

"Mia, you have to talk," Dr. Marshall said, closing her laptop.

I bit the side of my nail, tugging at the skin. Chewing my cuticles was the only form of self-mutilation I was allowed.

The burns on my arm I kept hidden by a gauze bandage had been discovered by the hospital staff. They were treated and wrapped and already starting to heal. Not that I made it easy for them. I picked at the new skin during my first night in the facility, smiling in the dark when I felt it oozing down my arm. I was so wrapped up in its comforting tenderness I gave no thought to what would happen when it was discovered in the morning. My sores were treated and bandaged again by a stone-faced nurse along with a notation to my chart. That night I was strapped to my bed rails, making it impossible to pick at the sores again.

Dr. Marshall watched me chew my thumbnail down to the quick, but didn't comment on my mutilation. "Mia," she prompted.

I looked up from my nail. "What?" I finally demanded.

"Can you tell me what you are feeling?"

I didn't answer right away, sticking my index fingernail between my teeth. "What I'm feeling? I traded one prison for another. At least in my old prison I wasn't surrounded by other crazy people who scream all night." My words came out faster than bullets.

"Do you miss living with Judy?" she asked, quirking an eyebrow at me.

I shrugged. "I'm sure you'll tell me it's wrong if I say yes."

"Mia, your feelings are never wrong. Can you tell me why you miss her? Judy did terrible things to you. Do you miss that?"

I had been pressured into this line of questioning so many

times. Why was it so important for Dr. Marshall to keep harping on Judy? She did "terrible things." I got it. I did leave though, so wasn't it obvious that I understood? Were the details really that important? "It doesn't matter," I said, glaring at her.

"Why do you say that?"

"Because it's true. Judy punished me and she had her reasons. Why does any of that matter now?"

She tapped her pencil lightly on the mahogany desk in front of her, contemplating her thoughts.

Tap, tap.

I wanted to reach out and grab the pencil. Break it into a million pieces and then throw them in her face. "Can we just move on," I said louder than before.

Tap, tap, tap.

Fuck that pencil. That's all I could think. I hated the stupid piece of wood. "You can keep looking at me, but I don't know what you want me to say," I said, crossing my arms.

Tap, tap.

"How am I looking at you?"

Like you want to be stabbed with the pencil, I thought. They'd probably strap me in a straitjacket, but it might have been worth it. Anger always seemed to be just below the surface for me lately, ready to boil over. "Can you please stop tapping the pencil?" I said through gritted teeth. I didn't recognize my voice.

The pencil abruptly stopped its thumping against the desk. "Is it bothering you?" she asked.

"You think?" I answered, my voice dripping with sarcasm.

"Mia, are you angry?" Dr. Marshall asked.

I was, but wouldn't answer her. I didn't want to give her the satisfaction. These silly questions weren't serving a purpose. I saw no point to them or these sessions for that matter. I was where I belonged and nothing was going to change that. Not her questions or her psychobabble.

"Mia, it's time we talk about the punishments."

"I don't want to," I said sullenly, like a child.

"It's time."

I stood up so abruptly I knocked my chair over and began pacing the room. "Why is it so important? So Judy hit me. People get hit all the time. You break a rule, you get punished. Nothing unusual there." My voice ricocheted off the walls.

Dr. Marshall didn't even blink as I stormed around her office, screaming my words at her. She was unfazed and if I wasn't so mad I'd even say she looked pleased. I could see nothing through the red haze of anger that clouded my vision.

"You did not deserve your punishments."

"You have no idea what I deserved! If you knew everything I did you wouldn't be saying that."

"Mia, I've seen the pictures," she said compassionately. "You did nothing to deserve what happened to you. Those marks on your back were not your fault."

I shuddered slightly. Would there be no end to my shame? I had scars. So what. Plenty of people had scars. "I deserved every single one of mine."

"Why?" she asked quietly.

"I was bad. All the time. Don't you see? Mother had rules and as long as I followed them she treated me fairly. If I would have just followed the rules she wouldn't have done any of this," I said, pointing at a scar on my shoulder.

Dr. Marshall sighed, rubbing the bridge of her nose. "Mia, people break rules all the time. Children test the boundaries their parents set. They get caught, but their punishments don't involve a leather strap or starvation. That woman took your naivety and used it against you, to make you believe you deserved her form of punishment."

"I did things," I said, waving my arms hysterically in the air.

"What kinds of things?"

I leaned against the wall. "In the beginning I cried a lot. I knew I wasn't supposed to. It was disrespectful after everything she did for me. I betrayed her time and time again."

Dr. Marshall's chair creaked as she sat back. "Everything she did for you?" she asked, raising her eyebrows. "You mean how she took you from your front yard? From a family who loved and adored you. A family who grieved the loss of you. Is that what you betrayed? Mia, don't you see? You didn't betray her; she betrayed you. She took you from everything you knew. Of course you cried. You were a scared little girl."

I slid slowly down the wall as her words began to sink in. "But, she saved me," I whispered. I pulled my knees up to my chest and slowly rocked back and forth.

Dr. Marshall stepped around her desk and sank down on the floor next to me. "Mia, what was she saving you from?"

I scooted away like an injured animal. I didn't want her close to me. I didn't want anyone close to me ever again.

Images of my time with Judy flooded my mind. Every scream, every beating, every swing of the leather strap. I felt my body wince in pain as if I were reliving years of punishments over and over again. "My sickness. I mean, I don't know. I'm just so confused," I said in a raw voice.

She shook her head, scooting close to me. "Mia, you weren't sick. She didn't save you. She was sick and she lied to you."

I closed my eyes. No longer angry. No longer sad. I was empty. There was nothing left to give.

"I trusted her," I said, trembling. My vision blurred from welled-up tears. Every emotion I had kept bottled inside began pouring out uncontrollably.

"I know you did. That's what she wanted."

Dr. Marshall pulled me tightly into her arms, allowing me to crumble into her embrace.

"I'm so sorry," I cried, repeating the words several times.

"It's all right, sweetie," Dr. Marshall said as she rubbed my back gently. "Everything will be all right."

• • •

My anger and sadness came and went in sporadic waves over the next few weeks as Dr. Marshall and I discussed my time with Judy in great detail.

"I've met with Judy," Dr. Marshall told me during one of our sessions. "We sat for an extensive interview. Her own childhood was far from perfect. She was raised by an abusive father who believed in corporal punishment. She used that same type of punishment to control you and bend you to her will."

I processed her words. Weighing them in my head.

"Did she ask about me? Is she even sorry?" I finally asked.

Dr. Marshall shook her head. "Unfortunately, remorse just isn't in her genes. The only thing she regrets is losing you. You must understand—Judy doesn't believe she did anything wrong. She is convinced to this day that kidnapping you was in your best interest."

Her words made the air stick in my throat. "So she hates me," I said knowingly, absently scratching at the skin on my wrist.

She reached for my hand to stop the clawing. "What Judy did is a learned behavior. Much like when you inflict pain on yourself. For so long pain has connected you to reality. These are learned patterns, but we can work on them together, with your family if you are open to it. None of us want to see you in pain anymore. You've had enough harm to last a lifetime."

Although I understood Dr. Marshall's intentions were only to help, at times I still found myself hating her for making me talk. For forcing me to see things I had been so blind to for so many years. She encouraged me to talk until I was sick of my own voice. All my secrets tumbled out as if an invisible gate had been lifted. Dr. Marshall's probing, though painful, made me finally accept and blame who was truly responsible for everything.

IT TOOK a month until I was comfortable enough to see Mom and Jacob. Dr. Marshall had been nudging me in that direction, preaching that I needed to "trust" them again. That was her key word. Trust not only my family, but myself as well. Trust that I could handle my life outside the hospital.

"I'm so excited today is visiting day," my new roommate, Trisha, said, bouncing on the edge of her bed.

I looked up from the book I was reading and shot her a look. When she was brought to my room five days ago she was lethargic and practically unresponsive. Her wrists were heavily bandaged and she had a vacant look in her eyes. Within two days of being on meds she was a completely different person. She was so damn chatty and happy that she seemed out of place here. At first I questioned if she even existed, wondering if my mind had once again conjured someone to distract me. Fortunately, Dr. Marshall verified her presence. During our numerous sessions at Brookville, Dr. Marshall and I talked about my time with Gunner at the hospital. It was under her orders that no one, including Mom and Jacob, intervene. She felt at the time that knowing the truth would be too traumatizing. Since my breakdown at school, I was now on a treatment plan to better cope with my stress.

Chatty Trisha was indeed real and evidently here to torment me. I'd say drive me crazy, but that ship had already sailed.

I set my book to the side and sat up on my bed. "I'm excited too," I said, knowing she wouldn't let it go unless I echoed her sentiments. I avoided looking at her wrists, which were still heavily bandaged. She had confided in me that she slit her wrists when the voices in her head wouldn't shut up. She did it to silence them, but her younger sister found her before all the blood could leak from her body.

Looking at her now, cheerful and happy, it was hard to believe that a week ago she had tried to end her life.

"You want to go down and wait in the rec room with me?" she asked, bouncing to her feet. She was like a damn kangaroo. "That way we'll be the first ones there when they let the visitors in." This wasn't Trisha's first stay at Brookville Mental Facility or *Broken*-ville, as some of the residents liked to refer to it.

I hesitated before answering, wiping my hands that were suddenly damp on my pant legs. "I guess," I said, climbing to my feet.

I wanted to see Jacob and Mom. I knew I was ready, but that didn't mean I wasn't terrified. What would they say? What would I say? I was a completely different person now. I knew I had a sickness, but I still didn't understand the inner workings of it. Dr. Marshall claimed we might never understand it, but acceptance was the first step. Talking about my past had been the second step, and from there we have been moving forward. Would my family accept me like this? I wouldn't know until I saw them.

"Yay, I can't wait to see my family. Baillie said Mom baked me my favorite cookies last night. Wait until you taste them. They practically melt in your mouth." Trisha linked her arm through mine as we left our room.

I was tempted to pull away. Everyone I thought I could trust since I had escaped Judy's had left me. Logically, I knew Trisha was different. She wasn't a friend my brain had conjured up. She was real, which made me want to pull away even more.

Other patients called out to Trisha as we walked down the hall together. None called out my name. Trisha had been back five days and already seemed to talk to everyone in the whole facility. I'd been here over a month and spoke only to Dr. Marshall, or on occasion in group therapy when they forced a question on me.

Trisha though never shut up. She was like Gunner and Heather rolled into a tiny magpie on crack. If she sprouted feathers, I wouldn't have been surprised.

Trisha dragged me to one of the tables where a checkerboard sat with the pieces scattered about. I sat down, lost in my thoughts as I idly flipped one of the pieces in between my fingers. The board brought back memories that didn't even exist. I thought Gunner taught me to play checkers, but it had been another trick from my brain. Dr. Marshall explained it as something I had most likely learned years prior. Judy punished me to repress any of my life before her involvement until eventually all my memories became buried. Gunner had a free pass on all those memories.

"Do you want to play?" Trisha asked, plopping her feet up on the empty chair beside me.

The red piece slipped from my fingers, rolling toward the edge of the table. "Not right now," I answered, catching the piece before it could roll off.

Trisha shrugged, jumping up from the table and joining a couple of other patients who were in the middle of a card game. She interjected herself in their conversation like she'd been a part of it from the very beginning. I envied her ease, her natural personality. If not for the stark white bandages around her wrists, I would say she didn't belong here. She wasn't like the boy sitting in the corner yelling at a speck on the wall or the girl three rooms down from ours who screamed all night. Sadly, they both showed traits I had myself. I'd done both.

The rec room became busier as visiting hours approached. Trisha came back to my table, chatting about the gossip she had gleaned from her brief time with the other group. I listened with half an ear, keeping my eyes on the door. I couldn't care less that one of the nurses had gotten fired for getting too friendly with one of the patients or what nurse gave out extra meds if you slipped her some extra cash.

I wiped my hands on my pants, wishing they'd stop sweating so much. I was being ridiculous. It wasn't like Mom and Jacob were going to bite me or anything. Dr. Marshall reassured me they were dying to see me. I'd argued that they didn't even know me, but she countered with the suggestion that this could be a new beginning for our family. As the minutes ticked by, I almost lost my nerve, thinking another time would be better.

Before I could make my move to leave they walked through the door. Mom's arms were around me instantly. "Sweetie, I've been so worried. Dr. Marshall told us you were doing better, but I wouldn't believe her until I saw you with my own eyes. She was right though. You look amazing. Healthy." She paused in her gushing, releasing me so Jacob could give me a hug.

"Hey, sis," he said, giving me a tentative hug like he was afraid I was going to break. "You look good."

Their words were kind, but I knew what they were thinking. *Crazy.* We all knew it. I wouldn't be here if it wasn't true.

"Why don't we go for a walk around the pond," Mom suggested as the noise level in the room rose.

"Okay," I agreed. I was ready to escape the crowds anyway.

The sun was shining bright as we stepped outside. Summer was just around the corner, but the humidity made it feel like it was already here. I didn't care. I loved being outdoors, spending the majority of my time there when I wasn't in my therapy sessions. The facility was fenced in, but well hidden behind trees and shrubbery that provided privacy from the outside world.

"How are you doing?" Mom asked, reaching for my hand.

My favorite question. I weighed my words, searching for the right answer. The question was simple, but required an answer that was heavy and cumbersome. How did I convey how I was feeling when it all felt so complex? "Better," I finally answered. Better was a safe word. In truth, it was the most appropriate word. I did feel better. At times I was terrified at the complexities of my mind and what it was capable of. Other times I felt huge waves of relief that my mind had gotten me to where I was now. Dr. Marshall said it made me strong. It gave me the will to survive.

"I'm so glad, sweetie. Are they treating you okay?"

I nodded. "Why didn't you tell me?" I asked as we looped the pond.

They didn't have to ask what I meant. The time to treat me like I was too fragile to handle the truth had passed.

"We should have. Dr. Marshall wanted me to admit you as soon as we realized your condition was persisting. I was the one who wanted to give you a chance to adjust at home. I hoped it would get better."

"Persisting? Is that a nice way of saying *still off her rocker*? I was talking to people who weren't even real. You guys just thought it would go away?"

My words were harsh, but Dr. Marshall had encouraged me to speak my mind. I kept my tone even so they would at least know I didn't blame them. They were in a tough position. I realized that. All my anger had been hashed out in therapy along with my embarrassment. I did feel bad for Jacob though. He was forced to endure all the repercussions of my fallout at school. I wondered if that had something to do with his uncharacteristic silence.

"I'm sorry about the whole school thing," I told him as we looped the pond a second time.

He shot me an incredulous look. I stopped mid-step, waiting for him to lower the boom. I wouldn't blame him. I had completely disrupted his life. "You're apologizing to me. Why don't you kick me next?"

I studied him in confusion. Aggravation I expected, but this was something else. This was self-loathing. "What? I am sorry. I wouldn't blame you for hating me. I left a mess behind for you to clean up."

Mom opened her mouth to interject, but Jacob held up a hand to stop her. "No, Mom, I stayed quiet long enough. All of you insisted you knew what was best for Mia, but I tried to tell you guys you were pushing her too hard. Asking too much from her." Jacob's voice shook slightly. "Mia, you think I'm mad at you? I'm not mad at you. I'm pissed at everyone else. We pushed you until you broke. I could see it happening and I did nothing to protect you. I failed you again." His voice broke and I was shocked to see tears in his eyes.

It was unsettling to see my big, strapping brother crying. He was too tough for tears, too emotionally stable for them. "Jacob, you didn't fail me ever."

He shook his head vehemently. "I did fail you. I told you I

was going inside to get us Popsicles and I never came back. I went up to my room to play with my cars. I was sick of playing house with you and your dumb doll."

My mouth dropped open over his admission. I had completely forgotten he was outside with me that day. That little stink had promised me a cherry Popsicle. When he didn't come right back out I thought about going in and hunting him down to demand my frozen treat, but I was having too much fun playing with Daisy.

A giggle escaped my lips before I could hold it back. Mom and Jacob exchanged looks, but again I giggled. They were sure to think I was off my rocker again and needed another dose of meds.

I clapped a hand over my mouth. This was not the time for laughter. "I'm sorry. I didn't mean to laugh," I said as another giggle escaped me. "It's just that I was so mad that day thinking you ate my Popsicle. I was going to come in and yell at you, but I was having too much fun outside. It wasn't your fault I was taken. It's no one's fault," I said, including Mom in my statement. "I always played in our front yard. I should have been safe. Little kids aren't supposed to be taken from the front of their house. It's no one's fault," I repeated. "Judy stole my childhood, but I won't let her steal the rest of my life." A huge weight lifted from my shoulders. Dr. Marshall had been trying to get me to this point for a long time. It was all about acceptance and moving on. No more hiding from the truth.

My words lifted the invisible wall Jacob had erected

between us. He pulled me in for a bone-crushing hug that threatened to cut off my air supply. This was real.

We spent the next few hours talking about all the taboo subjects we had avoided before. At times Mom cried, other times I cried. Dr. Marshall would have considered it a therapeutic session. It felt good.

When we returned I was shocked to find another visitor waiting to see me. He stood off to the side of the room looking extremely uncomfortable to be surrounded by patients. Jacob and I exchanged a look when we saw him. Mom didn't look surprised though. "Did you know he was going to be here?" I asked, standing in the doorway.

"He called earlier this week and asked about visiting hours. He wanted to come see you."

Jacob snorted with derision.

"Despite his faults, he's still your father," she chastised Jacob.

"Could have fooled me," he said, giving me a hug. "I'll see you next week, Mia." He turned on his heel and left.

Mom sighed but didn't call after him. "I know you're mad at your father, but give him a chance, okay?" she said as Dad approached. He looked as unsure as I felt.

"Mad at him? I don't even know him."

He flinched at my words.

"Blake," Mom greeted him.

"Tracey," he said.

"Mia, I'll see you next week," Mom said as she hugged me tightly. I clung to her for a moment. I'd missed her more than

I realized was possible these past few weeks. I needed her to know that.

Mom squeezed me one last time before leaving. Dad and I watched her go. An awkward silence swelled between us. He hadn't bothered to see me when I was at home, so what could he have to say now? I shifted my weight, glancing around the room, and spotted Trisha in the corner with her family. Her body language suggested that she was aggravated. Obviously I wasn't the only one with family issues. We would have to catch up later.

"Mia, do you want to sit?" Dad finally asked, breaking the silence. I pulled my gaze from Trisha. "I thought we should talk."

I shrugged but followed him to the far side of the room where it was quieter. We sat in the two solitary wing chairs in the corner although the silence once again swelled between us. I scratched at the thin skin of my wrist, waiting for him to speak. My aggravation began to grow. Why was he even here?

"You wanted to talk?" I finally asked sarcastically, anxious for this meeting to be over.

"Your doctor contacted me and suggested it." He raked a hand through his hair.

So, unless my doctor hadn't called him he wouldn't have come. Great. This was a staged performance. "And," I said, my frustration boiling over.

"Look, Mia. I'm not perfect. I know I've made mistakes."

I snorted much like Jacob had earlier. What Dad said was

an understatement. Not because of his absence in my life, but because of his absence in Jacob's life. He left Mom and Jacob when they needed him most. That was fucked up. Anger filled me as the thoughts took hold.

"You're an asshole," I blurted out.

"What did you say?" he asked, recoiling at my words.

"You're an asshole," I shouted, gaining the attention of most of the other occupants in the room.

"Mia," he started.

I held up my hand, stopping him mid-sentence. "Why are you even here? You stopped coming to see me when I was in the hospital and you sure as hell weren't there when Jacob and Mom needed you."

"I'm here because your doctor thinks it's vital to your recovery. I want you to get better. I need you to get better."

"You need me to get better?" I laughed with derision. "Is that why you stopped visiting me in the hospital? You knew I was broken? You knew that something was wrong with me and you wanted no part of that." He really was an asshole. He left Mom when she fell apart after I was taken. He abandoned his son, leaving him to grow up without a father, and even when we had been given a second chance, he ran again.

He avoided my eyes and I knew I had hit the nail on the head. "Do you wish I had never been found?"

"Don't be ridiculous, Mia. I'm not the monster here. Of course I'm happy you were found. I just wasn't prepared to deal with the aftermath. The constant onslaught of attention. Your picture splashed across every media outlet. That

criminal and all her abuse made public knowledge for everyone to see. You inventing people who don't exist. It was too
much."

I flinched at his words. "You think you were the only one
who felt the pressure? Some of us weren't given the luxury of
bailing though."

"I told you, I'm not perfect. I like structure. I thrive on
routine and normalcy. Our lives have been in a constant up-
heaval for the last ten years."

"Yeah, well, I'm sorry I got kidnapped," I said. My voice
dripped with sarcasm.

"So am I."

We slumped back in our seats, both having had our say. In
a way I had my answers. During our sessions Dr. Marshall
kept insisting that I was strong. I wondered what her opinion
of my dad would be. As far as I was concerned he was weak.
He bailed when things got rough. He let all of us down. That
was his cross to bear. Not mine.

"I'M GOING to miss you," Trisha said sadly as I zipped my suitcase.

I lugged the heavy bag off my bed and gave her an impulsive hug. "I'm going to miss you too, but you'll be out in a couple of weeks. And this time you're going to call me if the voices won't shut up," I said, looking down at the angry scars on her wrists.

"Promise we'll be friends once we leave these walls," she pleaded.

"I promise. Besides, you're the only friend I haven't made up," I teased, giving her another squeeze.

She giggled. "That's true, but what if you decide to replace me with someone better in your head?"

I gave her a nudge with my shoulder. "Bite your tongue."

"It's okay, you know? We can't help that our brains work on a different frequency," she said, parroting something Jill, our group leader, had said.

I snorted. "Jill would be so proud of you," I said, ignoring her statement. It was a Brookville motto to accept that we were different. I accepted my mind, but would do everything in my power not to relapse. I wanted to live in the real world, not the one I had built in my head. "Call me as soon as you get home," I instructed her for what felt like the millionth time.

Her lower lip trembled and I knew tears were close. "I love you, kid," I teased, pulling the handle of my suitcase up and wheeling it out of the room before she could flood the room we'd shared for the last six weeks.

I waved to a couple of my friends as I wheeled my suitcase past the rec room. With Trisha as a roommate it became impossible to keep everyone at arm's length. Before I knew it, I was being included in everything. I could now tell you which nurse carried a flask and which doctor got caught with his pants down. Literally. I would miss this place.

"Ready?" Mom asked, meeting me in the reception area. "I already filled out all your discharge papers."

"I'm ready," I said, gripping the handle of my suitcase tightly. A small bubble of fear lodged in my gut as I stepped outside and away from the building. I was ready for this. Even if everyone wasn't telling me I was ready, I would still know it was time.

"Where's Jacob?" I asked as I buckled my seat belt.

"He had to work so he's meeting us at home," Mom

answered, starting the car. With that, we pulled away from Brookville. I didn't turn around for a second glance. Looking back wasn't necessary.

"Does he like his new job?" I asked.

Mom laughed. "He likes the money he's earning."

I nodded. Maybe I would get a summer job too. Something to keep me occupied before I started classes in the fall. Thanks to Dr. Marshall's help, I had taken the appropriate exit exams from high school and would be starting classes at the community college in the fall. Mom told me that Dewy High had been more than willing to help make it happen. No surprise there. I bet my meltdown in the cafeteria would be the talk of the school for years. They wouldn't get a gripe from me. I'd had enough high school experience to last me a lifetime.

Jacob and Kevin were waiting with two pizzas when we got home. As soon as I walked in the door, Jacob stood up and slung an arm around my shoulder.

"Hey, Mia," Kevin greeted me, standing up and giving me a hug. I blushed slightly as my arms wove around his waist. I wasn't sure what I'd been expecting. Jacob told me on our last visit that Kevin had been asking about me. I figured he was just being nice, but the hug felt genuine.

"Hey, Kevin," I returned. It had been almost three months since I'd last seen him and the feelings that had just begun to form now sprung into high gear. It was silly. He was Jacob's friend and I was Jacob's sister, but the look he gave me didn't make me feel that way at all.

"Let's eat," Jacob said, saving me from my embarrassment.

Kevin winked at me, sending a warm feeling spreading through my body. It was good to be home.

Dinner bled into a game of cards and then Monopoly. Laughter and teasing filled the room with happiness. It all felt so very normal and right. For the first time in years, I felt in control. I was going to be okay. My family was going to be okay. We'd lived through the unthinkable and were stronger for it. My brain may have fault lines, but with Dr. Marshall's help those fault lines were now invisible from sight.

Kevin gave me another hug before he left, which earned him a razzing from Jacob, asking for a kiss for himself. Kevin responded by giving him a sock in the arm. I climbed the steps to my room, happier than I could remember. Nothing could take this feeling away from me.

I made a beeline for the bathroom so I could brush my teeth. Peering into the mirror, I was surprised to see that my eyes were bright and shiny. They looked as happy as I felt. Practically skipping to my bedroom to dress for bed, I switched on my television for some background noise as I dressed. The weatherman giving the seven-day forecast sounded a little too enthusiastic about the record high temperatures. His chipper tone would have given Trisha a run for her money. I climbed up on my bed with the remote to find a sitcom I could watch before I went to sleep.

Before I could change the station though, a familiar face filled the screen just as I was settling against my pillows.

I sat up abruptly and scooted to the edge of my bed. I hadn't seen Judy in almost six months, but she looked exactly as I remembered. Without giving conscious thought to it, I turned the volume up. I hadn't realized her court case was coming up. No one had mentioned it. Between Dr. Marshall and Mom and Jacob, I had been kept inside a cocoon of protection. I understood their reasoning for shielding me, but Judy was a part of my past that will never be forgotten. Seeing her face on the screen sapped away all the contentment from the day in one gigantic rush. I picked up my pillow and hugged it against my chest as the newscaster talked about the impending case. Though I should have been expecting it, I was surprised when my picture flashed across the screen, making me flinch.

I barely recognized the girl staring back at me. The girl on the screen looked sick with her sunken-in cheeks and limp hair hanging around her face in clumps. It was her eyes though that looked most shocking. They were lifeless and dead. Those were not my eyes. My eyes were bright and shiny and happy.

They were Leah's eyes, not mine.

"Of course they're my eyes," Leah said from the chair by my window.

"Leah?" I gasped, knowing it couldn't really be her.

"Hey, Mia," she replied, tucking a limp cluster of hair behind her ear.

I closed my eyes. "She's not real, she's not real," I muttered, rubbing my eyes hard. I opened them again, relieved to find the chair empty. It was just my imagination. I scooted up on my bed and lay back against my pillows, ignoring the churning in my stomach. Part of it was sadness, which made no sense. Leah was a part of me that no longer existed, I shouldn't be grieving her.

Sick of hearing the voices drone on from my television, I switched it off, along with my bedroom lamp. Darkness filled my room and the grief inside me slowly began to unravel. Even in the darkness though, I knew she was still there. I could feel her before the edge of my bed dipped down, her shallow breaths tickling my ear from the pillow next to me. A warm blanket of relief covered my body. She would always be there for me when I needed her the most. Why wouldn't she be? Leah was the strong one after all. Maybe one day I would be able to let the bad memories of Judy go, but for now this was enough.

I smiled as her hand moved toward mine, linking our fingers together. "I missed you, Mia," she whispered.

"I missed you too, Leah."

ACKNOWLEDGMENTS

Writing is said to be solitary. Authors floating on islands amongst themselves with only the voices in their heads to keep them company. In many aspects this is true. With a book like *Losing Leah* that island quickly grew to include many other people.

Losing Leah formed as a complete story in what I jokingly call my mind's eye. The story was there and all I had to do was get my fingers to keep up with the words as they poured out of me. These were my moments of solitude. For these brief moments Leah and Mia belonged to me and me alone. The moment they appeared on the pages though, they began to belong to so many others. Neither character would be who they are without the voices of encouragement and insights of others.

The following people deserve an abundance of accolades and all my thanks:

Kevan Lyon. You are the superhero of all agents. Without you *Losing Leah* would not be in the hands of readers. Your insight helped evolve Leah and Mia into the girls they are.

"Thank you" seems inadequate for always believing in me. You truly make me feel like a writer.

Jennifer L. Armentrout, Melissa Brown, Jamie Hall, and Hollie Westring. I will never be able to express my gratitude to all of you. You dared to read the roughest copy of *Losing Leah*. I owe you a debt of thanks for seeing beneath the rough edges and loving Mia and Leah despite their flaws. You loved Leah and Mia when they were still being discovered.

Anna Roberto. I could thank you a million times and it still wouldn't be enough. I am grateful beyond words that you saw the story I was trying to tell beneath its murky surface. Your wisdom and words helped shape *Losing Leah* into the book it now is. Thank you for loving Mia and Leah as much as I do.

Katie McGarry. You will never know what your thoughts on *Losing Leah* meant to me. You made me feel like I belong in this crazy world of publishing.

Ashlynn King. There simply wouldn't be books by Tiffany King without you. You inspired me to write my very first book and every single book that followed it. You made me the writer I am today. You are the dream of all daughters and I am thankful every day that you belong to me.

Ryan King, my boy. You give me life. You are the laughter that bubbles up through me and the inquisitive voice that sticks with me always. You are a bright light when the world would otherwise be dark.

Finally to my husband, Karl. Without you there would be no *Losing Leah*. You're not only my very first reader, but you are also the volume to my voice. You are my confidence and strength. Your voice of encouragement, love, and support has allowed me to be the person and writer that I am. Life is uncertain and scary, bumpy and twisty, but as long as you are by my side I will never feel alone.

Thank you for reading this FEIWEL AND FRIENDS book.

The Friends who made

LOSING LEAH

possible are:

JEAN FEIWEL PUBLISHER

LIZ SZABLA ASSOCIATE PUBLISHER

RICH DEAS SENIOR CREATIVE DIRECTOR

HOLLY WEST EDITOR

ALEXEI ESIKOFF SENIOR MANAGING EDITOR

RAYMOND ERNESTO COLÓN SENIOR PRODUCTION MANAGER

ANNA ROBERTO EDITOR

CHRISTINE BARCELLONA ASSOCIATE EDITOR

KAT BRZOZOWSKI EDITOR

ANNA POON ASSISTANT EDITOR

EMILY SETTLE ADMINISTRATIVE ASSISTANT

ILANA WORRELL PRODUCTION EDITOR

Follow us on Facebook or visit us online at mackids.com

OUR BOOKS ARE FRIENDS FOR LIFE.